THE EARTH KEY

The Elementals Book 2

Jennifer L. Kelly

This is a work of fiction. All of the characters, organizations, and events portrayed in this novel are either products of the author's imagination or are used fictitiously.

Library of Congress PCN: 2016918410

BoxerBull Books

Cleveland, OH

ISBN-10: 0-9977764-3-9
ISBN-13: 978-0-9977764-3-0

TO MY DEAR READER~
WHERE IS YOUR BEGINNING?
-J.L.K.

OTHER BOOKS BY JENNIFER L. KELLY

THE ELEMENTALS

ARMY OF FIRE

THE LUCIA CHRONICLES

THE PROPHECY
THE DISSENTIENT
THE BEACON
THE GIRL WHO WASN'T LOVED (NOVELLA)

STAND ALONE FICTION

THE FRACTURED LIFE OF JENNY MCCLAIN

PROLOGUE

You'd think 800 years is a long time, right? Think of all the advances that we as a society could make in 800 freaking years. Seriously. Flying cars—no, better yet, spaceships. Crazy sleek silver spaceships that could fly around the planet. Fossil fuels, gone out with the gas guzzlers. Houses would be like glass bubbles—maybe sustainable domes with their own vegetation and solar panels to eliminate the use for the now non-existent fossil fuels. When you wanted to hang out with your friends you'd take your spaceship and drive—navigate?—to their little glass dome home. Of course, the house itself wouldn't be glass, that would be too intrusive. The house itself would be made of recycled materials because we'd used up everything else long ago. Society's menial labor tasks would be conducted by robots. Robots that could walk and talk—maybe even look just like a human being with, you know, blonde hair and blue eyes or whatever. They'd do the jobs that no one really wants to do, like build the recycled homes or construct the spaceships that replaced the cars. Computers would be obsolete. Who would need them if everyone had a robot? Maybe even the frickin library would just be a robot. You walk up and ask it a question and it would just automatically answer. Even better, you'd have a chip embedded beneath the skin of your arm and the robot would just scan it and directly load the information into your conscious. *Bam!* Anything you ever wanted to know, downloaded instantaneously. What would happen with that kind of power?

Access to anything you ever wanted to know. Ever.

800 years is a long time.

Then why are we still living in stone houses and drilling for water?

Some say it's because the Imminent Darkness is keeping us from progressing. But no one seems to know why.

800 years ago the sun died and 3,000 people left Earth to populate a new planet: Xon 9, with its two moons, never-setting sun, pink sky, and balmy temperatures that never change. There was one catch: rogue elements that would affect our human physiology sometime after puberty. Once we reach our last school year, we have to pronounce an Element, a life-long affiliation. Fire is passion and impulsiveness like the uncontrollable flicker of a flame. Wood is steadfast and wise like the sturdiest of trees. Metal is brave and strong like an iron bridge. Water is intuitive and calm like a bubbling brook. Earth is reliable and nurturing like the ground beneath your feet.

I chose Fire.

Big mistake.

Turns out the Imminent Darkness had infiltrated some of the Elements and after Tristen created her Army of Fire, well, let's just say University is out indefinitely. (Everly, this one's for you. *Gulp.* Turns to bartender, "You know I still hate the taste of that stuff, thanks to you.")

I'd always thought I was ordinary and indecisive, but I was wrong. In fact, I am quite extraordinary. I found out I'm part of some kind of legend. Weird, right? Well, yeah, so the legend goes there's a girl (an *impossible* girl) who embodies all of Xon 9's Elements: Fire, Water, Wood, Metal, and Earth. But in order to protect her, Elemental Stones were thrown into the Elemental Abyss. So now, she has to retrieve these Stones from the Abyss, and with each retrieval a part of her now fractured personality will be returned. And once it's all returned? Watch out, Imminent Darkness, because you're going down.

Who, you might be wondering, would throw some strange magic rocks into an abyss? Well, it's strange what lengths we'll go to in order to protect the ones we love. You know, like traveling across the planet, trekking deep into a cavern, surviving an enchanted waterfall, and then leaping over a fiery chasm just to throw a few rocks into some portals that lead to other worlds. No big. Like I said, who would do that!?

Yeah, that would be my mom.

Novea Waylon.

CHAPTER 1

After our drink at the bar vendor, we head through the little alleyway to our ledge. I love the ledge. It looks out over the colony. Little lights sparkle in the distance. The warm breeze rustles my hair and kisses the back of my neck, caressing my now-healed Elemental Star tattoo. If only I'd known then how appropriate a tattoo representing all the Elements would truly be for me. It was impulsive, just like the Fire coursing through my veins, and I was drawn to the flash on the wall like a moth to a flame. Once a tattoo is bought, it's taken off the wall never to be used again. It's mine now, just like I have my Fire back. Now, I just need to restore what else is rightfully mine.

I tenderly push the thought aside. Not much time has passed

since my return from the Land of Fire and my boyfriend Sloan has practically had to stake me to the ground to convince me not to go rushing back to the Elemental Abyss for the next stone. Sloan is a few years older than me and used to be my teacher, which is weird in its own right, but then it got even weirder because I found out he had taken that position in order to watch over me and keep me safe. His mother, Bina, is an Unbalanced Metal with the gift of the Sight. She saw that the Impossible Girl was coming, but even she thought it was only a legend. However, as I got older she began to see me in detail and informed Sloan that I'd need a protector. He was up for the challenge apparently, not realizing, as he puts it, that he'd fall for the one he was protecting. Typical, right? We used to have a sort of love-hate relationship, but right now it's been more love than anything.

My leg is pressed against Sloan's as he takes a long drink of water, restoring his body's equilibrium. He turns toward me and the silvery-green scales on the right side of his face catch the pink light of Xon 9's sun. "You know, you really make Bernard crazy." He's referring to the bartender.

"Well, that one time, he totally tricked me! It wasn't very nice!" Once, I secretly followed Sloan into the Underground, to the outskirts of the Black Bazaar. And when I ordered a water at the bar, having never drank before, the bartender—Bernard—had tricked me. Let's just say my choking debacle not-so-discreetly attracted Sloan and his sister, Michaela's, attention.

Sloan chuckles at the memory. "I should be getting you home." He tucks a strand of brown hair behind my ear, green eyes teasing, expecting the protest before it even leaves my lips.

"I can get home by myself just fine!"

Normally, you'd expect an argument here. But not from Sloan. Even when I'm angry, he's calm as a pool of water.

"You know my responsibility. And I don't take it lightly. Especially now that we're…well, now that you're no longer just a student." He stumbles over the words, flushing slightly. "I made a promise."

"Speaking of which. I think it's time." He raises an eyebrow at me. "Time to retrieve the next stone. I'm fully recuperated." I pat my chest as if to prove my solidity.

"You don't have enough information. Just let me see what else I can find out. You don't know what the Imminent Darkness is capable of, and let me tell you, after your stint with the army of Fire, Tristen was less than happy." In order to protect me, Sloan has gone so far as to infiltrate the lower ranks of the Imminent Darkness. Risky indeed, but unfortunately, also means he misses out on some vital information. If he moves up in the ranks and is noticed, then he could put my life in jeopardy, the exact opposite of what we want. I look over his shoulder toward the alleyway. I am safer in the Underground. Bina told me so. What goes on in the Underground stays in the Underground. It's why the Black Bazaar is full of things you'd never see anywhere else: like fortune-tellers, tattoo shops, and bars. That doesn't mean they're invincible though. Nobody is.

"Waiting is just so frustrating!" I sigh. "You don't know what it's like. It's like I'm a broken dish and I can't put it back together because I don't have all the pieces."

His eyes sparkle. "You just compared yourself to a household item." I glare at him, but he just takes my hand and pulls me to my feet. "Time to get you home."

Before we head back, we stare out at the world below. It looks safe. However, I know that it's anything but. Secrets are hidden beneath the surface. Secrets that could change our society. Each other. Everything. His lips graze my cheek and I peer up at him.

"I promise you, we'll retrieve the next stone. Together. But it's too soon. They're waiting for something else to happen. And when it does, we'll have an even more difficult time getting to the Elemental Abyss."

I sigh, resigned. Often this is how the discussion ends. "Promise?"

"Always." And I know he's good for it because he's yet to break one. He wraps me in his arms, pressing my ear against his chest and I can hear the soft beat of his heart as he rests his chin on the top of my head. "And, Ka, you're anything but broken. I've never met someone more whole."

I don't reply. I know what he's saying. That I don't need the stones to be complete. But he doesn't understand. No one does. It's like I didn't realize I was even empty until my Fire was returned to me. And somehow the return of my Fire has emphasized the other four voids that much more. I don't just want the next stone, I *need* it.

. . .

I lie awake in bed staring at the ceiling. I should be in

University, adjusting to life with my fellow Elementals. But I'm not. I shut down that operation. Well, not me alone. I had Everly's help and Doran's. Everly is one of the first Fires I had met after initiation. She accompanied me into my Mindscape. A Mindscape is this super trippy thing where you're basically in your own consciousness, interacting with your own thoughts and dreams. Everly could only act as a witness, recording all that she observed. Only she had to lie about my Mindscape. Apparently, she saw things about myself that I didn't even know about yet, like the whole Impossible Girl thing.

One of the memories we traveled to was when I was just a kid. My mother had met with a Metal woman, whom I now know to be Bina, Sloan's mother. She was concerned because I'd shown tendencies for all the Elements. She feared that I was the legend come to life. Bina gave my mother five stones, one representing each of the Elements and instructed her to travel to the Elemental Abyss and throw each stone in reciting the mantra: Protection. Piety. Promise. With each toss of the stone, a piece of my personality was taken away…or rather I suppose put away for safe-keeping. Because now in order to defeat the Imminent Darkness I have to retrieve each of the stones.

I know my mom was only trying to help me. But how could she watch me be so lost all those years? I was always a plain kind of kid. I didn't excel at any one particular thing, not like my best friend Ahna who is a stellar student. No guys were ever interested in me, except Li, Ahna's twin brother, but that hardly counts because he's interested in everybody. For the last eighteen years I was just, I don't know, *there*. Not above average, nor below average. Just average. And that all changed when Everly told me she knew who I really was. She went to great lengths to protect me, even dying in battle, sacrificing her life to return the Fire stone to me. We were fighting side by side, then POOF! She was hit by a fireball from Tristen's army of Fire, and incinerated. As if she never even existed. Just a black smudge of soot on the stone floor.

My stomach recoils at the memory. I've tried to talk to Sloan about it. He tries to understand and I know that to some extent he does. After all his mother had a MindCleanse because of me. Luckily, it backfired because of her Sight and instead cleansed the mind of the person administering it. But not before Bina had a significant amount of her life energy drained. So, I know that he has just as much to lose as I do. But Everly died for me. Okay, maybe that's a little self-centered. She didn't die for me exactly, she died for what I represented to her.

Sloan put it best. At the University Complex is a great iron archway with the words: *divide et impera* scrolled across it in beautiful, metal calligraphy. I never thought much about it, but Sloan was my Universal History Teacher, so he's all into that sort of stuff. I just assumed it meant that if we divide ourselves we can conquer anything, not like Xon 9 is in danger of being attacked or anything, but I guess more like we could control the rogue Elements if we divided ourselves up, and chose our Elemental affiliation. But Sloan insists that's wrong. He says the motto is a reminder to the Imminent Darkness that they divide us in order to conquer us. That in order for them to exert control, they must create separation. Sure, we all get along more or less, any Element can marry another for example. My mother is an Earth and my father a Wood. A good, solid match. But Sloan and me…well, Water and Fire both complement one another, where I am passionate he is calm, but both are quite unpredictable. And an Unbalanced Elemental is a completely different thing. Unbalanced Elementals can be extremely dangerous. That's why I always thought Unbalanced Metals lived in the Underground. Because the rest of the colony put them there, but in actuality it is self-imposed. Metal is invasive and the most likely to become Unbalanced. Metals make up our entire military: they are brave and strong. But an Unbalanced Metal can be aggressive and deceitful, thus the nature of the Black Bazaar. Only recently did I learn that many people show qualities of more than one Element, yet they're forced to choose only one, and wear that label for the rest of their lives.

None of it makes any sense. Why would anyone not want our society to thrive? What would the Imminent Darkness gain from dividing us up into these little categories? I feel a headache forming behind my eyelids, pulsing inside my skull. I haven't slept much since I came back home. My nights are filled with dreams. Sometimes they're sweet, like Sloan and me swimming in a vast sea, the likes of which I've never seen except in my dreams. But usually they're nightmares. Everly's death replays over and over an endless loop. Or it's me drowning in order for the real me to survive the enchanted waterfall at the Abyss. Or Li telling me to run before the collective conscious registered that he recognized me, the veins bulging in his forehead as he tried to resist the fireball already conjuring in his hand. The black tattoo that was once golden filigree on the side of my roommate Rhian's face as she lay barely breathing after the explosion.

I finger the back of my neck where my Elemental tattoo is usually hidden by my long, brown hair. It's healed now. Smooth to the touch, except one of the star's points. As I was getting ready for my date with Sloan earlier tonight I noticed that it seemed…different. I leaned over my dresser, using two mirrors to inspect it closer. At first I thought my eyes were playing tricks on me. The point of the star representing Fire, realistic flames carefully drawn by my friend Zora, seemed to shimmer golden in the pink light from my bedroom window. Just like the beautiful filigree that adorns the faces of the Fires. Just like I thought it would inevitably adorn my own face.

Li and the others had been injected with something to rapidly expedite the Change, virtually eliminating the Transitional Phase all new Elementals go through. It could have killed them. It almost did. I move my hand to the right side of my face. Smooth. I can practically feel the Fire coursing through my veins, not burning like it did at first, but more like an aliveness, a sort of energy buzzing from the top of my head to the bottom of my toes. I turn onto my side. The curtains on my window blow in the warm breeze and the deep pink of the sun casts a perfect square onto the bedroom floor. I close my eyes and wait for sleep to come.

. . .

The first thing I notice is the smokiness in the air that burns my eyes. I squeeze them shut then open them to slits. The sky is black. Something hits the top of my head and I reach up and touch my hair. Something soft. I hold my fingers close to my face to better inspect them. Ash. I know where I am. I am in the Land of Fire. It's where I went to retrieve the first stone. Last time my friend Doran, Zora's brother, went with me. And I am thankful he did, because he was spared Li and Rhian's fate as Fire soldiers. This time I am alone.

I'm wearing boots and I can feel the hot ground permeating their soles. In the distance I can see the volcano which housed the Fire stone, on a pedestal. Its removal caused the eruption. I'm not sure why I'm here this time. If it's raining ash then the volcano already erupted. I shield my eyes and try to scan the horizon, but the smoke is too thick. I look down at my feet and now I understand why the soles of my boots feel like they're on fire. They practically are. Lava in the various stages of cooling is all around me. It's definitely after the stone's retrieval. But I don't know how long. I didn't pay enough attention in Science class I guess.

I decide to walk toward the volcano. I am wearing a jacket and I pull my hood up and over to try and shield my eyes, periodically lifting my gaze to make sure I am headed in the right direction. At first I think I am imagining it. Through the haziness I see a misty shadow that appears to be coming toward me. I'm aware that I'm dreaming and safe in my bed at home, but like all my dreams this one feels very real. The figure is getting closer and through the smoke I see that it is taking the shape of a small figure wearing a hooded cloak. My heart pounds in my chest. Is it a member of the

Imminent Darkness?

Soon the figure is close enough where I see gray eyes peering at me from beneath the hood and then a nearly toothless smile. Bina. "Ye visited this Land once, Girl, why do ye keep coming back?"

Her words catch me off guard. "How do you know I keep coming back?" I haven't told Bina about my nightmares. Or Sloan for that matter.

She ignores my question. "Ye need to move on. The answers you seek are no longer here. Ye got what ye came for." As if in response the volcano in the distance lets out a rumble.

"Well, then where do I find them?" I ask exasperatedly. The raining ash seems to come down in thicker swirls. And even though Bina only stands a foot away it gives her a strange ethereal affect.

"'Tis right in front of yer face! Ye will find the answers at the beginning not at the end."

"That doesn't even make sense!" I protest. But she just smiles and begins to fade away, although I'm not sure if she's truly fading away, or if it's just the effect of the ash and haze.

Her voice languidly floats to me through the smoke. "The beginning has the answers ye seek."

CHAPTER 2

"Wait. Tell me again what she said?" Ahna asks.

We're swinging on the swings in the park in between where we live and the school that we used to attend before Pronouncement. It's where Sloan—Teacher 4—is at right now actually. Despite the closing of the University Complex, most life has continued as normal. People still go to school. My parents, and Sloan, still go to work. Some kids, like my friend Doran, who is helping out his mom at her shop in the Black Bazaar, have jobs to bide their time until the University Complex reopens. If it reopens. I don't think Doran will be going back anytime soon. When I first met Doran I thought he was an insolent punk, but I was shocked when I saw the Fire Leader, Tristen, use physical reprimand on him, and more than once. She also used it on Everly, but I'd rather not think about that either. Not exactly on purpose, Doran ended up traveling to the Elemental Abyss with me. I ended up being glad he did too because he saved my butt on more than one occasion.

I had just finished telling Ahna about my dream. Ahna has been my best friend since before I could talk. Her long hair is jet-black and she wears it in a thick braid. She has tawny skin and deep brown, almond-shaped eyes. Not only is she beautiful, but she's also the smartest person that I know. Ahna chose Earth at Pronouncement. She was going to study Medicine. Earths are excellent nurturers, yet have the ability to make sound decisions, never letting their emotions interfere.

"She said, 'Ye will find the answers at the beginning not the end.'" I repeat Bina's words, accent and all.

"And you can't just go and ask her or Teacher 4, I mean *Sloan*, why?" She swings higher and higher, kicking her legs into the pink sky. Her words fade in and out as she gets closer than flies away again, so I can clearly hear about every other word that she says.

I twist the chains of the swing, inching myself up until my toes just touch the red dirt beneath me. And then I let go, spinning, enjoying the rush of dizziness as the world soars by in a blur of pink, gray, and white. The vegetation on Xon 9 leaves much to be desired probably due to the whole water underground thing, but all the foliage takes on a blah grayish-green foliage.

"Because even if I did go and ask her, she wouldn't tell me. She'd just say the same thing. And Sloan's still weird about the interfering stuff. I mean he's come around since we destroyed the Fire stone, but considering I practically drowned, he's not real keen on looking for the next stone without more information."

Ahna digs her heels into the ground and comes to a stop beside me. "Typical," she says and suppresses a smile. She claims she knew I was always Teacher 4's favorite, which he had a funny way of showing it, because to me it seemed like he was always singling me out. "Of course he wants more information. I see your point about Bina too. How's she doing by the way?"

"I haven't really seen her since she's staying with Sloan's sister, Michaela. And then Michaela moved out of the Underground. But from what he says she's become more forgetful. He also claims her Sight doesn't seem as strong as before the MindCleanse."

Ahna lets out a shudder. "That is so horrible. I can't believe they do that to people. Travel inside their mind then wipe it clean. I wonder what happens to them after that."

I shrug. I'd rather not think about it. "Well, I'm glad it backfired on whoever was doing it. Maybe they'll think twice before trying to wipe out someone's memories."

"Doubt it." We sit in amicable silence for a moment. "If Bina's Sight is weakened, then how do you know it was actually her in the dream and not just, well, a dream?"

I consider this. I tell Ahna everything, well, almost everything. I haven't told her about the super vivid dreams with Sloan before we truly got involved. I would dream I was in an ocean and he'd always be there, staring at me, just beneath the surface. Or not to mention the dream I had at the Elemental Abyss where he informed me I had to drown in the dream in order to break the enchantment and wake up in reality. I think it's safe to assume Sloan has some of his mother's abilities. "I just know." I recall Bina's steely gray eyes, the hooded cloak shielding her face from the raining ash. The Imminent Darkness wear cloaks too, but theirs are thick and velvety. Bina's was thin and raggedy. She's not one for frivolous things. Up until the attempted MindCleanse, she lived and worked out of her own trailer in the Black Bazaar. That's how I met her—before I knew she was Sloan's mother.

"Okay," Ahna draws out the word slowly and I can tell she doesn't completely believe me. I mean, I know she believes I had the dream, but I'm not sure she's convinced it was an actual visitation from Bina. "What are the answers you're looking for?"

I sigh. Where do I even begin? "Well, I'd like to know which stone to retrieve next."

"And?"

I scan the horizon. To our left are the concrete houses in the complex where we grew up. Small houses with three bedrooms upstairs, a small kitchen with a table, and a living space. Modest homes in a barren landscape. Our food is grown in greenhouses, but we also have nutrient pills that can supplement meals. It never rains. The sun never sets. Xon 9's two moons rise and set to mark a day's time. The temperature is always around 67 degrees Fahrenheit with a warm breeze. The ground is a hard sienna-colored clay dirt. Here and there are tufts of brownish-gray colored grass. There are no flowers.

There are no wild animals running about. However, we do have livestock, but they are contained and used as a food source, created using cells and embryos brought with the original 3,000 people who came to inhabit Xon 9. We can't fish because there is no surface water. Our fish, like all our food, is genetically modified, grown, and contained. I recall the one time I went to the Earth Building in the University Complex to visit Ahna. There was a gorgeous waterfall and lush green foliage. I notice the tiniest wisp of a green curlicue beginning behind Ahna's right ear, the signs of her beginning the Change. Soon it will look like my mother's: long green vines, like veins, running down the side of her face and around her ear. My mother.

"My mother. How did she know I was different? Why did she go to such great lengths to protect me? Did she know that someday I'd have to retrieve the stones? And why didn't she ever tell me who I was?" I can feel the burn of tears behind my eyeballs. That last question is the one that's bothered me the most since I found out about this whole legend of the Impossible Girl thing. How is it I found out from two complete strangers who I truly was and how was it that my own mother knew and never told me? For eighteen years I fumbled through school and through fitting in, Ahna and Li being my only friends really. Always indecisive, unable to make up my mind about what Elemental to pronounce until the last minute and even then making an impulsive, regretful decision. No, not regretful, I am thankful for the Fire that runs through me. Fire is the life force: energy, passion, aliveness. But I am sad it cost others so much for me to have it.

Ahna is quiet. "That's a lot of questions." My mom is like a second mother to her, what, with how much time we've spent together. "You need to talk to her, Ka."

I feel my shoulders sink. I know Ahna is right. It's just about the last thing that I want to do. I can already hear her protests now. That it's too dangerous for me to retrieve the stones. That it's better to leave well-enough alone. It was difficult enough to get her and my father to accept the fact that I was dating a guy four years older than me, let alone to get them to accept that I'm planning on taking down the Imminent Darkness. "I know."

"Sooner rather than later. I think that's what Bina was trying to tell you. Maybe what you need to know is something that needs to come from your mother. She's the one who started this whole thing, right? By seeking protection for you and throwing the stones into the Elemental Abyss." She turns to look at me and her eyes are contemplative. "Truly, you only saw one side of the story in your Mindscape. Bina isn't telling and you only saw things from your child-like perspective." As usual, she's right. In my Mindscape I was about six and playing with my wooden blocks in the living room while my mother met with a Metal woman. I only picked up bits of the conversation and my mother's worried body language. Maybe there's more to it than what I can remember.

"You know what they say," Ahna continues beginning to slowly swing again.

This time I swing too, pumping my legs so that we're in

unison. She reaches her hand out across the space between us and I do the same, our fingers barely touching. I can't believe that at one point I thought I'd have to do all this alone. Alone is the last thing I've been since all this started.

"No, what do they say?" I ask.

Ahna continues to soar and there's a hint of laughter as she says, "There are three sides to every story: yours, theirs, and the truth."

. . .

Usually, my mother gets home before my father. Today's no different. While the University Complex may no longer be open for students, it is still open for employees. All buildings were closed for a short time for inspections, but then reopened. Except Fire, which is closed indefinitely for obvious reasons. Lately, Mom has looked really tired. Dark circles rim her golden-brown eyes and gray streaks line her brown hair. I'm preparing some rice and beans for dinner in the small kitchen when she comes home. "Hey, Kata," she smiles, setting down her work bag. She kisses my forehead. Mom is a professor and researcher at the Earth Building. Mainly she researches sustainable ways of growing food. One of the original problems back on planet Earth, was the food supply was too low for the population—over seven billion people—how is that even possible!? Mom makes sure that never happens on Xon 9, even though our population is nowhere near that. In fact, our population hasn't increased all that much since the first inhabitants arrived here. Another one of the other mysterious workings of the Imminent Darkness.

I stir the beans into the pot of rice. "Mom? Do you have a minute? Can we talk?" Recently, she's been bringing home a lot of her research, holing herself up in the office down the hall from my bedroom, staying up well into the night. Her work tends to ebb and flow. She claims she is extra busy and has additional pressure when the department decides to bring in the scientists.

She sits down at the table and uses her index and middle fingers to rub her forehead while her thumbs massage her temples. "Are you having boy troubles?" I want to tell her Sloan is hardly a boy. Mom never approved of my hanging out with Li. Don't get me wrong she loves Ahna, but everything Ahna is her twin brother is not. Li is handsome, mischievous, and impulsive. But he helped me sneak out of the Fire Building numerous times on my missions and he tried to save my life, telling me to run away, but I refused to run when my friends needed my help.

I shake my head. "No, every thing's great with Sloan." I turn the flame down to simmer and pull out the chair across from her. After the incident at Fire, vague letters were sent to parents of students explaining that the University Complex was under investigation for endangering students. Of course, Mom knew a little bit more because she works at the Complex. She knew that the Fire Leaders had injected the newest Fires with some sort of serum to expedite the Changeling Phase. She knows that it somehow backfired and all their Fire was drained. She's seen the black, tattoo-like marks on the side of Li's face. She also knows that Fire is still under investigation for conspiracy to overthrow the Council of Leaders—a group of five Wood Elementals who act as our governing body. But that's where her knowledge ends. I didn't tell her that I'm the one who caused the army of Fire soldiers to be drained, that I'm the one who caused the scar Li will wear for the rest of his life. I also didn't tell her about my numerous visits to Bina or about my trip to the Elemental Abyss to retrieve the Fire stone. As far as she knows I've been simply biding my time until I can return to University.

"I was kind of wondering...well, about me." A flicker of recognition in her golden eyes, as if she'd expected this moment, but then it's gone almost as quickly as it appeared. She shifts uncomfortably in her seat.

"I'm not sure what you mean, Kata?" Kata is the nickname my friends and family use for me. Kata means *pure one*. But Ka, Ka means *Fire*. The irony of both is not lost on me.

"Well, a while ago, I visited a Metal woman with the Sight in the Black Bazaar..." I start. Her eyes flash with anger at the act of disobedience. My parents have never approved of the Underground or the Black Bazaar. Another reason they didn't like me hanging out with Li. But they don't know the Underground as I now know it.

"Ka, you know that your father and I don't approve of you going to the Black Bazaar—" But I cut her off.

"Like I said, it was a while ago. But that's not the point." She shifts again in her seat. It isn't often I've ever been disrespectful. In fact, I can't ever recall a time where I interrupted my mother or father when speaking. She runs her hand over the worn surface of the wooden table. "The point is what she told me. She told me: *You are all possibilities and yet you are impossible. You are the Impossible Girl."* I recite Bina's words exactly, forever ingrained in my brain. When I say them my mother freezes, her hand stops running over the table surface and her body grows rigid. She snaps her head up and the anger has not faded from her eyes, like little fires glowing from deep inside.

"It's nonsense. You can't trust a Metal, Ka. Especially one with the Sight." Her jaw is set and the words come out clipped. I'm not about to tell her that the Metal woman is Sloan's mother. Nor am I about to tell her that I've seen—*felt*—it for myself and know the words to be true. Her shoulders seem to relax a little and she lets out a placating smile, like you'd use with a small child who just said they saw monsters in their bedroom closet. "Kata, the Impossible Girl is just a legend. It isn't true. It's as legendary as the Old Earth stories, the gods and goddesses, the myths. Simply a story either told to explain naturally occurring things before we understood the science that explained them, or to assuage people's fears. The Impossible Girl falls into the latter."

This isn't going quite as I'd expected, so I decide that I need to pull out the biggest piece of proof that I have. "In my Mindscape I saw you meeting with a Metal woman." Her smile quickly fades.

"Your Mindscape is simply your own recollection of events and dreams. It doesn't mean it's true." She waves her hand dismissively.

"So you never met with a Metal woman when I was little?" I clearly remember it. I was there, both as a child and in my

Mindscape. Everly was there too. We both saw it. And, more obviously, Bina was there too. Bina wouldn't lie to me. Mom stands up, placing her palms flat onto the table.

"Maybe I did, maybe I didn't. I can't exactly remember every person I've ever had a meeting with in the last eighteen years, Kata."

"But I saw it," I mumble. I am not doubting myself, but I am doubting why my mother wouldn't be truthful with me.

"I think you saw what you wanted to see," she replies simply. "I have some work to finish. I'll be upstairs." She picks up her bag and disappears up the stairs.

I slump back in the chair frustrated. That's not how I thought it would go at all. My mother has never been so quick to put up a wall between us. Usually, she's all into talking about our feelings and all that junk. *I think you saw what you wanted to see.* I am more perceptive than she realizes. Her words said one thing, but her eyes said another. Her eyes said, *Leave it, Ka. You were never supposed to know. Its' my job to protect you and that's what I am doing.*

I get up from the chair and move toward the stove, continuing to absent-mindedly stir the beans. The answers to the end lie with the beginning. If my mother has the answers, but refuses to give them to me then how will I ever know? A frightening thought occurs to me. What if the Imminent Darkness is even more dangerous than I've realized? In order to protect me, my mother is willing to withhold me knowing my true identity, but maybe I am not the only one that she's protecting. The skin on the back of my neck prickles as if in agreement.

. . .

"She wouldn't tell you anything at all?" The next day Ahna, Li, and I sit at the playground on some spinning, merry-go-round type thing. I still have a hard time looking at Li and what I did to him, even though he's told me numerous times since the incident, that it's not my fault and he's just thankful to be alive, without Fire, scars and all. *Besides*, he'd said gesturing to himself, *who needs Fire when you've got this?*

I pick at some of the peeling yellow paint on the merry-go-round, not feeling very merry. "Nope. She basically told me I imagined the whole thing, and only saw what I wanted to see."

"Mindscapes don't lie," Ahna points out.

"How am I ever going to find out what the heck Bina meant? If my mom won't give me the answers I need, then how am I supposed to find them?"

"I don't know," Ahna bites her lip. She's just as frustrated as I am.

"Really?" Li looks at both of us in disbelief. "You are two of the smartest people I know and you can't figure out where people go to find out answers?" We look at him quizzically. He stares at us and shakes his head like he can't believe our own dumbness. "You go where you always go to find answers."

"The Black Bazaar?" I ask, confused.

"No, silly, the library."

CHAPTER 3

The Earth Building has a beautiful library hidden behind large wooden doors with cast iron-ringed handles. As we navigate down the built-in steps that spiral along the dirt walls, Li gapes at the gigantic waterfall, the likes of which he's probably never seen before. It's his first time in the Earth Building, my second, and the effect of the rushing water in its place of honor and the atrium above it letting the pink light trickle in, have a sort of stunning affect. I nudge him and he continues to follow Ahna down the stairs.

When we reach the bottom a few people pass us. They have green vines with tiny green leaves that cover the right side of their face and climb down their necks, just like my mother. Ahna nods a greeting and expertly navigates her way to the library. The last time I was here was after my initiation into Fire. New Elementals are not really suppsoed. to interact with others outside of their Element.

One, in order to create a cohort of sorts and two, because the Transition Phase can be on the unpredictable side as new initiates try to harness control of the changes in their physiology.

We reach the doors and Li makes a grand gesture of pulling one open and ushering us in. "After you, madams," he grins cheekily. I roll my eyes and enter into the library. The library has a circular center area with a librarian positioned behind the counter along with several hovering monitor screens. Li and I follow Ahna past corridors of books. The wooden shelves go from floor to ceiling. Iron chandeliers casting a golden glow hang from the dirt-packed, beam-reinforced ceiling. The aisles of books are broken up with areas containing long wooden tables with chairs for research and study.

"The entire library is climate controlled since it's underground," Ahna explains as we make our way to a far corner. She stops when we reach a wooden door tucked inside an archway. It has a metal plaque nailed to the front reading: *Restricted Area: Ancient & Rare Texts*. "Li got me thinking after he suggested we come here. We're not just looking for answers about your mother. We're also looking for answers about the Imminent Darkness. Who they are and what they want."

"Don't forget The Impossible Girl," I add. "We want information about her too."

"You don't know yourself?" Li quips with a grin.

"You know what I mean."

"Right, so as I was saying," Ahna continues, "I have a feeling in order to find that information we'd have to delve a little deeper.

Both literally and figuratively." She smiles at her own joke before pulling open the door to the *Ancient & Rare Texts*. We're greeted by a rush of cool air. At the bottom of a short staircase I can see the glow of light. A wooden handrail lines either side of the staircase, which is also narrow, only able to fit one person at a time.

Ahna descends and I follow with Li behind me. He pulls the door closed and I feel the hair on the back of my neck prickle. We quickly reach the bottom of the staircase and are greeted by a giant mahogany desk. A woman with shiny black hair past her shoulders and almond shaped eyes sits behind it. "Hey, Mona," Ahna greets her.

"Oh, hey Ahna. I see you've brought some friends."

"Yeah, you know. I'm always doing research, whether University is in session or not! This is my brother, Li, and my friend, Ka."

"Pleased to meet you guys. Listen, Ahna, my shift ends soon, so if you could just turn the lights off on your way out that would be great."

"Sure, no problem, Mona!" Ahna replies brightly. We wave good-bye to Mona. It doesn't surprise me that Ahna is on a first-name basis with the librarians or that they'd trust her in restricted areas without supervision. She's a very dedicated student and I think books are a sort of sacred space for her.

We walk past sections with labels like: *Old Earth Classics*, *Ancient Earth Religions*, and *Ancient Earth Mythology*. We stop at a section labeled *Original Settlements*. "What's that mean?" Li asks gesturing to the sign.

"These are all the journals, notes, and documents from the first settlement of Xon 9."

"Do you really think we need to go back that far? Ka's only eighteen."

"Yeah, but the Imminent Darkness has been around much longer than that," I say finally catching on. "Even Sloan has said that our society hasn't progressed to nearly where we were on Earth before we left. Supposedly that's the work of the Imminent Darkness."

Satisfied, Ahna smiles. "Exactly, so if we want to find out more about the Imminent Darkness we have to find their first mention." She starts pulling out books. Large books, thick books, small books, thin books. Some are so old they look like they'd fall apart if you so much as looked at them. As she pulls them she hands them to either me or Li. Finally, once she's satisfied we move to a battered wooden table. There are about thirty books total. We each pull several from the pile and begin scanning for any mention of the Imminent Darkness.

The first book I open has a journal entry from an agriculturalist. There are lots of entries about the greenhouses, as well as failed experiments, but no mention of the Imminent Darkness. I close it and place it off to the side. The next book is about the establishment of the Leadership Council and how it came to be that only Wood Elementals should govern. It then continues into the Laws and Amendments of Xon 9. I can feel my eyelids begin to slide closed. I have no idea how Sloan taught History for so long, nor how I ever stayed awake in his class. Li yanks the book out of my hands and adds it to our growing discard pile. "If I don't get a nap, you don't get a nap," he says handing me a new book. I scowl at him.

The book is thin and frayed all around the edges. The cover is a soft, supple leather. The binding is worn and it almost looks like a small journal. The title is embossed in a pretty golden calligraphy: *The Five Goddesses*. There's no author listed. Intrigued, I flip gently through the book. The inside text is hand-written, furthering my suspicions that it's a diary or journal. At the back, there are also hand-drawn illustrations, done in now-faded watercolor. I return to the beginning and read the first page: *In the beginning there were five sisters. The sisters were the beautiful daughters of Katayun and Raj.* I pause. That's funny. Her name is sort of similar to mine: Kata and Katayun. I shrug it off as coincidence and return my attention to the book. *The sisters were happy children who roamed the Universe. They traveled anywhere they pleased and all of the Universe was shared betwixt them. One day the five sisters met a weary traveler. He appeared elderly and wore a dark hooded cloak that covered much of his face. 'I have traveled long and far to come to you,' the traveler explained. 'I have brought a gift for each of you.' The sisters chuckled and the eldest replied, 'Dear, Old Man, but what could you give to us that we do not already have? We have the entire Universe shared betwixt us.' The old man proceeded to pull objects from his bag and with each object he handed it to one of the sisters. The objects were beautiful stones. 'To the eldest the stone of Fire. May you rule your land with unbridled passion. To the second eldest, the stone of Water. May you rule your land with the calmness of the sea at sunset. To the middle sister, the stone of Wood. May you rule your land with the firmness of the oak tree.' He continued handing objects. 'To the second to youngest, the stone of Metal. May you rule your land with the same ferocity from which iron is forged. And to the youngest, the Earth stone. May you rule your land with the balance of sky and sea.' The sisters were confused. They did not rule separate lands. They were daughters of the Universe itself, birthed from the galaxies. 'Dear, Stranger, we thank you for the gifts, but we do not rule separately, we roam the Universe together in harmony.' Then a peculiar thing happened. The stranger began to laugh and it was a horrible, disconcerting sound. 'Divide et impera' He replied before disappearing in a poof of smoke. The sisters regarded each other uneasily. It didn't take long for the stones to begin to have their effect. Each sister became more and more possessive of what they felt fell into the realm of jurisdiction for their stone. The happiness betwixt them faded and the sisters became suspicious and jealous of one another until Raj finally had to intervene. He created five portals and within each portal he created a land that would belong to each of his daughters: a land of fire, a land of water, a land of wood, a land of metal, and a land of earth. Katayun was saddened to see her daughters go their separate ways and as a farewell memento each daughter gave their mother a kiss, and with each kiss a piece of their element placed itself inside her heart, the only place where the sisters resided in harmony. And thus, the Five Elemental Goddesses were birthed.*

I flip to the back of the book where the illustrations are located. There is a full-page portrait of Raj and Katayun, kind of floating among the stars of the Universe. It's quite beautiful, even though it is faded, I can still sense its ethereal qualities. There are also portraits of each daughter. The Fire Goddess has flowing red locks and amber-colored eyes, flaming filigree lines the right side of her face. She reminds me a little bit of Tristen, but a much prettier version. The Water Goddess's face is adorned with the telltale scales and her eyes are a piercing violet. The artist conveyed her potential for both calmness and fierceness, just like her Element namesake. The Wood Goddess has brown eyes and brown hair, tendrils of bark lining the side of her face, she appears plain compared to her sisters. The next page is the Metal Goddess and the image is striking. The silver threads, the same as Bina and Zora, intertwine along the side of her face. Her eyes are a steely gray and her hair is white, close-cropped, and spiky. She looks more like a warrior than a goddess. I turn to the last page and feel the color drain from my face. Looking back at me is a water-color portrait of my mother.

. . .

"Woah," says Li leaning over my shoulder. "It's Mrs. Waylon."

Ahna leans in from my other side and studies the water-color portrait. "Well, I wouldn't say it's exactly Mrs. Waylon." I study the picture. The golden brown eyes, shoulder-length brown hair, and small round nose are almost identical. The curve of her lips, merely similar. The freckle below her left eye, also identical, as well as the curlicues of green vines and tendrils coursing the side of her face.

"If it's not my mother," I find myself saying, "then it appears she has an identical twin."

"I'm just saying, there are theories that say there are only so many human facial templates. Supposedly, in the Old Earth days when there were billions of people, there would be someone somewhere else in the world who could appear to be your identical twin, or sibling. And the people wouldn't even know each other existed. There's been studies on it."

"Who reads up on this stuff?" Li asks.

"When I have spare time, I like to look into the various theories of humanity. You know, for fun."

"You have a strange definition of fun, Sister." Li says, taking the book from my hands, and flipping it back to the beginning. "There's no author."

"I noticed," is all I can manage. My mind is reeling about a bazillion kilometers a minute. Is it just coincidence, some kind of human template twin, as Ahna explained, or is this an actual portrait of my mother? The logical side of my brain puts the brakes on that almost immediately. First of all, I think I'd notice if my mother was a goddess. Secondly, I went to the Land of Fire and didn't run into any Fire goddesses. The woman in the book does slightly resemble Tristen. But Tristen's nose is pointier and her eyes closer together. At best, if the portrait in the book is based on actual people, at best they'd be cousins.

Li continues to study the book. "You know this guy here, the bad guy, didn't you say members of the Imminent Darkness wear this kind of cloak?"

"It's probably just a coincidence. All the wicked witches in those fairy tales we read as kids had hooded cloaks. It's like standard bad guy protocol." I have an uneasy feeling settling in my stomach and Li's observations aren't helping.

"Oh-kay. But what about when he says 'Divide et impera.' That's what the arch at the entrance to the University Complex has on it."

"Li's right. And didn't you say that Sloan said something about it not meaning what we think it means? I always thought it meant, like, divide your troubles and you can conquer them together. Kind of like that old saying about dividing your sorrows and multiplying the joys. But Sloan said it means that if they divide *us*, then they can control us more easily," Ahna adds getting into it.

"Something like that," I mumble.

"And, Ka, what about the most obvious. Katayun. I mean really?" Li asks waving the fragile book around. I grab it out of his hands before he can damage it, and slip it carefully into my messenger bag.

"Again coincidence," I respond with a little more confidence. "The Earth Goddess portrait can be explained…maybe it's a distant relative or like Ahna said, just one of the human templates for facial features. And maybe the Imminent Darkness got the whole idea from this story, just like my mom could have gotten my name from the story. It's obviously really old."

"Then how come we've never heard of it?" Ahna asks.

I throw my arms up in the air helplessly. "How should I know? Are you implying that my mom is an ancient goddess and that I'm some kind of queen of the Universe?" Even weirder, that would make me both my mother's mother and my mother's daughter. I may not be that great at science, but I'm pretty sure that's biologically impossible.

"Of course not. I'm merely suggesting that the situation needs further investigating. The number of coincidences are a bit unsettling." I don't bother to tell Ahna about the portals in the Elemental Abyss and how they correspond to the ones mentioned in the story. I need to sort this out myself. Figure out fact from fiction, fiction from fact. She gathers up several of the books and puts them into her tote bag. "Normally, they don't loan these out, but I'll leave a note for Mona telling her I borrowed them and will bring them back tomorrow."

"Wow, rebel twin, watch out," Li quips.

Ahna glares at him. "Besides I need something to do while we're on hiatus from University." She disappears out the door to leave Mona a note at the desk. Li and I get up to follow. We stack the remaining books neatly, push in the chairs and turn out the lights. Li gestures toward the door with a smirk on his face.

"After you, Your Royal Highness Queen of the Universe."

. . .

By the time I get home, it's late and my parents are asleep. The light is on in the study upstairs, so I peek in the doorway to be sure my mom isn't up working late again. Honestly, she's the last person I feel like seeing right now. But she just forgot to turn the light off. The story of the five goddesses rests like a lead weight in my bag. There are books on the desk and I find myself unable to suppress my curiosity. I close the door softly behind me and tiptoe over to the desk, careful to sidestep the squeaky part in the middle of the floor. Her desk is beneath the window. "The least I can do if I'm working from home is to be able to look out at the world," she'd explained to me once. The window is open slightly and the warm breeze rustles the curtains.

The books are stacked neatly to the side. I look at the spines. *Sustainable Best Practices, The Plight to Feed Seven Billion, A Full-Report of Xon 9 Food Sustainability.* Just boring, old research. Nothing suspicious there. I feel a slight pang of disappointment. The curtains sway in the breeze and the white light of the moon catches something. I turn. One of the desk's drawers is pulled slightly open. The light has caught something old and bronze colored. I go to pull the drawer further open, so that I can get a better look at the object, but the drawer is stuck. Which also explains why it doesn't close all the way. I yank on the metal knob again trying to get the drawer to open. I sit down at the desk chair and brace my foot on the underside of the desk then grip the knob again and pull with all my might. The drawer comes loose, sending me off balance and tipping back, I grab the edge of the desk to steady myself, and the chair falls back with a soft thud. I hold my breath, waiting for my mother or father to come running down the hallway at the prospect of their house being broken into. I wait a beat and neither comes. I place the pulled-out drawer on top of the desk and turn the chair upright. Luckily, it fell on top of the woven area rug which had softened the sound.

I return to the drawer's contents. I can see now that the object that caught the light of the moon is a tarnished, bronze-colored key. A very old key…what did they used to call them? A skeleton key. It's heavy in my hand and has elaborate interlocking circles on one end—five of them—and two jagged teeth on the opposite end. I don't know why, but I find myself slipping it carefully into my bag. Something tells me that it could be important, but I'm not sure why just yet.

I continue to rummage through the drawer. There are some pens and pencils, message tubes (all with red lights indicating no messages), a magnifying glass, and several blank notebooks, as well as several pieces of loose coin. I'm placing the drawer back into place, pushing carefully on the bottom to ease it back in gently when I notice that the bottom of the drawer isn't flush with the sides. Most likely the reason that it wouldn't close all the way. I try to jostle it around and when I do the bottom slides over, but the rest of the drawer stays in place. The drawer has a false bottom. It's not very deep, maybe enough space for some papers or something. I slide it out slowly. Inside is a folded up piece of paper and a medium-sized burlap pouch. The pouch is empty, but I recognize it almost immediately. I feel around in my bag and pull out my own pouch that is identical. My pouch contains a speckled feather, a crystal, a pack of matches from The Old Tavern and the Sea, and a vial of clear liquid. Gifts from Bina to help me destroy the Elemental Stones and restore the fractured pieces of my personality. I enclose both sacks in the palm of my hand and hastily unfold the piece of paper, which I can tell has been folded, unfolded, and refolded many times.

It's a map. I recognize our colony, the Underground and University Complex clearly marked, the rough-drawn mountains of

Xon 9, behind the mountains a cavern. Inside the cavern a small lake with a waterfall, which I happen to already know is enchanted. A large crevice and then a cavernous area with five doors, clearly labeled: Fire, Earth, Wood, Metal, Water. It's a hand-drawn map of the Elemental Abyss. Written in my mother's neat print in the bottom right corner are the words: Promise. Piety. Protection. *I think you saw what you wanted to see.* I carefully refold the paper and place it inside my bag with the two pouches and the key. So it is true. *Well, Mom, maybe you're the one who's seeing what* you *want to see.* Or more apt, what you *don't* want to see.

CHAPTER 4

Bina has a trailer in which she lives and works located in the Black Bazaar. While she recuperates from the MindCleanse attempt, she's staying with Michaela. Michaela is also a Metal and she lives on the outskirts of the Underground, straddling the rest of the community. The colony of Xon 9 was originally created with 3,000 people from Earth. Since our arrival, the population hasn't really grown much more than that. If it's because we learned the error of our ways or some other force, like the Imminent Darkness, is at work I've yet to determine. Besides at the University Complex, we don't reside strictly with our fellow Elementals. Ahna's family and my parents live in angular houses constructed of concrete and stone. I make my way past the Underground and toward a community that's a more eclectic mix of wooden and stone houses.

Sloan's house is also made of stone. Where my parents' house is angular, his is all curves. The doorway is an inviting wooden door that opens into a spacious main area with smaller pods for the bathroom, bedroom, and kitchen off the larger one. The ceiling is high and arching with a window at the very top that lets in the natural light of Xon 9, casting the house in a warm pink glow as the never-setting sun's light bounces off the stone's light-colored walls. Even though he's expecting me, I knock anyways. He answers the door in a t-shirt and sweatpants, barefoot. It isn't early, but he looks like he's just woken up, brown hair askew.

"Rough night?" I ask, entering and closing the door behind me. He disappears into the kitchen pod and I make myself comfortable on the worn sofa in the middle of the space, dropping my bag onto the round table that's directly beneath the sky light. Sloan's house is simple, yet cozy. Kind of like he is.

He reappears from the kitchen pod with two steaming stoneware mugs. He hands me one. "You've no idea. It's not easy working all day then going to these secretive Imminent Darkness meetings. I didn't get in til the moons were almost down."

I take a sip of the coffee, inhaling the earthy aroma. "Did you learn anything interesting?"

He sighs, running his hands through his hair. "No. And that's the frustrating part. Tristen is still suspended. Apparently, whoever runs the show never approved of her whole army of fire side project."

"Some side project," I scoff.

"Eoin completely put everything on Tristen, saying he had no idea what her true intentions were." Eoin had seemed so nice when I first met him, the day I completed the Ritual of Fire. Little did I know he would actually end up being Tristen's accomplice. "Other than that…" he shrugs.

"So what exactly happens at these meetings?"

"Well, I'm pretty low on the food chain, as I've explained before. Tristen and Eoin, they're kind of beneath the ones in charge, whoever that is. Kind of like Imminent Darkness minions."

"If Tristen and Eoin are minions, what's lower than a minion?"

He chuckles. "Dunno, peasants? The Imminent Darkness is sort of divided into factions in order to ensure that nobody knows too much information at any one time. Different factions conduct different assignments from the top. Kind of how you were on the assignment table because you were turning eighteen on the hundredth solar alignment."

I swallow nervously. I know Sloan would never hurt me, in fact, he's taken a vow to always protect me. But that doesn't mean he can necessarily stop those who want to hurt me from doing so. "Am I still on the table?"

"Since Tristen's debacle, a lot seems to be on hiatus. She jeopardized the trust of the entire colony and aroused the suspicions of the Council of Leaders."

"If everyone knows that the Imminent Darkness exists then how come no one has tried to stop them?"

"Ah, a history question," he smiles. "Because of our Law of

the Land which was established upon our founding, in which groups have the right to form and assemble as long as they do not cause damage or harm. That's why Tristen kind of messed up the agenda. But don't let the non-action fool you, the Imminent Darkness recruits more members every day."

"What makes it so alluring?"

"Power, prestige, forbidden knowledge, the usual. Think of any sort of ancient society or membership, all the way back to the Freemasons or Knights Templar." I can feel my eyes starting to glaze over from all the historical references.

"Sorry, we were just covering Religions in Universal History," Sloan smiles apologetically. "What about you, find out anything interesting?"

"Well…" I pull out my bag and first hand him *The Five Goddesses*. "This for starters." He flips through the book, scanning the pages.

"Interesting. Katayun and Raj. Those names mean queen and king in other languages." He raises an eyebrow at me.

"It's just coincidence right? I mean, I know my name means *fire* and my nickname, Kata, means *pure one*."

He nods. "Could be coincidence." And I believe him. Slow, methodical, collect all the facts before jumping to conclusions. He continues to scan the book until he gets to the illustrations in the back.

"There." I flip to the last goddess, the Earth goddess. "This one has an uncanny resemblance to my mother. Down to the freckle right there." I point to the black dot beneath her eye. "Also coincidence?"

He studies the picture a minute before looking up at me. His eyes often give away his emotions. They're a brilliant green; often calm like a glassy sea, but can be turbulent like the tempest in an instant. Right now they're very deep as if I'm looking into an oceanic abyss, an abyss I'd much prefer to the Elemental one I have to inevitably return to. "How many coincidences before something is the truth?"

I'm not sure if he's asking me for an actual answer, but it seems an impossible question to answer. Almost like a riddle. Then it hits me and I feel my stomach drop. I chose Fire. But the box at Pronouncement, recommended Water. We have free will, and at the time, I was unsure of Sloan and who he really was because I didn't yet know. I chose Fire. Was it coincidence that Tristen was a Fire Elder? I stopped the army of Fire with the Fire stone. Another coincidence. The Metal woman who saw my future was the same who had helped my mother. Yet another coincidence. The son of that Metal woman is my sworn protector. Coincidence yet again? My head is spinning. He must see my shock because he slowly sets the book back down onto the table.

"My mother is the ancient Earth Goddess?" I whisper. He strokes my cheek softly and pushes a strand of my hair behind my ear.

"I don't know if that's necessarily true, but at this point, I'm not sure that it can be ruled out."

"I didn't think goddesses were real." His hand finds mine and enfolds it.

"At one time we didn't think the Legend of the Impossible Girl was real either, but here you are sitting on my couch. And trust me, you're definitely real." I give him a tentative smile. It's true. I've had dream meetings, been to enchanted waterfalls, and seen the spirits of Earth and Fire manifest in front of my very eyes. Who am I to say what's real and what isn't?

Before I can show him the key and the map, there's an impatient knock at the door. I can tell he isn't expecting anyone because he smooths out his hair and catches a glance in the mirror, running a self-conscious hand over his scales. As soon as he pulls the door open, Ahna comes rushing in, practically knocking him to the earthen floor.

"Oh, thank goodness you're here! Actually, I figured you'd be here. And it's even better that both of you are together because you aren't even going to believe this! Well, actually you will believe it because I have the proof right here. That book you have isn't the only one that mentions The Five Elemental Goddesses. There's another." She holds up a large leather bound book with the title *Mythology of the Ages* in shiny gold letters. "And your mom's in this one too!"

. . .

This book isn't just a story. It also has profiles of the various gods and goddesses from numerous traditions, Celtic, Greek, Roman, Norse, Egyptian, you name it and this book covers it. "See, right there it says, she goes by the names Anuja, Kesara, or Novea." Ahna glances up at me, but continues reading. "*She is the youngest of the five sisters, so the variations of her name mean youthful or young. Contrary to some belief, she does not represent the planet Earth, but rather the ebb and flow of life. Just as the tiny seed, sprouts into a tiny green stem before it blooms in all its glory, and then wilts and dies only to be reborn again, so too does the Earth Goddess.*"

"According to this your actual mother may just be one incarnation of the Earth Goddess," Sloan explains.

"*If* she's this Earth Goddess," I object.

Ahna ignores me and continues reading: "*The Earth Goddess is believed by her sisters to be the favorite of Katayun and Raj, the Queen and King of the Universe itself, which is why they had no more children. After the trickery of the Codger, and the resulting split betwixt these so-called Daughters of the Universe, each was given their own land to rule. The Land of Earth is filled with lush greenery, bubbling brooks, and various animals that could have been found on the Planet Earth. Some even theorize that planet Earth was the Land of Earth given to Anuja/Kesara/Novea, but archaeologists have yet to prove this to be true. The Earth Goddess is also known in various other myths as the Maiden, Mother, and Crone. It can take hundreds of years for her to cycle through these various incarnations.*" Finally, Ahna stops reading and looks up at me. "You have to admit, Ka it almost makes sense."

"Almost. But if my mother is a goddess then what does that make me?" I ask.

"Half-goddess, I'd say," grins Sloan, trying to gently ease my shock as my brain grapples to make sense of it all.

"Actually, all jokes aside, he's right. Bina said so herself that you're the Impossible Girl of the legend. It only makes sense that a mother with a lot to lose would go to such great lengths to protect her daughter."

"Speaking of Bina," I say snapping back to reality. "I have proof that my mother not only met with her, but traveled to the Elemental Abyss." I reach into my messenger bag which is still on the table and pull out the empty burlap sack and the antiquated key.

"That's one of my mother's talisman bags," Sloan says. He takes the key, turning it over in his palm, inspecting it. "I've never seen the key before though." My heart sinks. It's part of the reason I brought it here, since they were stored together I was hoping that maybe Sloan would recognize it.

"Oh and this," I say reaching back into the bag and into one of the little compartments. I pull out the map, unfold it, and place it on the table so we can all see it. Since I'm the only one who's been there I point out, "It's a map of the Elemental Abyss."

Ahna traces her finger along the pathway from the University Complex and out over the mountains, down through the cavern to the enchanted waterfall. "It all seems surreal."

"Tell me about it," I say and slouch back against the soft cushions of the sofa. "And the more answers I find, the more questions I have."

Sloan puts a reassuring arm around me. "Just don't forget: no matter who your mother is or who you are, you're still Ka."

Ahna puts an arm around me from the other side. "Yeah, and you're still my best friend." I let them hug me from either side, a warm ring of comfort, temporarily easing my worries.

If only it were all that simple.

Ye will find the answers at the beginning not the end.

CHAPTER 5

The scene that greets me when I return home is not what I expect. The door is slightly ajar which sets my heart a flutter in my chest. Each step is quicker than the last as I approach the door. I push it open until the door hits the wall. "Mom?" I call into the house. Afraid to go in, but knowing that I have no choice. Why did I turn down Sloan's offer to walk me home? Ahna had headed back to the library to return some books and do more research, so I'd went the rest of the way alone. I close my eyes for a second, worst case scenarios running through my mind. None of them pleasant.

I step across the threshold. The house is in total disarray. Immediately to my left is the kitchen and all the cabinets are open, their contents spilled across the counter top and floor. To my right is the living room and all of the couch cushions have been slashed, their stuffing littered about the floor. Someone was looking for something.

I take the stairs off the living room two at a time, calling: "Mom? Dad?" Panic rising in my chest. How is it that our bodies know something is wrong before our minds? Intuition? Sixth sense? I don't know how, but I know something is very, very wrong.

I reach the top of the steps and I hear a low groan. Crap. I didn't even think that the intruder could still be in the house! I have nothing to protect myself except my messenger bag and it's non-threatening contents. I reach and pull the old key out, securing it in my fist. At the very least it would hurt to get stuck in the eyeball or throat with a heavy, brass key. It's the best I can do. I head down the hallway in the direction of the moaning. The house somehow feels different, as if I can physically feel the violation of its trust and security. My skin prickles. The moaning grows louder. It's coming from the office. The door is open a crack. I'm not exactly one to go in all guns a-blazing so to speak, so I tentatively peek through the crack and feel my stomach drop to my feet.

I throw the door open and am half-crawling, half-sliding to get to my mother as quickly as possible. She's laying in the fetal position in the middle of the carpet between the door and the desk. A large, dark stain is forming beneath her. Her brown hair is matted to her head. Blood. So much blood. Bile rises in my throat and I swallow it back down. Her eyes are confused and cloudy, but she continues to moan. "Mom, oh, I don't know what to do!" I pull a sweater from my messenger bag and try to wrap it around her head, applying pressure to a spot just above her right ear. "I have to get you to the hospital." She mumbles something that I can't quite make out and I lean down closer to better hear her.

"No."

"No? If I don't, you'll die!" I protest. I pull her up into my arms so I can apply better pressure but also hear her at the same time.

"They came. They know. We need to leave. Now." The few words seem to take all of her energy and her face grows paler with each fragmented sentence.

"But what about Dad?"

"No time."

"Where do we go?" I think she may be losing it. Post-traumatic stress from the attack or something. I still think I need to take her to the hospital, but how do you rationalize with the irrational? She replies but it comes out gurgled. She closes her eyes for a second. The sweater grows warm in my hand where her blood continues to spill out. When she opens her eyes, they're a fierce, bright golden color. More gold, less brown. Brighter than I've ever seen them before. Alert. Clear.

She tries again.

"Key."

The key is still clenched in my fist. When I open my palm, little half-moons from my fingernails are dented inside. She gives me a small smile and places her hand over mine. Everything goes black.

. . .

I've felt the sensation before, of hurtling through time and space.

When I was with Doran and we traveled through a portal from the Land of Fire back to the Elemental Abyss. They're not like the pods at the University Complex that use your brain wave frequencies to drop you off at your exact desired location. The sensation now, as with the portal, is like being sucked through a vacuum. There's no sense of time or space. No light, no sound.

I can feel my mother's hand still wrapped around mine. I can feel the key secure in my fist. I also get bits and pieces of my mom's thoughts. The same happened with Doran. I saw pieces, like a puzzle, of his past. Little glimpses. The cost of space-time-traveling with a companion I suppose. Doran's pieces appeared linear, while my mother's are more jumbled. I see my mother's worried expression as she meets with Bina when I am a small child. It then jumps to her as a little girl, a gorgeous little girl with four sisters, laughing as she skips among the stars. A codger handing her a stone. A beautiful forest with birds and a stream that ends in a little waterfall. The images come so fast they're almost a blur.

The last image before we fall through the portal is of a hooded figure. I can't see his eyes, but his mouth forms a snarl as he bends over my mother's lying form before disappearing in a swirl of smoke and fire.

...

I land on my back with a hard thud, knocking the wind out of me. I lay there feeling the warm breeze. I hear the chirping of birds. And if I concentrate I can hear the gentle flow of water. Although I landed hard, the ground beneath me is sort of soft and spongey. And damp. Kind of itchy. Even though it causes pain, I manage to push myself up so that I'm resting on my hands, legs outstretched. I'm on grass. But not like Xon 9's sparse patches of grayish-colored grass. This is *real* grass. Green, dewy grass. Around me are trees, the tallest trees I've ever seen in my life, so tall the tops disappear into the blue—blue!?—sky.

I look at my hands. Moisture and tiny green blades of grass stick to my palms. A mist hovers just above the ground. Precipitation. We don't have rain on Xon 9, but I know what happens when a warm surface encounters a cool one and the reaction that can occur. It rained recently. As if on cue, I notice the dampness seeping through my cargo pants. My mother.

The thought re-energizes me and I hurry to my feet. I don't see her anywhere. When Doran and I went through the portal from the Land of Fire back to the Elemental Abyss, we were holding hands, and we landed on the other side together. The key. It's no longer in my hand. I get on my knees and feel through the blades of lush grass. No key. It's gone.

I stand back up slowly, wiping my damp hands on my pants. Okay. No Mom. No key. No Xon 9. So where am I then? Did the key bring me here? More importantly, where and why did it take us and how did my mother know that it would? I assess the situation and decide there's no point in staying in one spot to wait. Besides, I'm curious and want to explore.

I follow the sound of water, the light tinkling sound. It's warm here, but different than Xon 9. I can feel the moisture hanging in the air as if it's clinging to the air particles themselves. I push my shirt sleeves up and put my hair into a sloppy bun. I'm in a forest and the ground is a combination of the lush grass and a dirt path with sporadic rocks and boulders. I pay attention, careful to step over any tree roots that have crept up from the earth below. The birds continue to chirp, but I hear other things too. During our early lessons of Old Earth, we listened to what the teacher called *nature sounds*. Back then, the sounds seemed to come from magical creatures, most of which we don't have on Xon 9: frogs, wolves, birds, whales, monkeys…but now I recognize some of them. I can hear the deep drum of some kind of frog and the buzz of something in my ears. The entire forest seems to vibrate with life.

The tinkling sound grows louder into a bubbling as I round the bend and the forest opens onto a narrow stream. Suddenly, I'm overcome with thirst. But I remember the enchanted lake in the Elemental Abyss and I hesitate, kneeling beside the stream. I can see my own face looking back at me, the stream is so crystalline. My reflection appears peaceful. Calm. Not panicked like I'd expect it to be. A little winged creature with a jewel-like blue body hovers just above the image of my face, as if telling me it's okay. I dip my palm into the stream, making a little cup and bring it to my mouth. The water is cool and refreshing. Now I understand why when he's teaching Sloan carries a big jug of it around. Being a Water, his equilibrium is even more sensitive than that of non-Waters. Almost immediately I feel energized. But what's the hurry when you don't know where you're going?

There's a large boulder beside the stream and I climb onto it, slipping my messenger bag over my head and setting it down beside me. The sound of the stream is soothing. I feel calm as I look around and notice my surroundings. There are small furry creatures playing on the other side of the stream. Maybe a rabbit and a squirrel, but I can't be completely sure. I turn my face up to the sky. There's a glowing golden orb and I can feel its warmth even so far below. The sun. That's why we came to Xon 9. The sun died. But how magnificent! The warmth! It's as if I can feel it permeating my skin and traveling down to my very bones, like it's warming me from the inside out. I remember from Science about how the sun made the conditions on Earth perfect for all the life that thrived there, that and the amount of surface water was conducive for various crops, animals, vegetation, and of course humans. I snap out of my reverie.

So this must be Earth. Well, not the real Earth, of course. Maybe, it's the Land of Earth, like the Land of Fire and I somehow bypassed the Elemental Abyss. The key. Mom knew I had it. Is that what the man in the cloak was looking for? The key? My stomach stirs at the thought. It seems quite the coincidence that I find out my mother's true identity—or at least what could be her true identity— and unearth her lies just when someone who looks like the embodiment of the Imminent Darkness breaks into our house and leaves her for dead. What if I hadn't come home at that moment? What if I'd been home earlier—could I have prevented the attack? I almost laugh. Not likely. According to Sloan the Imminent Darkness is both very old and very powerful. But what if I'd come home later?

Would my mother still be alive? Is she alive now?

I look around at all the colors and beauty surrounding me. This beautiful place teeming with life. Yes, if my mother knew to come here then she must be alive. But where did she go? As if in answer the little blue-winged creature returns. It lands on my finger and I get a closer look. It has a gorgeous sapphire blue body that is long and skinny like a stick, and although its wings are translucent, they too have a blue sheen to them that glitters in the sunlight. It has four wings, almost equal in size. Its tiny feet tickle the skin of my finger. "What are you?" I ask it, racking my brain for images or names from my youth, but coming up empty. It flies off my finger and hovers in the air just in front of my face. It darts away and then comes back, as if to say, *This way! Follow me!* And since I used this creature as a sign it was safe to drink from the stream, I figure why not?

I grab my bag, dropping the strap over my head, and get to my feet. The little creature seems to dance excitedly in the air around me. I have a mother to find and, if this truly is the Land of Earth, then I have an Elemental Stone to find here as well. The little creature stays close, dancing majestically in the air. "I don't remember what you're called," I explain. "But since you're going to be my guide, I'll call you Cyan. It's the name of a shade of blue about the same as you." As if in reply, Cyan swirls in delight.

CHAPTER 6

At home, assuming that this place is not my home, the sun never sets. On Xon 9, the moons rise and set, indicating the passage of time. This place is different. There was a spectacular array of pinks, oranges, and purples as the golden globe in the sky slipped behind the horizon. The sky continues to fade from light to dark and little pinpricks of light begin to dot the sky. Above, in place of the sun, is a single moon, glowing like a white beacon. It's becoming increasingly difficult to see Cyan, although the moonlight occasionally glints off the translucence of her wings.

We are still walking along the stream and I can see tall, purple mountains in the distance, like jagged shadows against the now-darkening sky. I'm hungry. Earlier, along the way we passed some bushes with bright red berries. Cyan hovered, even landing on one of the bushes, as if to let me know it was safe to eat them. So I did.

They were sweet and tart at the same time and I ate a couple handfuls, savoring the flavors. But now my stomach growls. I dig in my bag. Just as I suspected, at the bottom is a bottle of nutrient pills from my last trip to the Elemental Abyss. The passage of time was odd in the Land of Fire and at the Elemental Abyss. I'd been pretty sure Doran and I had been gone for two or even three days, but when we returned it was the same night we'd left, only later. I wonder if the passage of time here will be the same. I wonder if my father is in a panic and has contacted the authorities. What would he think of coming home to a ransacked house and his wife and daughter gone?

The path along the stream breaks into a clearing. The branches of the trees hang low, providing some cover, but otherwise it's pretty open. I suppose Cyan's telling me to take a rest. "Okay," I say, "But only for a couple hours. We need to find my mom. And the Elemental Stone." Before I can even finish the last of what I say, I'm yawning. I lay down on the soft grass and use my messenger bag as a pillow. The sky is so bright even though it's dark. It seems as if there are millions—no, billions—of stars. Little winking dots of light. I hear all sorts of sounds, most of which I cannot name, but none that seem frightening. I feel Cyan's tiny insect feet land on my forearm, as if protecting me. My eyelids grow heavy and finally slide closed.

. . .

I know that I am dreaming. I'm in the basement of the Fire Building. The torches that light the wall cast eerie shadows and small pools of light across the stone floor. My body continues as if on autopilot. My feet lead me to the room of doom. The room where

Everly was punished for lying about my Mindscape. The room where I found Doran, literally brought to his knees. The room where I found Li as a soldier programmed to bring about my demise. I feel nauseas as I round the corner and enter through the doorway. *Maybe this time it will be different*, I find myself thinking. But it never is. No matter how many ways I try to change it, it always ends the same.

Everly is already huddled behind the flipped over table and I run to join her. Fireballs rain down around us. I get the bright idea to use a torch to fight off the fireballs, but it only extinguishes them and temporarily disables the fire-generating capacity of the individual throwing them. I'm backed into a corner. Three soldiers approaching me, all conjuring fireballs at the same time. There was a hole in my bag and I see the Fire stone on the floor. I call to Everly. She picks it up and throws it to me. As soon as it leaves her hand she's hit with a fireball, a shocked expression on her face and she disintegrates, just a black smudge of soot on the floor. Gone, forever, in an instant. I didn't even know if she had a husband, or kids, or anything. I knew nothing about her. I swallow the guilt and in a last ditch effort throw the stone. A wall of fire surrounds me, and as quickly as it appeared, it's gone. The army of fire, my friends and fellow initiates, lay scattered about scarcely breathing. I have to get to the door. When I get to the door, that's when this nightmare stops being relived. Blank eyes watch me, chests barely rising and falling, black tattoos ingrained where the filigree of Fire had once marked the right sides of their faces. I know the last one I reach will be Li.

But the dream is different this time. It has its own agenda.

Cold fingers wrap around my ankle. I pause, afraid to look down. Whose face will I see? Everly? Bina? My mother? I slowly look down and it feels as though my heart has been doused in ice. Green eyes stare back at me. I drop to my knees. "How? This isn't possible!" I cry. There's the hint of life far, far behind the green, but there's a cloudiness, an uncertainty. I put my hand beneath his head, cradling it. His chest rises and falls slowly. "You aren't even a Fire! You're a Water!"

"I will protect you." Is all he says before, as if on cue, his body melts and my hands are immersed in a puddle of cool water. A puddle that just seconds before was my boyfriend.

. . .

I start awake frightened. It's still dark out, but I can see the sun just beginning to rise on the horizon. I look to my left. Nothing. I look to my right. Eyes. Glowing yellow eyes, not friendly, peer back at me from the bushes. I'm on my feet and running as fast as I can, which I'm not sure is the brightest idea, but also not sure what other choice I have. I can hear the soft pad of feet behind me. Fast. Much faster than me. I run as hard as I can, my heart pounding as if it will explode, my legs going numb. I hear a snarl and feel a yank on my messenger bag, I go down hard, reeling backward. A large creature with pointy ears and a bushy tail, matted fur. Long white fangs. A wolf.

I can't leave my bag. It has the items from Bina, the map, the key, and the book. The strap is still secure around my middle and my fall must have surprised the wolf because he backed away unsure, but now he stares at me, fur bristled, haunches high, ready to pounce. I stay very still. When I ran, he ran too. Maybe he thinks it's a game. When Li and Ahna and I were little we used to play a game called Statue. You had to stand as still as possible and the first to move or laugh would lose. Then the first person out would try and make the other two laugh. So it was very difficult to win. I pretend that I'm playing Statue now and grow so still that I think even my heart may be playing as well.

The wolf continues to stare at me unsure. Perhaps just as frightened as I am. When I ran, I headed toward the mountains and the stream flows from that direction, so inadvertently I'm still beside it. There's a splash and I see a shimmer of silver in the morning light. I look down and the stream is full of fish. The wolf tentatively approaches the stream, swats into the water and a fish flips onto the bank. Breakfast. I don't stay long enough to see how breakfast goes down. While the wolf is distracted, I head toward the stone-strewn path where the stream trickles down from the mountains, but not before grabbing a few medium-sized stones to use just in case. I slip one in my messenger bag, which now has yet another hole, luckily the first hole is patched and these are smaller, tooth-sized holes. I hold the other stone in my fist.

I see an insect fluttering in the distance, hovering in the middle of the path. "And where were you?" I accuse Cyan. Not that an insect could have been all that much help. She flies in a circle and lands on my shoulder. "I suppose I accept your apology," I reply. "Where are we headed?" Excitedly, Cyan flies from my shoulder until she's about a foot in front of me, heading up the path that leads into the mountains. "Well, I hope you're right this time because I am not sleeping out in the woods again." I say before heading up the path.

. . .

The sun is bright and high in the sky when the path widens. We round a corner and Cyan stops, hovering in the air, beckoning me to look. I shield my eyes from the sun and look up. In the distance, further up the path I see a beautiful, white castle. The path leading up to it is lined with trees that have white bark and bloom with tiny pink flowers. Juxtaposed with the white of the castle and purple of the mountains, it's breathtaking. And the way the mountains are, until you round the corner, you've no idea it's here. Unless of course, you already know. Cyan hovers in front of my face and does an excited backflip. "I'll take a castle over a fiery volcano any day," I smile.

We continue up the path and as we approach the castle I can finally appreciate its size. It's not huge, like the ones I've seen in books, sprawling on forever, but it is large. It has a main building with a stained glass window at its peak and two smaller buildings with small turrets flanking either side. The stained glass window is multicolored but is divided into six distinct portions: a white circle at the center and then wedges, like rays, that are narrower near the circle and widen as they approach the glass's edge: sapphire, amber, emerald, ruby, and a brilliant turquoise color. I pause. Is it possible? But before I can think too much on it, Cyan lands on my nose, causing me to go cross-eyed and urging me to continue up the path.

In front of the castle is a small stone water fountain, in its center is a stone statue of a man and a woman intertwined. The water pours from their heads, coalescing down their bodies, and then into the pool below before being recirculated. Cyan hovers on the edge of the fountain before fluttering around the heads of the man and woman, then continuing up the steps of the castle.

The steps are far apart and I have to stretch out my legs to reach each one. And there are a lot of steps. I'm not sure it's really necessary, up in the mountains, without a lot of people around, to have so many steps. When we reach the top, the wooden doors are slightly ajar. A soft, flowery fragrance wafts out of the castle and Cyan disappears inside the door. I need a little more space so I gently pull the door and it opens easily. The light inside is dim, but sunlight pours in from the windows that line the entryway. I'm standing on a narrow purple carpet. The floor is polished white stone. The hallway is long, but at its end I can see a single throne. A purple upholstered, sturdy wooden chair with a high back. I want to call out, see who's home, but it somehow doesn't seem appropriate.

Cyan continues to flutter down the hallway until she reaches the throne. She settles down on the velvety upholstery. "So, you fancy yourself a queen, do you?" I ask. Around the throne the sunlight filters through the stained-glass causing an array of colors on the white stone floor, a swirl of color with the throne smack dab in the middle of the white circle. It's quite magnificent. I turn around to admire the stained glass from the inside of the building. "It's quite magnificent, isn't it, Cyan? And for some reason the colors remind me of the five Elements from home."

A voice, like a melodious song yet also strangely familiar, answers. "Actually, it has to do with the Five Elemental Goddesses. And, yes, I do fancy myself a queen of sorts, but you can still call me Mom."

. . .

I whip around. "Mom!?" She's sitting on top of the throne, where Cyan was only moments before, looking healthy and well. Her golden eyes are sparkling and her brown hair is thick and lustrous, tumbling to her shoulders in soft curls. She wears a long golden cloak over a sapphire blue dress that pools around her barefeet. I quickly close the distance between us, but pause just before the step up to the throne.

"It's okay, Kata," she says and her voice still has the same song-like quality to it. I take the step and throw my arms around her neck, checking her head to be sure that, indeed, she is healed. Once I'm sure that there's no longer a head wound, I pull back.

"You sat on, Cyan," I tell her, feeling sad that my new friend was squashed like a bug, quite literally.

"I *am* Cyan," she replies.

"You were a bug?"

"More specifically, a dragonfly. You couldn't tell? I thought I did a fairly good job of portraying motherly qualities."

"Like letting me sleep where a wolf could eat me alive?"

"Well, last time I was here there weren't any wolves who would want to eat any human children. Although I do wonder where the fish in the stream came from." I think about my dream and

Sloan's words that he'd protect me. "Anyways, I'm here now and that's all that matters. It's actually the first time I'm proud of you for disobeying me." I raise my eyebrow and walk back down to the beautiful colored wedges of light. "You taking the key. If you hadn't had the key I'm not sure what would have happened. I may have died."

"Goddesses can die?"

She gives me a little shrug. "In human form, why not?"

"Are you not in human form now?"

"Yes and no. Coming home has healed me and taking the dragonfly—"

"Cyan," I correct.

"Taking Cyan's form used a lot less energy so it sped the healing along quite nicely. I still have a bit of a headache though."

"Why did the Imminent Darkness come to our house?" I ask.

"For the key, which luckily you had already taken."

"Why?"

"Because the key has a living memory. It can remember the last place that it was and take you there."

"So it can take me home?"

"Eventually."

"And why did you have it?"

"So I could come…here."

"You told me it wasn't true. You told me that I imagined it."

She lets out a long sigh. "Yes, well, Kata, I quite underestimated you. I thought that you still needed protecting, that you were still just a child. Sometimes, I still wish that you were." She takes me in from head to toe. "But you're not a child anymore. You're a woman now. And I suppose you need to know the truth."

"I have a protector."

She nods slowly. "I know. He's taken an Everlasting Vow. And a very serious one at that."

"You lied to me."

"I know. I shouldn't have. I was wrong. I put us in more danger than if I'd just told you the truth when you asked. I hope that in time you can forgive my choice."

"Who are you?"

"I'm Novea, born of Katayun and Raj. Goddess of the Land of Earth. The youngest of the five sisters. This is my home."

"What about Dad?"

"Your father knows what he signed up for."

"And me?"

"You…well, you are part human-part goddess. But, oh Ka, you are so much more than that."

"How could you stand it? All this time watching me be so average, and knowing the whole time who I truly was and what I'm destined to do?"

I can see her eyes brim with tears. "It wasn't easy. But I also wanted you to have as normal and safe a life as you could. I suppose part of me wished the legend wasn't true, that the Impossible Girl was just a story. Maybe I wished for a little too long."

"Why did you name me Ka? Is it after Katayun?"

She smiles gently. "No, it was a peace offering to my eldest sister, the Goddess of Fire. And although you share her passion, your name doesn't strictly mean Fire. More specifically, it means *illumination.*"

"As in illuminating the dark?"

"Something like that."

"I've been to the Land of Fire and I didn't see anyone there. Just a giant volcano."

"That was her. Celosia, is her name. And she was the volcano."

"She erupted on me."

Novea shrugs. "She can be a bit temperamental."

"So then it's all true? The whole goddess thing and I'm the Impossible Girl meant to somehow stop the Imminent Darkness." She nods. "But how do I stop the Imminent Darkness when I don't even know who they are?"

"Well, for starters, you have a part of each of your aunts inside you, gifts bestowed upon you at your birth. I just wasn't expecting you to show such aptitude so soon, so I needed to protect you. That's where Bina and the Elemental Stones came in."

"Couldn't you just pop in and out like we did with the key?"

"Not quite. I had to do it the…human way. No Goddess-of-the-Universe short-cuts, otherwise it wouldn't work. And it did work, until you disobeyed me and went to the Black Bazaar with Li and met Bina."

"Were you ever going to tell me?"

She shrugs. "When I thought the time was right. And to answer your other question, I'm not so sure myself. The Imminent Darkness is an ancient force. My first encounter being with the old codger who tricked my sisters and me with the stones."

"How did Bina get the stones?"

"The stones were the gifts. Even though each of my sisters decided to rule our respective lands, we decided on a truce of sorts at your birth. Each sister gifted you with their Elemental Stone, knowing that it had the potential to give you great power. We trusted that you'd be able to use that power to stop the Imminent Darkness." Her eyes get a faraway look. "It's not just on Xon 9. It's everywhere. We say our Elements can become Unbalanced, but I suspect that's so because the Universe itself has become unbalanced. I don't know who or why, just that they need to be stopped."

"Why did you come to Xon 9? Why there?"

"Well, Celosia and I had a bit of a spat and she extinguished the sun."

"Wait, when Earth's sun died it was because of my aunt!?"

"Not exactly. Maybe a little. She played a bit of a trick on me. I'm not only the youngest, but also the most gullible, and Celosia was still angry at me for getting what she thought was the best stone. So she gave me the sun to sustain the Land of Earth. But the sun was a star. And stars die out."

"But billions of people died. We can't live without a sun."

"This is true. Celosia was quite regretful, not realizing so much life would thrive in my Land, unlike her Land which is dark, fiery, and barren. So she gave me Xon 9, which is similar to Earth, but because she had my sisters' help, we have the various Elements. This Land is the last piece of Earth that I have. But it's not like true Old Earth, this Earth bends to my will; whereas the old planet, as well as Xon 9, bends to the will of its inhabitants. That's how I created it and that's how it should stay."

"Unless the Imminent Darkness gets its way."

"Exactly. Now, we have a stone to find, don't we?" She gets up, smoothing her gown. "Don't suppose I can wear this."

"You can change back to Cyan."

"You'd rather me a dragonfly?"

"It was kind of cool." I pause unsure, feeling silly for what I'm about to ask next. "What do I call you now? Your Majesty or something?"

"Of course not," she clucks disapprovingly. "Like I said before, you call me Mom."

She spins around and the skirt of the gown flows out around her in a cloud of blue. When she stops spinning she's still wearing the golden cloak, but underneath she has on a black shirt and black cargo pants. Her feet are no longer bare, but inside a sturdy-looking sandal with a rubber bottom. "There. Better."

"How will we find it? The stone?"

"The same way we find all things, my Kata. With our hearts."

CHAPTER 7

I have to admit this isn't how I thought the mission to retrieve the second stone would go. No way did I think that my mom would be the one to accompany me. Although, now that the pieces are starting to fall into place who better to guide me through the Land of Earth?

As we walk I admire the beauty that's around me. The clear blue sky, towering trees that provide shade from the sun, and beautiful flowers of every color lining our paths. A small, red bird lands on my mother's shoulder. It chirps and she surprises me by responding. "Oh, no. I'm not sure." She listens for a beat. "Of course not. I'll be sure to monitor the situation." The bird gives a final chirp and then flies away.

"You speak bird?" I ask.

"Of course. I speak all the languages of the creatures that

inhabit my Land. A gift which did not extend to me on Xon 9."

"So what did he say?"

"The other animals are worried about the wolf. Here, in the Land of Earth, all the animals get along. Sure, there's the order of the food chain, but no animal acts out of malice, like how the wolf tried to attack you."

"It grabbed my bag." My mother pauses at a tree to our right, it's on the other side of a wooden picket fence, and she picks off a bright golden apple. She hands it to me and I take a bite, savoring its tartness. It tastes almost other-worldly, like the berries from the other day.

"Like I said, the Imminent Darkness is a very ancient being. It can travel where it pleases and take on many forms."

We continue to walk on a dirt path, the orchard and the forest opening up onto a vast meadow with tall wildflowers reaching for the sun. "But what does it want?"

"What all our egos want."

"And what's that?"

"Power."

. . .

We walk for what feels like hours. We've already been gone a day's time. At least in this world. I wouldn't be surprised to return home and find out my absence has gone unnoticed. The wolf has me more frightened than I'd care to admit to my mother, her Royal Highness. If the Imminent Darkness can shape shift, and take on the form of an old man or a ravenous wolf, what else can it do? And is it one being or many? The wolf had clearly grabbed onto my bag. It has the fang marks to prove it. I think about the bag's contents. The key is gone. At least for now. The book and the map are both still in my bag. As well as the empty burlap sack from the drawer and the other burlap sack filled with the items Bina gave me. What would a wolf want with a pack of matches, a feather, a vial of liquid, and a crystal anyways?

Mom said we'd follow our hearts, but my heart hasn't told me anything yet. As we've walked, the landscape has changed numerous times, from the meadow to sand dunes to a pink sand shoreline with beautiful waves crashing. I take off my shoes and the sand squishes between my toes and the water is cool around my ankles. It reminds me of a sea I've seen before, but that's impossible, of course. I pause, looking out at its vastness, at the sun hovering above the horizon. For a second, I think I see green eyes peering back at me from the tranquil waters, but I blink and they're gone. We continue walking and I have the feeling that we've traversed many miles much faster than we would have if we were at home on Xon 9.

"You're lucky, you know," Mom says breaking the silence, pausing to stare out at the sea.

"I don't feel all that lucky. Intimidated, unworthy, hesitant, confused…those are all things that I feel among others, but lucky isn't one of them." There's a washed up log on the shore and I sit on it. She sits beside me.

"I always just wanted to feel normal."

"Welcome to the club."

My comment gets a small smile out of her. She pushes the hood of her cloak back and the sun illuminates her brown hair, giving it a sort of effervescent crown. "I wanted to feel human. I wanted to feel human emotions. My Land is the only one where human life could exist and thrive. The conditions were just right for it to happen. Stardust and evolution. It's more complex than you'd realize, the exact conditions needed to produce human life. Oh, and to watch the progress! Sure, I witnessed horrible things. But there were beautiful things, too. I was willing to experience the bad things in order to feel the good things. Like meeting your father, like love."

It's an odd feeling to know that your mother is older than all of humanity. I remember what Ahna said about the maiden, mother, and crone. I want to ask how old she is, but instead ask, "How long have you been human?"

"As long as you see on my face. Forty-eight years. And I feel every single one. It's not like here where I don't feel time."

"I noticed your head wound healed quickly."

"Yes, taking Cyan's form, and just being here, in a place created of my own essence, helps me to heal quickly." I feel a pang in my heart and I ask the question, the thing I'd feared since I'd found her on the floor of the study, lying in that pool of blood.

"Will you die?" I whisper.

She turns to me and her eyes are very sad. She is careful with her words. "My human form, yes, it will die. And I wouldn't want that any other way. I wouldn't want to live in human form for all eternity without your father." She turns back to the sea. "But me, as a daughter of the Universe itself? No, I will go on and on until time ends. If it ends."

"That would suck," I say before I can stop myself.

She smiles at me. "We find ways to pass the time."

I snort. "Yeah, like creating entire worlds."

"Yes, there's that, but as you've noticed time here is much different than time on Xon 9."

I nod. "Yeah, I've noticed. The same thing happened in the Land of Fire."

"When I said you're lucky, Ka, I was referring to the fact that you are so loved. Your father and I love you, Ahna and Li love you. And, of course, Sloan. You have people who will protect you and help you, stand by your side. Sometimes it's lonely without my sisters, you won't ever have to experience that."

"Why don't you just, like, meet for a cup of tea or something?"

She laughs. "*Divide et impera.* The stones didn't just create an emotional rift between my sisters and me; it created a physical one. By collecting and destroying the stones you not only restore each Element to your soul, you also will destroy the barrier that separates my sisters and me. But it must be all of the stones."

"So, you have an ulterior motive? It's not just about me getting my essence, as you called it, back? It's about you being able to spend all eternity with your sisters?"

"Yes and no. I'm working on being more truthful with you, Ka, but there's a lot at stake. When I gave birth to you, I practically turned the Universe on its head. I admit, I was reckless, and unsure what would happen. Either way, my sisters cannot have children of their own, so as I told you before, they bestowed you with great gifts, the gifts of their Elements. Those Elements are trapped in the stones, the stones that were given to us by the Imminent Darkness and which are the same stones tossed into the Elemental Abyss. Five stones, five worlds."

"Five sisters. Five goddesses."

"Destroy the stones, restore your gifts, and dissolve the barrier. You were created out of love, not just of your father's and mine, but also of my sisters, of the entire Universe. You were born simply to be loved."

"And why does the Imminent Darkness want you and your sisters separated?"

"With love there can be no division, and love is the antithesis of power. While power feeds on deception and greed, love is true and there is always enough. The Imminent Darkness is as old as the Universe because there needs to be balance."

"Just as with each Elemental there are good and bad qualities. Like how Fire is passion, but also can be destructive."

"Precisely. And right now, there is an imbalance that needs restored." She shivers as if in confirmation. "Ready to keep moving?"

I nod slowly. The whole scenario is much more complex than I'd realized and I wonder if even Sloan realized. He took an Everlasting Vow to protect me, but did he realize exactly what he'd signed up for?

In the distance, further down the beach, I can see a towering object, wider at the base, and narrower at the top. The top shines in the setting sun. I've never seen anything like it. As if on cue, my heart drums against my chest and I can feel a fiery energy surging through my veins. As we get closer, I can see that the object is a pyramid and that the tip is golden which is why it shines like a beacon on the beach. Closer. *Thump, thump.* Closer. *Thump, thump, thump.* It's as though my body knows before my mind. "There!" And as I say it, a giddiness comes over me. Just as I was drawn to the volcano where the Fire Stone waited for me on a pedestal, I'm drawn to the pyramid where I know I will find the Earth stone.

. . .

"Are you sure, Kata?" Mom picks up her pace in order to keep up with me.

"Yes. The best piece of advice you ever gave me is one I didn't listen to: head or heart. Well, I'm listening now, and my heart tells me the Earth Stone is in that pyramid."

In actuality I thought that the pyramid was much closer than it is. We seem to walk a fair distance before it rises up before us, like a giant in the sand. I remember learning about the Egyptians in Universal History—Sloan would be proud—and how laborious it was to build them without advanced technology. Everything was basically done with simple machines and human hands. I stare up now at the monument towering before me, its golden tip glimmering in the now setting sun. Its entrance is flanked by two large, intricately carved columns of stone. There is a large wooden door with iron supports blocking the entrance.

"Did you create this?" I ask.

"Sort of. This Land was created by Raj and Katayun. But it contains some of my own manifestations." She approaches the door and places her hand on it, palm flush against the wood. She bows her head slightly and closes her eyes. There's a golden burst of light and the door slowly opens. "There are some benefits to being a goddess," she shrugs sheepishly. I step forward but she puts her arm out, barring me across the chest. "Be careful, Kata. The Imminent Darkness is in this Land and can take many forms."

"Can't you put an enchantment on the Land or something?"

"Not unless I want to keep everything that is out, out and everything that is in, in. The Imminent Darkness can come here, but it cannot stay too long because it is draining to its energy. It always has to go back to the darkest corners of the Universe where there is no light, in order to replenish itself. We must be on our guard."

I nod and swallow down my fear. I enter through the door first and am greeted with darkness. There's a flare of light behind me and I turn. My mother is holding a small, golden orb in her hand that is emitting a soft light. The light dances off the stone interior of the pyramid. It provides enough light to softly illuminate our surroundings. We are in a sort of tunnel with stairs leading up. I guess I was expecting something a little more majestic in the entryway to a pyramid, kind of like at the castle. Something grand and magnificent.

Mother nudges me forward and I head up the stairs with her

right behind me. There is no railing and there must be a hundred crumbly stone steps. The stairwell is narrow and feels as though it is squeezing me in from either side. Even still, it's better than running through a precariously erupting volcano, so I'll take my chances. When I reach the top, my mother steps up beside me and holds up her glowing orb. We're in a gigantic room. Correction: we're in an opulent, gigantic room.

The walls are lined with jewels, alternating rows of sapphires, amethysts, rubies, emeralds, topaz. You name it and it is in here. The ceiling looks to be of the same gold as the tip of the pyramid. The floor is made of glass. I'm almost afraid to take another step because without the soft glow, all I see beneath me is blackness. In the center of the room is an ornate pedestal, in a similar style to the pillars at the entrance, in the center of the pedestal is a golden-yellow, velvet pillow with tassels. In its center sits a plain stone. *Thump, thump, thump*. My stone. The Earth stone.

"Go my Kata. Go and retrieve what is yours." My mother urges, but I'm afraid to take a step. I know the floor is just an optical illusion, but still. She sees my hesitation and hands me the small orb. It hovers just above my palm and I can feel a warmth emanating from it. I decide to just concentrate on the stone and ignore the floor. It's only several steps away. Instead, I focus on the sparkle of the gem-covered walls, how the colors seem to grow more vibrant with the passing light of the orb in my hand. Two more steps. One more step. This almost seems too easy. I mean, sure, it was a lot of walking. But compared to traveling through the Elemental Abyss and into the center of an erupting volcano, and almost dying a handful of times, this is a cakewalk. The hair on the back of my neck prickles. I grab the stone.

It was too easy.

There's a crash and I whirl around in time to see a gilded cage appear out of thin air and materialize around my mother. She grabs at the bars. "Ka!" Then quickly pulls away as if she's been burned. "It's a trap!"

I hear footsteps coming up the steps. There's only one way in and one way out. When I grabbed the stone I must have set the trap in motion. "You have to find the hidden door!" My mother's saying. "It's the only way."

"Hidden door?" I screech unable to hide the fear in my voice. My mother's voice is calm and still melodious.

"Yes. There's another stairwell that goes down to the burial chambers. This room is to store the gems and treasures that go with the deceased to the afterlife. You need to find the door that leads to the other stairwell. Then, from there you can exit the pyramid through a tunnel."

"What about you? Can't you, like, evaporate out of there or something?" I ask.

"I'm a goddess, not a magician, Kata. I will find a way out."

"I can't leave you!"

Whatever was coming up the stairs has reached the top. I hold up the orb and gape in horror. It's a mummy. A real, live—is that an oxymoron?—mummy. The first thing I notice is the stench. It smells old, ancient even, and I remember my mother saying that the Imminent Darkness is as old as the Universe. It *is* ancient. The second thing I notice is the eyes: glowing yellow eyes. Like the wolf. The linen rags are deteriorating and some flap around the mummy's body. It walks toward me with slow, jagged steps, like it's drunk on something from the Black Bazaar.

"Hurry, Kata! Try the walls, look at the floor! See if you can find the door!" I move the orb so that it shines on the glass floor and I peer down, no longer afraid of what lies below and more afraid of what stands in front of me. The mummy is getting closer as it closes the distance between us, arms outstretched. And that's when it truly hits me, that retrieving the Elemental Stones is about so much more than having my identity back; it's about restoring balance to the Universe. To everything.

The orb's light falls on a ladder beneath the glass. Above the ladder, the glass has a small loop handle and an almost seamless hinge. The stench is growing stronger as the mummy inches closer. I slip the Earth stone into my messenger bag and use my now free hand to pull up on the small door. I slowly inch my way inside until I'm standing a few steps down on the ladder and I peer back at my mother.

"Mom!" Not Earth Goddess, not Novea, Her Royal Highness, or any of those names. Just Mom.

"Go, Kata!" The mummy is leaning toward the door. And just behind him and off to the side in her gilded cage, I see my Mom wave something at me. But I can't quite make out what it is. "I love you!" she calls and then I see another flash of white light. And she's gone, leaving behind an empty cage. I swallow back my tears and confusion, and turn my attention back to descending to the burial chambers. I pull the glass door closed with a matching looped handle on this side, but the mummy has grabbed the handle on the other side.

I pull as hard as I can without losing my balance, and while holding the orb in my other hand. Like heck I'm going down there without a light. The mummy may be slow and smell bad, but he's strong—stronger than me—and I'm losing the battle for the door. Does it really matter? I'm much faster, so I can still probably beat it out of the pyramid. But what happens then? I decide I'll have to take my chances. I descend the ladder as fast as I can one-handed and when I reach the bottom the mummy is still trying to wiggle its way through the door. My light shows me that the tunnel only goes one way, so I make like double-time and run, my messenger bag thudding against my legs in time to my heart pounding in my chest. It seems odd that the Imminent Darkness wouldn't be able to just appear wherever it wants. Like ahead of me further down the tunnel. I've seen it as a wolf and now as the mummy. Maybe it cannot be formless when it's in other worlds. Maybe that's why it needs to recruit humans to its side on Xon 9, to do the work for it.

I run as hard as I can, the tunnel turns left, then right. I can feel the steady slope downward, but it's disorienting. Finally the tunnel stops. I've reached the bottom. I lift the orb and see a large stone table in front of me. Perhaps the mummy's final resting place before the Imminent Darkness decided to animate it. I swing the orb to the right and I see a wall. I swing it to my left and the light falls onto a very tiny, discreet stone slab doorway with a metal handle. I'm overcome with the stench of something rotting and I know the mummy is almost to the bottom of the tunnel. I make my way to the small, half-size door and pull on the metal handle, but nothing happens. I need both hands. But then I'll be in total blackness with a rotting, Imminent Darkness mummy behind me. What choice do I have?

I toss the orb to the side and it goes out as soon as it hits the floor, it must somehow feed off the life force of the person holding it. I'm immersed in complete darkness now. I grab the metal handle with both hands and pull as hard as I can. Nothing. I hear shuffling across the floor and the overwhelming rotting smell. I brace my right foot on the wall next to the door and pull. Still nothing. Oh, come on! The shuffling is getting closer and again, the hair on the back of my neck prickles. I close my eyes even though it's dark, bracing myself. I take a deep breath and, with my foot still on the wall I pull with all my might and it's all I can do to not go tumbling into the mummy that I know is behind me. Just as the door opens I feel fingers wrap around my wrist, but light from the sun just kissing the horizon spills through the doorway, the fingers loosen and then are gone. In the remaining sunlight I venture to peer behind me and all that's there is a pile of linen wraps. Nothing is there.

I don't wait to investigate. I emerge onto the beach. And then as extra precaution, pull the door closed behind me. Then I half-stumble, half-run down the beach trying to put as much distance between myself and the pyramid. My face is caked with dirt and tear-stained. The adrenaline is starting to wear off and the sun has slipped below the horizon. I'm exhausted. The single moon is high in the sky casting beautiful light onto the placid sea; the sea that is the opposite of the tumultuous emotions inside me. I plop down on the beach and stare out. No green eyes look back at me.

How do I get home? Where's my mom? Then I realize what it was she was waving at me. She had the key. The key with its living memory, remembered the last place she had been was the castle. It took her home. Well, to one of her homes, but will she be back on Xon 9 when I get there? If I get there. I hope that she is, but maybe it's too dangerous now. In human form, she could die. But here…she could live forever. I could visit or something, couldn't I? But Dad's at home and he must be worried. And Sloan. I have so much to tell Sloan, Ahna, and Li when I get back.

I'm so tired, I just want to lay back and rest in the soft, pink sand. Just for a few moments. I lie down. Just rest for a minute. And when I lie back and peer up at the star-speckled sky I see it. There's a circular area where there are no stars, just blackness swirling in the middle of the sky, just a little bit above the beach. A portal to the Elemental Abyss, just like the one that appeared in the Land of Fire to whisk Doran and me to safety. I jump up, suddenly rejuvenated, and approach the swirling portal. I reach my fingertips toward it and the familiar upward pulling motion takes hold, yanking me out of the Land of Earth, my mother's true home, and pulling me back into the abyss of time and space. My way home. Well, almost.

CHAPTER 8

I am hurtling toward a door. I can see the door clearly even though everything else around me is dark. Light seems to emit from around the door. I hope I have enough momentum to burst through it because I know I won't be stopping anytime soon. I close my eyes for the impact. My shoulder hits the door first and it bursts open. I tumble to the floor and catch my breath. Patting my legs and chest to make sure that all of me has returned. Of its own accord, the door slams shut.

I sit up slowly. Five doors hover in the air in front of me, the one through which I just busted through labeled Earth. To its left is the one labeled Fire. Been there, done that. Not going back anytime soon. Three more doors. Three more stones. I know that I've returned to the Elemental Abyss and I'm not looking forward to the journey back alone. I silently curse my mother for her stupid key. I wish I was back in the castle or better yet home. Instead, I have to cross the fiery chasm and get past the enchanted waterfall then hike home from the mountains. Mom is probably sitting on her throne eating royal candies or whatever it is goddesses do when no longer in human form.

Still sitting on the stone floor of the cavern, I decide to check my messenger bag and make sure all my belongings made it back with me. Nutrient pills, half-drank bottle of water, the Earth stone, the goddesses book and the map I found inside the hidden drawer. The map. I pull it out. I'm not in a hurry. I mean I want to get home, of course, but it's nice to have a rest after being chased by the living dead. An eerie blue-white light emits from an orb on a pedestal, last time it helped open the door to the Land of Fire—its own key of sorts—and right now it provides enough illumination for me to peek at the hand-drawn map.

The five doors are clearly labeled as well as the fiery chasm and enchanted waterfall. I look closer and follow the line out of the cave and into the cavern which opens into the mountains. The path she took home is round about and far. It would easily take two or even three days' time to make the trek. Normal days, not Elemental Abyss days. I sigh. Not as helpful as I'd hoped. I recall how when Doran was with me we used the blood of a Fire to build a smoke bridge across the chasm and how we then used the Earth Elemental's help to get home, harnessing the power of the wind. I assume those weren't one time deals. At least I hope not.

I climb to my feet and walk over a ways to the chasm, leaning between the battlements on this side and peering into its depths. Fire roils and bellows below. Flames leap and dance. It seems as though it has no bottom. I don't have a pocket knife or anything else to offer my blood to the fiery beast, but Fire is temperamental, just like the Goddess of Fire, Celosia. Doran had reasoned it was to provide the Fire our blood to show that we were one with the Fire in the chasm. If I can't summon the smoky monster from before, there's no way for me to cross the chasm. It's too wide to leap with the battlements. Not to mention risky. So, I lean over and spit into the chasm. It's the best I can do, hoping it's enough for the beast to sense the Fire that is now part of my DNA.

At first nothing happens, but then a billow of smoke rises out of the chasm, creating a grotesque attempt at a beast-like form. Glowing orange eyes peer back at me as if to say, *Why do you wake me?*

I stutter. "Um, I'm sorry to disturb you, O' Fiery Lord, but I wish to pass to the other side of the chasm, O' Exalted One." Maybe it's a little superfluous, but this is Fire and flattery will get you everywhere.

It stares at me unblinkingly and then swiftly contorts itself into a bridge across the chasm. I take a deep breath, side-step through one of the battlements, and run across the chasm, willing my head to imagine the bridge is something solid and not merely a vapor. I make it to the other side and no sooner does my foot hit the ground before the smoke reconfigures into the giant beast that towers above me. "Thank you for safe passage, Brother of Fire." I say and bow slightly. Seemingly satisfied, the smoky beast blinks and then disappears, as if sucked back down, into the fiery chasm.

I wipe the sweat from my brow with the back of my hand and continue down the corridor. The soothing sound of the enchanting waterfall meets me before I round the corner. The small wooden rowboat is staked to the ground. But how can that be? I didn't come into the Abyss this way, so the boat should still be staked on the other bank, near the entrance to the cave. I hear a splash and see the glint of a fish tail disappearing beneath the water's surface.

The enchanted waterfall is a magical—and dangerous—place. Its beauty is unlike anything I've ever seen. Turquoise water and a light that seems to originate from behind the falls, along with the soothing rush of water are both beautiful and deadly. The enchantment lures you to sleep and takes you to your preferred place of comfort. There are two ways to wake up. One way is to get far enough away that you can no longer hear the waterfall. The other is you have to die in your dream-like state in order to wake up in your real life. Drastic I know. As well as terrifying and not all that pleasant. But it works. Personally, I'd rather just not fall asleep. Which is going to be all the more difficult since I'm alone. Not that having someone here helped the last time, as Doran and I both drifted off to dreamland.

I climb into the boat and untie the rope, tossing it into the bottom. I take the oar—there used to be two, one lost to the fiery chasm and this one seemingly returned by the creature that had snatched it—and begin to row myself from out behind the waterfall, trying to occupy my mind with anything I can. I hum a song my mother sang to me as a child, a silly little thing that she'd sing if I was frightened or scared, or just as we walked around the colony:

You are many things to me

But of all the things you will be

Kata is my favorite

Loving, steadfast,

Strong, Wise, and True

All of this is inside you

If you will just look inward and see

You are all these things to me.

I repeat it over and over, humming in time to my rowing. Down, up, over. Down, up, over. I can feel my eyelids growing heavy with fatigue. Not only from the enchantment, but also the day's adventures taking their toll. My head begins to lull forward, my chin lowering closer to my chest. My rowing gets slower and my breathing deeper. The oar slips from my fingers. Last time, my mind took me to a beautiful beach and Sloan was there. It would be so nice to see Sloan right now. His impish smile and the way he looks at me like he can't believe I'm real. Yes, it would definitely be nice to be on a beach with my Water Elemental boyfriend. As if in answer to my desires, my brain starts to manifest. I can see the white sand and the beautiful, glistening sea, but it's as though I'm still hovering above it. I just need to get my feet on the ground. I can hear myself still humming the silly song, but it sounds garbled and far away as if traveling through a long tunnel. I'm getting closer to the beach and I can almost feel the sand between my toes like on the beach in the

Land of Earth. Maybe my comfort place is actually Old Earth which is a strange thought because Earth is as foreign to me as, well as, having a goddess for a mother.

I can see Sloan already in the water waving at me and I wave back excitedly. My feet are just about to hit the ground when suddenly I'm hit with a blast of cold water and am jostled awake. My eyes fling open and I'm in the wooden rowboat in the middle of the lake with the enchanted waterfall rushing behind me. There's a bit of water in the bottom of the boat and my clothes are sopping wet. I ring out my ponytail and push the wet hair out of my eyes. My oar is floating in the water beside me. Not very useful. I still feel groggy so I shake my head as if I could shake the magical place I was just dreaming about straight out of my ears. It felt so real, but I know that it wasn't reality, at least not my reality. Last time I asked Sloan what happens to the people who never wake up and he said they stay there forever until they die at the enchanted lake, but they're none the wiser because they're in a place of comfort. I shudder at the thought. To die lost in an illusion seems a cruel twist of fate. The Elemental Abyss isn't for the faint of heart.

I peer over the side of the boat. The water is dark and I can't see below, but I also need my oar in order to get to the other bank and get home. I reach a tentative hand over the side and reach for the oar, but before I can get it a cold slimy hand closes over my wrist.

. . .

A man, and I use that term loosely, peers back at me, his head just above the water. His eyes are a pale green and he has a tuft of greenish-black hair on his head. Instead of being confined to the right side of his face, his silvery green scales take up more than two-thirds. The fingers locked around my wrist are webbed and scales run down his arm as well. The lake is home to Unbalanced Waters, more fish than man. An Unbalanced Water can be a dangerous thing: narcissistic, calm like the sea one moment, rage like a tsunami the next. Sloan has warned me, but this isn't my first encounter with these creatures. "Sleep is dangerous, Princess," he says picking up the oar and dropping it inside the bottom of my boat.

For some reason the thing I think to say is pretty stupid. "I'm not a princess."

He smiles and his teeth are pointed and sharp. "Oh no? Who else would travel to and fro in the Elemental Abyss if not for The Impossible Girl, the daughter of the goddess and grandchild of the King and Queen of the Universe? Does that not make you a princess?"

"You woke me up."

He nods. "Twice now. Once when you were with the boy and again just now."

"Why?"

"We are made to protect the lake. Not all those who pass are worthy."

"So I am worthy?"

"As I said before, Princess, we must all abide by Raj and Katyun's word." I recall how Raj created each of the lands for his daughters. Did he create this place too?

"What's your name?" I ask.

"Brooks."

"Ironic."

"Tell me about it." He's not that old and I wonder how he became Unbalanced. It isn't something that can be controlled. The Element kind of goes rogue and takes over, or sometimes, a person's body even rejects the Element that's been claimed.

"Well, thank you, Brooks, for waking me up and for retrieving my oar. I suppose I should be on my way before I fall asleep again."

"Oh, and you dropped this." He hands me a wet piece of paper. "Anytime, you need help in the Enchanted Lake, just call my name and I'll be there." And with a flip of his tail he's gone, disappearing beneath the surface.

I look at the piece of paper. It's the map. I must have still had it in my hand when I crossed the bridge and somehow dropped it in my haste to get to the boat. Except, it's different. My mother's drawings are still there, but other markings have appeared up and down the sides. Like notes. The rush of the waterfall grows louder in my ears. First, I need to get out of the cavern.

I shove the paper into my pocket and row across the lake as quickly as possible, carefully making my way out of the boat, and leaving the remaining oar inside. I take the rope and wrap it in a knot around the stake on this side of the bank. I then stick my fingers in my ears and run as fast as I can down the tunnel leading out of the cavern until I no longer hear the rush of the waterfall. Once I'm sure

I can no longer hear it, I slow down to a jog, and then back down to a walk, catching my breath. I reach the entrance to the cave and step out onto the narrow ledge.

This high up the wind whips my damp hair into my face. I sit down to rest, taking out the bottle of nutrient pills and swallowing one with the warm remains of the water. In the distance I can see the twinkling lights of the colony, shimmering a golden-pink against the red sky. I never knew Xon 9 was so vast, had so many nooks and crannies. Our colony only takes up a small portion of the land I can see. We never expanded to the base of the mountains. Perhaps because of the Imminent Darkness or perhaps because we never had a need. I can't be sure.

The moons are high in the sky, flanking the sun. I pull the map back out. It's still damp. The hand-writing is also my mom's. She's written things around the map:

-Time is not the same. Xon 9 time vs. E.A. time

-Unbalanced Waters in the lake (good not bad)

-Medeis seaweed to block the waterfall's enchantment

-Zephyrus seeds to summon the wind

-Ignis Flos to appease the beast in the chasm

There are other notes, but they're more difficult to make out. As the page dries, the words begin to fade. Medeis seaweed, Zephyrus seeds, and Ignis Flos? I've never heard of any of those things. I'll have to ask Bina because if anyone would know, it would be her.

I place the map back into my messenger bag, tucking it in next to the Earth stone. I don't have any Zephyrus seeds, whatever those are, to summon the wind. Last time Doran and I just asked politely, the theory being that all the Elements are interconnected anyways, all stemming from the same earthly origins. I scoot to the ledge and close my eyes. I silently ask, Elemental to Element, that the wind take me as its own and provide me safe travels home. If what Brooks said is true, not the part about being a princess because that's just ridiculous, but that the word of Raj and Katayun are law, then the wind should be willing to help me again.

My ponytail whips in the breeze and then suddenly stops. For a moment the breeze dies down and everything grows very still before the wind picks up again with a vengeance. I feel myself being wrapped in imaginary arms and I find myself being lifted from the ground. It's an odd sensation, but I feel coddled and protected, like the tiniest of babies being carried. The wind continues to swirl around me. As suddenly as it began, it stops. My eyes are still closed and when I feel my feet set on the ground, the lights of my colony are brighter and I can see the perimeter. I feel one last playful gust of wind swing my ponytail and then it's gone. I turn, clasping my hands together, and bow my head in thanks. Mom has her way and I have mine.

CHAPTER 9

I decide that my best bet is to stop at Sloan's. It's probably a better idea than to return home alone. Just in case. From the height of the moons I can tell that it's late. Most likely it's the same day as the one I left. I pass almost no one on the streets as I make my way toward the familiar stone house. But then I hear voices coming from behind me. Who would be out this late? I turn as if headed to one of the complexes and once I'm sure they've passed me, I fall into step quietly behind them. Two figures, both wearing the long hooded cloaks of the Imminent Darkness.

"I heard that she took down the entire army of Fire by herself!" says a female voice.

"Nonsense," replies a male voice. "She's just a girl, surely she had help."

"I don't know." The woman's voice drifts back to me. "If the legend is true, and she really is The Impossible Girl, she's going to be near impossible to defeat. Half-human, half-goddess? With all the Elements running through her veins." There's a hint of disbelief in her voice.

"Legends are just misconstrued stories. Besides no one could stop the Imminent Darkness. You can't stop something as old as time itself."

I let more distance fall between us. Clearly, they're talking about me. And I take the woman's sense of awe as a sign of weakness. If people in the ranks of the Imminent Darkness are questioning what I'm capable of then they must not be as strong and powerful as they think. As my thoughts take over, I'm not paying attention to where I'm walking and I trip over some loose rocks on the pavement. My hands break my fall and I hurriedly crawl into some bushes, trying to hide myself.

"What was that?" asks the man. "Did you hear that?"

"It sounded like someone was behind us."

I peer through the branches of the bush. They turn around and I see the glint of silver on the woman's face: a Metal. Then I notice the ingrained markings on the man. A Wood. Hard to believe a Wood would betray the Council of Leaders. Woods are known to be steadfast. "I think it came from over here," the Wood replies and they backtrack to where I'd just fallen.

"Odd," says the woman. The man kneels down, inspecting the prints left in the dirt by the heels of my hands. He gives a disinterested shrug, and just when I think they're about to brush it off and turn to be on their way, the Wood man looks right at me through the bushes. There's nowhere for me to go.

"Well, well. What do we have here?"

. . .

He grabs me roughly, pulling me up by my armpits, the branches of the bush scratching at my bare arms.

"Yuck. Look how dirty she is!" exclaims the woman.

"Were you following us?"

"Who? Me? Of course not." *Be quick, Kata.* "I was just walking home."

"At this time?"

"I was in the Black Bazaar." I've never been good at lying and it surprises me at how easily the words come tumbling out. It's believable. The Black Bazaar is open late, but I really have no sense of the exact time.

"Don't you know there's a curfew?"

"I'm a University student."

"No, a curfew was instated earlier today. There's been a rash of break-ins and the Leadership Council decided a curfew should be instated for everybody." Break-in sounds like an understatement. More like attempted murder, I think but bite my tongue.

"No, I, uh, didn't know that." The woman and the man exchange a glance and I can tell from the look in their eyes that they aren't going to let me go. I remember how Zora told me the people in cloaks appeared to outsiders as a sort of civilian law enforcement. No one actually believes in something as ancient and powerful as the

Imminent Darkness—or wants to believe, so they have to tell themselves whatever lies and half-truths to make sense of it all.

"Unfortunately, there's a penalty for disobeying the curfew," the woman replies.

"Oh? Is that so? And what's the penalty?" I ask as innocently as possible.

"This." I feel a sharp prick in my left shoulder. Then everything goes black.

. . .

When I come back around everything is blurry and out of focus. The lights are dim and I can almost make out the hooded figures as my eyes adjust. My body feels heavy like it's full of sand. I'm lying on a hard surface and my ankles and wrists are bound.

"We found some very interesting things in your bag." The voice belonging to the man from earlier comes drifting over to me. "An interesting ancient text, a stone, and a map."

Oh, no! The map. He waves it in front of my face. The notes have disappeared, vanishing again once the map is dry. I yank on my restraints. "Haven't you ever heard of personal property?" I yank again. "Where am I?"

"Where you are is irrelevant. More important is *who* you are."

"I know who I am. Who are you?" I retort. I can feel my reclaimed Fire pulsating beneath the surface of my skin.

"We are the Imminent Darkness."

"The Imminent Darkness is ancient and formless. A more accurate term would be peasants of the Imminent Darkness or maybe minions." There's the sound of chuckling from several people.

"Well, that seems an unfair advantage, doesn't it? You seem to know who we are, so who are you? Barely a woman, almost a child. Wandering around late at night, dirty, yet smelling of the sea. An ancient text of the five goddesses—not to mention one of the earliest mentions of the Imminent Darkness—and a strange stone in your bag."

"It's just a stone. A rock. Big deal." The room is coming into fuller focus and I try to notate every detail. I'm lying on a wooden table and the restraints are leather. The man talking to me is definitely the same one from before, brown eyes almost black, wood grain lining the side of his face. He is standing close and I can see the black stubble on his chin and the creases of his face. His eyebrows rest above his eyes like bushy caterpillars. Above me is an elaborate iron chandelier with glass jars holding lit candles. I almost laugh because I can't tell if it's all for show or if the dungeon affect is intentional. It reminds me a bit of "Tristen's Funhouse" in the basement of the Fire Building. Every building has unknown tunnels and chambers. I could be virtually anywhere.

More laughter at my words. There are several people in the room. "Your map was quite entertaining. The Elemental Abyss, a place of yore, of legend."

"It's just a game my friends and I made up. You know like tag or something." I yank at my restraints again. I'm beginning to panic. People who carry unknown substances and then inject others with them aren't the kind of people I'd like to stick around with. "You know, what you're doing isn't only theft of personal property. It's also called kidnapping!" I yell. More laughter. Oh, how I'm getting sick of being laughed at.

"You are quite fiery, aren't you?" The man smiles. His teeth are yellowed. "Prepare her for the MindCleanse. It will tell us what we want to know and rid her of the things we don't want her to know." A woman in a hooded cloak—the Metal woman from earlier—steps forward. In her hands is a medieval looking device. It's metal and kind of looks like a crown but has bolts. She moves toward my head and I thrash against the restraints as she begins to place it on top of my head, tightening the bolts until they're flush against my skin.

"You really shouldn't get involved in games that are over your head." The woman says gently. "The first part shouldn't hurt much. As your mind is cleansed it replays your memories backwards, starting with the most recent." She bites her lip. "Although after a certain point, the older memories are harder to extract and it will become a little painful." Then her face brightens. "You're young though, so it shouldn't hurt too much." I remember how Bina looked when I saw her after her MindCleanse, which luckily didn't work, but she appeared ill and frail. If they take my memories how will I ever know who I am or who I am meant to become? Will I even recognize my father, my mother, Ahna, Sloan?

The woman inserts a tube into the top of the odd crown now on top of my head. A crown for the princess. It dawns on me that my extracted memories will be pulled into the tube by the crown and that the Imminent Darkness will then have them to keep. They'll know who I am and who my mother is. They'll kill me. If the MindCleanse doesn't kill me first.

She presses a button. People eagerly surround the table, ready to watch the show. A bunch of sadists. No, not sadists, minions. Minions for something older and more powerful than they could ever dream of being. I roll my eyes to look up and back. A brilliant blue light emits from the crown, some kind of current. Then a sharp pain. The memory of following the man and woman comes rushing into focus, being pulled up by my armpits, hiding in the bush, falling into step behind them. I want to scream out in pain as I feel it physically being pulled up and out of me, but it's like I am paralyzed and no sound comes out. I am watching my life in reverse.

I pull against the restraints, try to kick my legs, anything. But nothing happens. Landing on the ground, the wind swaddling me in its arm, lifting me up. These aren't theirs to take! *Give them back to me!* Looking at the map. *No!* They can't know my mom's notes about the map. The map that was tucked in safely next to the Earth stone. Slipping...slipping away. I begin to hum my mother's song in my head. Maybe if I can distract my mind, it will make it harder to pull the memories. I close my eyes focusing on the words:

> *You are many things to me*
> *But of all the things you will be*
> *Kata is my favorite*
> *Loving, steadfast,*
> *Strong, Wise, and True*

All of this is inside you
If you will just look inward and see
You are all these things to me.

Over and over again. *Thud. Thud.* My blood is pumping in my veins and I can feel the heat from before beginning to percolate just beneath the surface. What happens when you apply an electrical current to Fire? The heat can't dissipate as quickly as it generates. *Look inward and see.* Fire is inside me and I'm not just anybody. I'm the freaking Impossible Girl. And I am ticked off. Fire can be passion, but it can also be anger. And I am angry right now. Angry that I had to see my mother bleed. Angry that I was chased by an ugly, rotting mummy. Angry that these people took my stuff. Angrier that they are taking my memories in order to leave me a lifeless shell with no clue who I am. I spent my whole life so far not knowing who I am and like hell, these people are going to take it away from me.

I feel the heat growing hotter inside me. Behind my eyelids I see red dancing. There's a hissing sound coming from the direction of my head.

"What's happening?" An unfamiliar, panicked voice calls out.

"I-I don't know!" replies the woman. I open my eyes. The woman reaches out to touch the crown, but quickly pulls her hand away as if burned.

Smoke. I can smell the smoke. "She's combusting or something!" a voice calls.

"Let's get out of here!" calls another.

I can hear the crackle now, but I'm not afraid. I know my

Fire will take care of me. I don't feel the sharp pain anymore. The crown on top of me is igniting and I'm still bound to the table. I feel the restraints loosen. I look down and there's a young woman unbuckling the restraints. Pins and needles rise to the surface of my hands and feet as together we unbolt the crown. I take it and throw it to the floor. There's a curtained partition to my left and it immediately catches up in flame.

"Thank you."

Her face is kind, tiny green vines run up its side, and her eyes are gray and gentle. She bows her head slightly, shoves my messenger bag into my chest, and runs out the door. Maybe Sloan isn't the only one who's infiltrated the Imminent Darkness.

The map is on the floor beside the table, dropped in the haste to get out. I grab it and sling my bag over my head, running in the direction the young woman ran. The fire is spreading and I can hear it behind me as my feet pound up the stone stairs. I begin to cough before I reach the top. The door is already open. Everyone is gone and I see the red lights of a safety crew headed in this direction. I run into the protection of some trees to get my bearings. Where am I? The low building I just came out of is a mix of sleek lines and glass. Transparency. *The people shall see clearly who their leaders are and what they do.* It's Council Hall. Where the Leadership Council of Wood makes decisions on our behalf. It's our government building, the Xon 9 equivalent of the White House or the Taj Mahal, depending on how you look at it. The Imminent Darkness conducting dirty deeds right beneath their feet. I emerge on the other side of the trees and begin to run as fast as I can toward Sloan's. A scary thought occurs to me as I round the corner, the cluster of wooden and stone houses appearing in the distance: *What if the Imminent Darkness and the Leadership Council are one and the same?* The skin on the back of my neck prickles in response.

CHAPTER 10

The first thing Sloan says when he sees me is: "What happened to your hair?" Quickly followed by: "Where have you been? Where's your mother? Why are you so dirty?" Then followed in quick succession by: "I'm so glad you're okay." I respond by bursting into tears. He holds me for a while, letting me cry, and then he gets up without a word and draws me a bath. He hands me a fluffy towel and pulls the door closed, leaving me alone.

I climb into the warm bath, which he's laced with essential oils. It feels therapeutic, as if I can wash away the day and night's events. I splash water over my face and down my arms. There are marks on my wrists and ankles from the leather restraints. Once my skin is pink and I'm satisfied that I can't scrub myself completely raw, I take the fluffy towel and dry off. I slip into a t-shirt and pair of shorts from Sloan then use the towel to wipe the condensation from the mirror. There are big bags underneath my eyes and scratches on my face from who-knows-where, but the real shocker comes from my hair. I now understand why it was the first thing out of his mouth because it's definitely the most jarring thing about my appearance. The fire must have singed parts of it because a portion of my ponytail is missing and some of it is short and sticking out at odd angles. The other part is long and the bottoms are singed. I bite my lip and try not to cry.

There's a knock on the door and I pull it open. One look at my quivering lip and Sloan disappears, returning with a pair of scissors. Without a word he sits me on the toilet and goes about my hair with the scissors. He gently takes my chin and moves it side to side examining his work. Finally, satisfied he lets me look in the mirror. He stands in the doorway his arms crossed and a small smile on his lips. Surprisingly, it actually looks good. The back is pretty short, revealing my tattoo now, but he left the front longer, the pieces falling just past my chin.

"Well?" He finally asks and it's the first word he's spoken since I first appeared on his doorstep.

"It's not my first choice of haircut," I begin and his face falls slightly. "But it's not my last choice either." I'm quick to amend, wrapping my arms around his waist. "Thank you." And I've never felt so thankful. "For everything. Always. In the past and in the future."

"Woah. That's a little much don't you think?"

"You don't know what I've been through."

"Let me get you a cup of tea and you can tell me about it."

. . .

When I knocked on his door, he appeared to have been sleeping, but he admits it was more like tossing and turning. He'd heard about the attack on my mother. My father, who is staying with Ahna's family, assured him that I was in safe-keeping if I was indeed with Novea and that my mother had a way of working things out. Turns out I'd only been gone since the afternoon, now it was the wee hours of the next day.

I explain everything to Sloan starting with discovering the map and key. The map is still in my messenger bag, so I pull it out along with the book and the stone. I tell him how I discovered my mom bleeding and how we used the key to travel to the Land of Earth, completely bypassing the Elemental Abyss. I describe in as much detail how it was like a miniature planet Earth. I tell him about Cyan and the wolf and elaborate on my mother's explanation of who she really is, how I came to be, and what exactly the Imminent Darkness is all about. I describe the pyramid, the mummy, how I escaped and how my mother disappeared. Then I tell him about Brooks and how I used the wind to get home, only to be caught following the man and woman. He mentions something about my curiosity being the death of me, and then I go on to tell him how I escaped the MindCleanse by causing the device to overheat and catch fire, thus explaining my hair. I even tell him about the young woman with the gray eyes. The moons have set and the sky's grown bright pink by the time I'm done explaining it all to him.

"I don't even know what to say."

"And you were there again. Before I woke up and the wolf was there, I was dreaming and you said you'd protect me and you did. The wolf got distracted by some fish in the stream. I guess even the Imminent Darkness can't override basic biology. A wolf's still gotta eat."

"It's hard to explain…" he begins. "I wasn't really there of course, but it's like, like a piece of my soul travels with you to protect you. I know it sounds crazy." His cheeks flush and he picks up the Earth stone turning it in his hands, trying to distract himself with inspecting it.

"It's not crazy," I say putting my hand over his. "You took a vow to protect me. Maybe that's how you've always protected me, even when I'm not near. Before we even knew it."

He shrugs and holds the stone up. "Looks like any regular old thing doesn't it?"

I take it from him, turning it in my own hands. It does look like just any regular old stone you could find on the ground. The Fire Stone was obsidian and almost gem-like. The Earth Stone is plain in contrast. "It does."

"Will your mother come back?"

"I'm not sure. I can't imagine she'd leave my father. I mean falling in love was the whole reason she took human form."

"Maybe she'll take him back to live in that castle with her."

I shrug. "Maybe." But then she'd be leaving *me* behind. I push the thought aside. "Guess, the whole thing is a bit more than you thought you were signing up for?"

He wraps an arm around me and pulls me in close. "What? A half-human, half-goddess who is supposed to take down an ancient force meant to balance the Universe? Nah, piece of cake. That I can deal with." He squeezes me and kisses the side of my head. "Now, the look on your face and your hair when you appeared on my doorstep? That kind of stuff is a whole other thing." We both laugh and it feels good to feel normal again, if only for a moment. All my life, I'd wanted to be extraordinary, not realizing how extraordinary I truly was. And who knew that once I became extraordinary I'd long for moments when everything was ordinary.

. . .

Sloan says he has to check on Bina and Michaela, so while he's gone I curl up in the little pod that makes up his bedroom. There's no door, but he has a heavy curtain that can be slid across, more to block out light than anything. The mattress takes up the entire pod and he has a thick blanket and several pillows. There's a shelf at the head of the mattress with some votive candles on top. I use the pack of matches lying on the shelf to light the candles and I pull the curtain closed to block the light that spills in from the main room.

I haven't slept in almost two days and it will be good to finally get some rest. When he returns he promised we'll go to Ahna's to see my father. I run my hand over my newly shorn hair. So much for concealing that tattoo. My fingers find the smooth surface of the Fire filigree then runs over the rest of my Elemental Star where each remaining part feels like familiar skin. I don't want my messenger bag out of my sight, so it's at the foot of the bed. I take out the Earth stone, turning it over in my hands. It has to be destroyed using one of the items Bina gave me, the small burlap sack in the zippered compartment of my bag. I place the stone underneath a pillow and lay my head down. Sleep comes almost immediately.

I dream of my mother. Ever since I was a small child I remember my mother being obedient. Average. She didn't stand out in any way. She followed the rules. She wasn't overly beautiful, not like she appeared in the Land of Earth, where her radiance was unbound. She went to work. I remember how worried she was when I pronounced Fire, asking what I had done. Maybe it was because of her love-hate relationship with her sister Celosia, or maybe it's because she wanted me to be a Water and be safe under the protection of Sloan's Everlasting Vow. Images of my mother flash through my subconscious, coming to rest on the vision in my Mindscape which started this whole mess. The first time I relived this was as an observer, watching myself as a child. But now I find my perspective has shifted. In fact, it isn't even *my* perspective. It's my mother's.

I sit on the wooden chair in the kitchen wringing my hands nervously. The strange Metal woman sits across from me. I watch as Ka plays with some wooden toys in the main living area. "You've brought me here too late," Bina says. "They already know who she is."

"It just started recently," I say in a worried whisper. "I don't know what to do." I hold a handkerchief up to my eyes and dab at them.

"There's nothing ye can do," the woman replies.

I feel my stomach lurch at her words. "But if I can take away her gifts…temporarily, just hide them for a bit. Keep them safe. Maybe they will lose interest." I watch my precious little girl, oblivious of her magnificence and the potentiality with which she's been created.

"Ye are foolish. Ye come here thinking yeh can live a mortal life, but ye cannot. It is not the natural order of things. Now ye have put yer daughter, yer family, even yerself in jeopardy." Her words sting. Maybe it was foolish of me to meddle in human affairs, but I wanted to feel as a mortal feels. I wanted to feel the pang of grief and the ecstasy of love.

"I didn't think…"

"Exactly. Yer kind never do. That's why yeh and yer sisters were so easily tricked, seduced into yer own hunger for power." Bina glances over at Ka. "It will not be easy to split her personality. The Elements are strong inside of her."

"But, surely, I mean, there must be something. Anything. Please, Bina. I will do anything to protect her."

"The child of the eighteenth moon on the hundredth solar alignment. It's already been seen and once it is seen there is no undoing the Sight"

"Please."

"There is something," She studies me scrutinizing, the silence extending awkwardly long between us. "A mother's love knows no bounds, mortal or otherwise. I would do the same to protect my own son or daughter." She lets out a long sigh, reaching into her bag and pulling out a handful of stones. Stones that were given to her long ago. Stones that I've seen before. She hands me a smooth obsidian one. "Fire." Then she hands me a beautiful light blue stone with tan

cracks in it. "Earth" She picks up the next one and holds it up. It is opalescent like a beautiful seashell. "Water." She hands it to me. The next stone is gem-like, rough-hewn amber. "Wood." And lastly she pulls out a stone that is gray and sparkling in the afternoon light. "Metal."

Together they barely fit into the palm of my hand. "She will need protection. Each one represents the five elements. On each of five full moons, ye must take one and repeat this phrase: Protection, piety, promise. This phrase must be repeated five times, one for each of the Elements. Then cast the stone under the light of the two full moons into the Elemental Abyss."

"And then she will be protected? They won't be able to find her? That's the most important thing. It's vital that the Imminent Darkness cannot find her and harm her before it's too soon."

"Yes, the eighteenth moon on the hundredth solar alignment appears to be an auspicious time. The balance will have shifted by then and the Imminent Darkness will be at a penultimate of power." She closes her eyes as if sensing something from the future, that in my limited human form I am unaware of. She sniffs the air as if the ancient dark energy is present in the room. "An Everlasting Vow."

"Who?"

She opens her eyes. "My son. He is a few years older than yer daughter. On his sixteenth moon, I will explain the situation to him and perform the ceremony. He will be her protector. Close enough to protect, but distant enough to allow her free-will. He will watch over her, guide her if possible into making the safest choices."

The idea makes me feel better and it is a great sacrifice for Bina to bring her own son into the situation, but I have my doubts. "And what if he says no?"

She looks at me surprised. "An Everlasting Vow is a great honor. He is already showing great talents in dream travel and transmutation." She smiles. "He clearly takes after his mother."

"And this will protect her?"

"For as long as she needs protecting, it shall protect her."

"And what happens when she no longer needs protecting?" I feel my resolve begin to falter slightly. I look at the back of Kata's head, the long brown hair that tumbles down her back. She's just a child. I want her to enjoy being ordinary, if only for a little while. It's what I risked everything for—to feel normal-to have a clear beginning and end. A human life.

"Then the world as we know it will come to an end. A decision will be made that cannot be undone."

"Whose decision?" I ask desperately.

She wrinkles her brow. "It's not a set point in time. So it remains unclear. What I can see is that the decision will affect all decisions that are yet to come."

"What does that mean?" I ask, clutching at the stones, holding them to my chest, close to my heart, as if I could somehow pour additional love into them in order to protect her.

Bina rubs her forehead as if in great pain. "I don't know."

. . .

I wake up confused as to where I am and then I remember I'm at Sloan's. The dream comes rushing back. That's not exactly how I remembered it in my Mindscape. There were other parts, extra parts. Maybe it's like Ahna said: there's three sides to every story: yours, theirs, and the truth. So if I know my side and my mother's which one is the truth? I hear the front door open and close. I shake my head, telling myself I'll decipher the dream later. I push the curtain aside, allowing the light to come in. "Feeling better?" Sloan asks as he slips off his jacket.

"A little," I nod and change the subject. "How's Bina?"

"Better. Staying awake longer. Complaining as usual." He grins. "I think it bothers her that she can't go back to her trailer. But it's still not safe." His eyes cut to the sleeping pod and he pulls out my messenger bag and tosses it to me. "Speaking of, ready to see your dad?"

"Yes!" We head toward the door. "Oh, wait." I go back to the sleeping pod, yank a sweatshirt over my head, then pull the Earth stone from underneath my pillow.

"Hoping that the way to destroy the stone would seep into your dreams?" Sloan smiles.

I shove the stone deep into my bag. "Something like that."

. . .

The Solloman house is a mirror image of our own since we live in the same community. All the houses are a bleak concrete stone. Ahna's room is located where mine is, which was always fun growing up because we thought that made us some sort of soul sisters. Li's room is where my mother's office is located. Mr. and Mrs. Solloman and my father are seated around the large kitchen table when we arrive. Whereas our house is sort of plain and non-descript, the Solloman house is like an explosion of life. Colorful, woven tapestries adorn the walls, their table is made from intricately carved wood, and there are candles, statues, and all other sorts of oddities throughout the entire house. I always thought it was amazing to come to Ahna's because it was everything my house growing up was not. Maybe my mom took the whole ordinary thing a little too literally.

"Kata!" My father stands up and embraces me. He pats my shoulders and pushes me away to inspect me. "Your hair?"

"Yeah, I had a bit of an...incident."

"It looks lovely, Ka," Mrs. Solloman smiles. Ever since we were small, Mrs. Solloman has always been quick with a kind word, which is lucky for Li and his mischievous personality. "Here, come sit. I'll go fetch the twins."

I take Mrs. Solloman's seat and Sloan leans against the stone countertop. My father sits back down and his face is very solemn. "And your mother?" If you never looked in my father's eyes, you'd never know what emotion he was feeling. Sometimes his eyes say one thing and his words say another. This time his words indicate no worry as if he just asked how a day at school had gone. But his eyes belie his words. The deep brown is cloudy, revealing his worry.

"She's fine." I look over at Mr. Solloman and my father nods, urging me to go on. "When I found her, she was bleeding badly from the head, but I'd found the key and we used it." I'm not sure how much the Sollomans know about my family's unique situation.

"And will she be returning home?"

"I don't know. We got separated. I think she wants to come home, but maybe she isn't ready? She said something like you knew what you signed up for." I shrug, but I know the words might sting.

He nods curtly. "That I did. Well, I'm glad she's well. Was she happy to return?"

"Yeah, actually, she seemed really happy." I recall how radiant and almost effervescent she seemed sitting on the throne. "It suits her."

A faraway look replaces the cloudiness of worry. "That it does."

There's a pounding down the stairs and Ahna bounds into the kitchen. She throws her arms around my neck. "Ka! Oh, my gosh. When we heard what happened I was so worried! Your dad said you'd be okay, but still. And that one—" She glances over at Sloan who's still casually leaned against the counter. "Forget it! He was more worried than all of us!" A flush creeps up his neck as the rest of the room laughs.

There's another set of footsteps and Li jumps down the last few stairs, landing lightly at the bottom. "Kata. Glad to see you in one piece." He looks me up and down with his usual flirtatious attitude, not caring about Sloan's presence, which must be weird since all three of us were in Universal History together. "I like the hair."

I run my hands over it self-consciously. "Thanks, Sloan cut it for me."

Li nods approvingly. "It suits your new fiery personality." He wiggles his eyebrows and I roll my eyes.

"You're such an idiot," Ahna says. "Listen I have some stuff

I want to show you."

"Ahna, let her be with her father," Mr. Solloman scolds.

But my father is quick to intervene. "No, no. Kata is safe. Novea is safe and well. Go and be with your friends. I need to return to the office for a bit anyways." My father is a Liege to the Council, meaning he acts as a clerk for the Council of Wood. Also meaning he's going to the Council Hall. My stomach feels gripped in ice. I put a hand on his forearm.

"Be careful." My words sound ominous, despite the pleasant reunion He looks at me curiously, gets up from the table and kisses me on top of the head.

"Such strange words," he says with a raised eyebrow. He bows slightly to the Sollomans as a show of respect to their hospitality then turns to leave.

"I've heard stranger," I half mumble in reply, but he's already closed the door on his way out.

CHAPTER 11

Ahna's room is very un-Ahna like. There are open books everywhere: on the desk, on the floor, on the bed. Frankly, it's a mess. It's also the first time I notice the dark circles beneath her eyes. "I was worried when you disappeared," she begins, shutting the door behind Li as he ambles in. "Your father reassured us that if you were with your mother everything would be fine. But I overheard some law enforcement Metals speaking with your father, and I know that there was a blood stain in the study, which I naturally assumed couldn't be good. So I got to thinking."

"So what else is new?" Li mumbles. Li has always been the adventurous, non-committal child; whereas, Ahna is the studious, well-meaning twin.

She cuts him a glare. "Knowing what we know about your mother that your father doesn't know that we know—"

"That wasn't the least bit confusing," Sloan whispers. I can't help but smile because this is Ahna. When she gets excited and her wheels start turning, she latches on to an idea and there's no stopping her.

"Anyways, as I was saying, if it's true that your mother is the Earth Goddess then who would go after her with the intention of harming her? Naturally, I theorized it would be the Imminent Darkness, so I asked Mona, the librarian, to pull any books with the mention of the Imminent Darkness, thus the mess in here." She moves around a pile of books and papers, bends over, and picks up a book. "This one is especially interesting." She hands it to me.

It's bound in leather and the title is etched into the leather: *The Impossible Girl*. "It can't be." Sloan leans over my shoulder.

"I'd say it's impossible, but I don't want to seem facetious." I give him a small smile and turn it over in my hands.

"Go ahead," Ahna urges. "Read it. Out loud. Li hasn't heard it yet and it isn't long."

Li slides some papers off the bed and plunks down. Sloan and I push some more books out of the way and carve out a space on the floor. Ahna sits on her desk chair. I open the book. The pages are yellowed and there are beautiful swatches of watercolor designs on each page, but no actual illustrations. It isn't hand-written like the other book, *The Five Elemental Goddesses*, but appears to have been typed on a word processor of some kind. I clear my throat. I really don't like reading out loud, even if it is just my friends. "Here," I say thrusting the book at Sloan. "You're a teacher. You read it."

He raises an eyebrow. "Are you sure? It is *your* story, after all."

I nod. "I'm sure. I want to listen without being distracted."

"Suit yourself." As he reads it's immediately clear the book appears to have started where the other book ended.

There once were five sisters, born of the Universe. They would play together happily, until one day a codger came and tricked them, offering each sister a magical stone. The stones created division amongst the sisters and soon all they would do was fight and bicker. Each daughter refused to share her stone and refused to give up her stone. Not being able to see their daughters in such contention, Raj and Katayun, the Mother and Father of the Universe, decided to give each sister their own land which corresponded to their stone. Celosia received the Land of Fire, Constancia was to rule in the Land of Wood, Isa the middle sister would receive the Land of Metal, Tullia would dwell in the Land of Water, and the youngest sister, Anuja, would make peace in the Land of Earth. Goddesses of their own land! What more could a sister ask for?

Everything, is what the youngest Anuja would answer. Anuja was lonely. She appreciated having the entire land of grass, rivers, and mountains, but was sad that she had no one with whom to share it. One day the loneliness was especially difficult, so wearing her golden cloak, the youngest sister decided to explore. She took her magical key, this way she could always return home, and traveled to the beach. She was young and maybe foolish, but she was also observant. Over many days and nights near the pyramid of sand, she had noticed the change in the vibrational energy. Each day she would go to the beach and then return to her castle and record her observations. She noticed the birds and other animals would not go near this energetic field and at night there would be no stars in this peculiar circular piece of sky. She suspected, knowing the vastness of the Universe, that perhaps her father's creation of the Land was imperfect and that he had made a mistake. Either way today was the day she had planned to find out.

She arrived at the beach before sunrise and stood directly beneath the energetic field, feeling its hum in her fingertips as she reached up. There was a strong pulling sensation. She brought her fingertips back down and touched the key that sat securely in the pocket of her cloak. She could always come back, couldn't she? With a smile she reached up and was pulled through the portal. Bits and pieces of her childhood memories spun by as she hurtled through the tear in the fabric of time and space.

A door came into focus and she used her arms to cover her face as she tumbled through it. Another world? She got up from her hands and knees. She was in a large cavern and there were five doors, each leading to the Land of her sisters. An odd glowing orb was located in the center of the room, acting as a beacon to guide them. No, not another world. Simply her father's hopeful nature. He probably hoped that one day they'd want to visit each other's Lands, not realizing the capacity for their stubbornness. She turned and saw a fiery chasm and a tunnel leading to who-knew-where. On one side, she could visit any of her sisters now, but on the other side, adventure waited. The youngest sister chose adventure. And this is where the story of the Impossible Girl begins.

Sloan pauses and looks over at me. "Are you okay?"

My throat has gone dry. Some of this I knew already, from both my mother and the book, but here I am listening to what I imagine will be the story of how my mother met my father. *Your father knows what he signed up for.* The words come tumbling back to me. My boring, play-it-safe mother was anything but boring. It's almost like when she took human form she became the exact opposite of who she truly was. Did she do it on purpose? *Head or heart, Kata?* Obviously, she followed her heart. And she wanted me to follow mine too. *Oh, Kata, what have you done?* I'm immediately reminded of a children's rhyme we used to tease each other with when Li, Ahna, and I were kids. *Secrets, secrets are no fun. Secrets, secrets hurt someone.* What secrets will this story reveal to me? What other secrets is my mother hiding? "Yeah, yeah, I'm fine." Sloan looks at me, eyes searching. I put my hand on his forearm gently. "Really. Keep reading." He shrugs and obliges.

Anuja transmuted to a small cyan-colored dragonfly and crossed the fiery chasm undetected. Her little wings fluttering, she continued down the tunnel until she saw a large lake and waterfall. The sound of the waterfall was melodious, the most beautiful song of any she'd heard in the Universe. She flew across the lake easily. The confused creatures beneath the surface wondered how she was not affected by the waterfall's enchantment, which would lure any mortal to sleep. After reaching the other side of the lake she continued down another tunnel which opened into a large cavern full of stalagmites and stalactites. Still in her dragonfly form she flew to the opening and peered out. The landscape was red and rocky and the first thing Anuja noticed was the lack of water. She loved her bubbling brook at home that ran the length of the Land, not to mention the beautiful sea where she'd first noticed the portal. The second thing she noticed was the sky. It too was red like the terrain with a large red sun hovering high. Compared to home this land seemed dark The color of the landscape reminded her of blood.

In the distance she could see an outcropping of buildings. She decided she would stay in dragonfly form to reach the small city. On the outskirts of the city she transmutated back into a woman, pulling her cloak around her to shield herself from the strong breeze that seemed to blow across this place. She entered into the city and was amazed to see people walking about. Regular, normal, mortal people! The city itself was nothing fancy: mostly stone buildings with other more peculiar buildings here and there. She noticed an iron archway with the words divide et impera intertwined in the scrolls. The archway led to an array of buildings, but what caused her pause was the familiarity of the words. She'd heard them before. Only she couldn't recall when.

"Excuse me, are you lost?" a deep male voice jarred her from her memories.

She turned toward the voice and let out a little gasp. The deepest brown eyes stared back at her. They were set in a tanned face with an angular nose and thin-set lips. The man had black hair that fell into his eyes. He was tall and slender. And young, much, much younger than she was, but how does one compare mortal years to immortal ones?

"Oh, um, no, not yet. I was just admiring this archway."

He squinted at her, a small smile at the corners of his lips. He thought she was being funny. "Ah, yes, divide and conquer is the peculiar creed of Xon 9." She surmised Xon 9 was the name of this place. He gestured to the archway. "I never did care for it much myself." They stood awkwardly for a moment before the man continued. "May I walk you somewhere?"

Anuja smiled. "Yes, I was just walking this way." She pointed ambiguously.

"Excellent. I'll go with you."

And so began the love affair of an immortal and a mortal.

It wasn't long before Anuja fell in love with Absalom. Anuja was happy she was no longer lonely and she had no desire to return home. More importantly, Absalom didn't question her about her past or where she came from. Eventually, Anuja married the handsome Absalom. On her wedding night she sent messages to the heavens, asking for the blessing of her celestial parents. One night, in a dream, Raj and Katayun visited their youngest daughter. And they said to her: "We love you, Anuja, and if it is your will to be with Absalom then you have our blessing. However, our blessing comes with a condition. While living amongst the mortals you will take mortal form. You will age with your new husband into a wise crone and when your mortal body dies you will return to the Land of Earth. After this you will no longer be able to make trips to the mortal plane. If you somehow violate this condition and return to the Land of Earth before your mortal death, then you may never return. It is with our deepest love for you that we grant you your mortality."

The next day Anuja woke up. She didn't feel any different, but when she looked into the mirror she noticed some of her celestial radiance had diminished. She was still beautiful of course and the change was so subtle even Absalom wouldn't notice. Over time, Anuja and Absalom decided to have a child. Secretly, Aunja knew this could come with great risks, so she decided to visit a Seer. One night, while Absalom slept soundly, Anuja grabbed her cloak and snuck out of the house.

The Seer was located in the Underground. Anuja had quickly grown accustomed to her new home. She now knew that her sisters, and herself, somehow affected the physiology of the humans on this planet. Absalom had beautiful wood grain lining the side of his face and she herself had gorgeous green vines that curlicued from her neck and up the side of her face. It was their pronounced Elementals: Wood and Earth. It was a proper balance and secretly reminded

Anuja of her home. The Seer was a Metal woman. The Metals always frightened Anuja, with their unpredictable natures and silver threads on the sides of their faces. Metal was easily Unbalanced, but they were both revered for their strength and feared for the same reason.

Anuja entered into the Underground and found the Metal woman with the Sight. The woman was reportedly eerily accurate, a true gift of the Sight, unlike some of the other scamming Unbalanced Metals in the Underground. The woman had wild, curly gray hair and a couple of missing teeth. As soon as they sat down, the woman took her hand. A smile crept across her face. "Ye are not of this plane. Ye come from far seeking companionship. A child. Ye will have a child." She began to rock back and forth as the visions came quicker, trying to put the pieces together. "Earth. Wood. Metal. Fire. Water. Impossible. A child will be born to restore the balance. She will show signs at a young age of her aptitude, but it must be hidden. The Imminent Darkness will search for her. A debt to be repaid." The Metal woman's eyes flung open. "Ye shouldn't have come here, daughter of Raj."

Anuja startled. "How do you know who I am?

"I am with the Sight, the Sight does not have secrets."

"What is the balance that you speak of?"

"The balance of the Universe. Good and evil, light and dark, yin and yang. There is an unbalance happening. Yer unborn daughter is going to be the one to restore it. She will be the perfect storm of mortal and immortal."

"And the debt to be repaid?"

"Ye were given a stone. But yeh became greedy. The codger wants to be repaid for providing you with this life of companionship, for putting into motion the chain of events that led ye here."

136

"*I provided myself with this life!*" Anuja protested.

"*Tis whatever ye tell yerself. I am only a messenger of the future.*"

"*How will I recognize the signs you spoke of?*"

"*Ye will know. She will show signs of impossible things. She will be the Impossible Girl.*"

"*And how will I keep her hidden from the Imminent Darkness?*"

"*When ye notice the signs, find me. Now go, Your Highness, Daughter of the Universe. Go and enjoy your mortal life and make the debt to be repaid worth the cost of your daughter's life.*" Abruptly, the woman got up from the table and disappeared behind a curtain. The meeting was over.

Anuja left some coins on the table as payment and, pulling up her hood, re-entered into the night. Her heart was swirling with the human emotions she had so longed for: fear, sadness, happiness, and excitement. As she walked home to her sleeping husband she tried to push the thoughts of fear and sadness aside. There would be time to deal with those things later. But to think she'd be a mother! And have a daughter!

Nine months later the Impossible Girl was born.

CHAPTER 12

Sloan stops reading and looks up.

"Well, go on then," says Li.

"I can't. That's it," he replies.

"What?" I ask sitting up.

Ahna nods from her perch on the desk chair. "The last part of the book has been torn out." She plucks the book out of Sloan's hands. She turns to the back and shows us the remnants of the last few pages of the story.

"Ugh," I moan feeling defeated. "Just when I was starting to learn about my mother and myself, someone has to go and ruin it." Li leans over the side of the bed and hits me in the face with a pillow.

"Get over yourself, Kata. I mean, it's *your* life. I'm pretty sure you know how it turns out."

"As much as I hate to admit whenever Li is right, it's true,"

Ahna agrees.

"So your Royal Highness, what next then?" Li asks.

I take the pillow and turn around, whacking him with it. "I told you not to call me that." He's smiling when he pulls the pillow out of my hands and for a moment—the briefest of instants—I remember how things were before, when we were excited to be in Fire together and when there was so much hope for everything. Now he bears the scars on his face of my own doing. Things have changed so much and so fast.

He notices the change in expression. His smile quickly dissolves into a frown. "Don't look at me like I'm broken."

"I'm not."

He grabs my wrist. "You are. It's not your doing." He lets go. "I'm out of here." Before anyone can say anything he jumps off the bed and disappears out the door without another word. I start to go after him, but Sloan puts a hand on my shoulder.

"Trust me. Let him go." I nod, biting my bottom lip. "He's right, you know, it's not your doing."

"How is it not my doing!?" I exclaim. "In order to save him, I practically killed him. I'm lucky that I *didn't* kill him."

Sloan's face grows serious and anger flashes in his eyes, but only for a second. "And if you hadn't, he would have killed you." The silence is almost palpable until Ahna breaks it.

"He's been kind of moody lately. I think the loss of his Fire has been hard on him. But Teach—I mean Sloan, is right. It's not your fault. Li knows that, I know that, everyone knows that. Except you." I look down feeling a bit ashamed. If everyone else, including Li, can look past what happened and forgive me, why can't I forgive myself? Sloan takes my chin in his hand and moves my face so that I'm looking him in the eye.

"Sometimes, Kata, we have to hurt the ones we love in order to save them."

. . .

After dinner, of which neither my father nor Li is in attendance for, Sloan heads home. It wouldn't be appropriate to stay with him when the Solloman's have already offered their hospitality to my family. Ahna and I are in her room and it reminds me of the sleepovers we'd have as kids. We're laying side-by-side in her bed and it's comforting to have her here.

"Do you think your mom will come back?" she finally asks.

"I'm not sure," I answer truthfully. Now that I've heard the story, she'd be breaking the condition of Raj and Katayun if she returns, and then what would happen? Would her immortal form die too? She'd be gone forever. My father would be a widow. I'd rather not think about it. "Do you think Li will come back?"

Ahna laughs. "Eventually. Honestly, Ka, he really doesn't blame you...at all. If anything, he's been really hard on himself because *he* tried to kill *you.*"

"That wasn't his fault! He was programmed!" I protest.

"Exactly. And you saving your own life isn't your fault either. You both survived. And to me, that's all that matters."

We both grow quiet and I think she's fallen asleep when she

quietly asks. "Can I see the stone?"

I completely forgot that the stone was in my bag. I'd shown Sloan earlier, but then forgot all about it. Ahna's done so much for me: from helping me locate the Elemental Abyss to researching the Imminent Darkness, the least I could do is show her what all the trouble's been about. I turn on the light and grab my messenger bag. The corner now has two holes where the wolf's fangs grabbed it. I reach inside and pull out the plain stone and hand it to her. "It was inside a pyramid, just sitting there on a pedestal, in a room where all the walls were lined with any gem or jewel you could imagine."

"It looks kind of ordinary," she says and I can tell she is trying to hide her disappointment.

"It does, doesn't it?" I say taking it back and turning it in my hands. It's not very heavy. Smooth and brown-colored. "Hey, wait a second. In my dream Bina said turquoise. This isn't turquoise!"

"What dream?"

"I had a dream and it was a memory from when I was a kid, except instead of my perspective it was my mom's. It was when my mother first received the stones." I rack my memory from earlier. "Obsidian, turquoise, opal, amber, and hematite. None of the stones were an ordinary rock!"

"Sure looks like an ordinary rock. Are you sure you didn't get the wrong stone?"

"I was chased by a mummy."

She lets out a low whistle. "Okay then, that's not weird."

"You think that's weird, but your best friend being part

goddess, owning a magical key, and traveling to distant lands isn't?"

"Good point." She takes the stone back and turns it over and I can see the wheels spinning. Her eyes light up. "What if it's protected?"

"With an enchantment?"

"No, more like with armor. What if the ordinary rock part is just a shell protecting the inside rock, the turquoise one you saw in your dream?"

"So how do we get it out of its shell?"

"I'm not sure. Maybe it just needs washed?" I doubt it could be something so simple, but Ahna gets out of bed and disappears, returning with a clay bowl of water and a cloth. We immerse the stone in the water and begin to rub it with the cloth. Nothing happens. We rub more vigorously. Still nothing.

"I don't think that's going to work."

"Do you have a better idea?"

"At the moment, no." We sit in silence with the Earth stone still submerged in the bowl of water between us. "Wait, I have this." I reach into my bag and pull out the little burlap sack Bina gave me. I open it and pull out the speckled feather, the crystal, the vial of clear liquid, and the pack of matches.

Ahna looks at the items. "Not exactly the most helpful group of things I've ever seen." She picks up each item, inspecting it, and then sets it back down. She holds up the vial. "What's this?"

I shrug. "Bina didn't say. And I have a feeling that even if I ask now, she still wouldn't say."

Ahna unscrews the top and takes a whiff, immediately wrinkling up her nose. "Disgusting."

"Let me smell." She hands the vial toward me and as I'm about to take it from her, the bedroom door opens, startling me, and I spill some of it. "Crap."

Li comes waltzing in, a smug smile on his face. "What's going on, Ladies?" he slurs.

"Someone's been to the Black Bazaar," Ahna says at the same time I say, "Look what you made me do!"

I hold up the blanket where a drop of the liquid spilled. There's a tiny hole in it. "Woah! You're really lucky that didn't touch your skin!" Ahna says. Li comes over and sticks his finger through the hole. I smack his hand.

"Go away, you're dangerous!" I screw the cap back on the vial. No more accidents.

"Oh, come on, Kata, I just want to help," Li pouts.

"You should do as she says, Liwald. Look at you! If Mom sees you like this, good luck getting out of the house again anytime soon!" Ahna scolds. Ahna, the responsible twin, Li, well…he's Li.

"You guys are no fun!" he groans.

I hand the vial to Ahna and push Li towards the bedroom door. I get him into the hallway and am about to pull the door closed when he turns and leans in close. I can smell the bitterness of alcohol on his breath. My heart beats a little too fast. A kiss from before Pronouncement—before Sloan—comes rushing back to me. "How about it, Kata?" he whispers. "If you're truly sorry…" But I'm too used to Li's manipulative ways. I know he cares about me, but it's not in the way that I want or need.

"If you're truly sorry, you'll go to bed before I make you sorry!" I growl and shut the door in his face.

"Party pooper!" he calls from the other side.

I lock the door.

"He's so embarrassing," Ahna complains.

"Normally, I'd agree, but he's been through a lot. Let him sleep it off." I pick up the blanket and inspect the hole. "Sorry, about that."

"It's okay. At least now we sort of know what the liquid is." I sit beside her and she unscrews the cap again. "I don't think it's acid, but I'm not completely sure. Science wasn't my strongest subject."

"Every subject was your strongest subject."

She opens the bottle and pours a tiny drop on the rock's top. It still sits in the bowl of water, unperturbed. We watch as it begins to bubble and fizz. Ahna dips her fingers in the water and splashes it over the rock. Suddenly, the chemical reaction begins to froth and foam. She splashes it again. The foam disappears. She takes the cloth and scrubs at the spot. "Ka, look!" She squeals with excitement. Beneath the spot where she scrubbed is the most beautiful blue, like the sky of Earth. Gorgeous, clean, and shiny.

"Turquoise."

. . .

My first inclination is to dump the whole darn vial of liquid on top of the stone and let it foam away the hard outer shell, but

Ahna is a little more leery. And practical. "That's probably not the best idea. We aren't exactly sure what the liquid in the vial is and we aren't sure about the exact chemical process that's occurring. Obviously, it's abrasive…" *Blah, blah, blah.* I can feel my eyes begin to glaze over as she goes all scientific on me. "That being said, I think we could use the entire vial, but in a more methodical way." She disappears for a moment and reappears with two bowls, one empty and another with water, a pair of metal tongs, a pair of latex gloves, and a pair of goggles.

"Who has this stuff just lying around their house?"

"Well, when your mother is an Earth and your father a Water it's kind of inevitable that science junk will be a staple in the household." She hands me the stuff, scoops the books and papers off her desk and drops them on top of a bookcase, and then I place the items on the now clear desk. "Even Li picked up the science gene, in his own way of course. He's into technology and all of that, but my parents and I are more into the experimental part of things."

She puts on the goggles followed by the gloves. She then carefully empties the vial into the empty dish. I hand her the Earth stone and she grasps it with the tongs. She dips it into the liquid and it begins to bubble and fizz. She waits a few beats longer until almost all the liquid in the dish seems to have been used up, then dips the rock in the dish of water where it immediately begins to foam. I bring over the other bowl and she dips it into the third bowl to wash away some of the foam. She sets it carefully on her desk. I hand her the cloth and she carefully begins to scrub at the Earth stone's armor.

The more she buffs, the more layers of dirt are wiped away. The work isn't quick, but Ahna is methodical. After a bit, the majority of the outer layer of ordinary rock is gone, revealing a gorgeous turquoise stone that is smooth with has tiny lines and speckles of tan that run through it. It reminds me a bit of Cyan, but lighter, somewhere in between Cyan and the colors of the sea.

Ahna scrubs the last of the armor away and holds up the stone, proud of her efforts. "What a beauty! I've never seen anything on Xon 9 like it."

She hands it to me and I take it, feeling its texture which is both smooth in some parts and bumpy in others. "That's because it's not from Xon 9."

She snaps off the gloves and pulls the goggles over her head. "So what happens now?"

I shrug, still mesmerized by the stone's color. Sure, the gemstones in the pyramid were brilliant, but something about this stone and its earthiness, the mix of blue like the Earth sky and brown like the dirt, somehow it seems so much more beautiful to me. I know what I must do and the last time, with the Fire stone, it nearly killed me. If Sloan hadn't been there, I surely would have died. It's going to be more difficult with a stone that reminds me so much of my mother. But it's the only way to restore the qualities of Earth back to me: steady, loyal, and wise.

"We destroy it."

CHAPTER 13

Ahna, Li and I sit on the swings. I sway back and forth, absent-mindedly rubbing the turquoise between my index finger and thumb. Li's more or less returned to a normal state. He didn't apologize for the previous night and I suppose I wouldn't expect him to. Sloan is at work. Everyone is at work, except us displaced Elementals. The entire point of the University Complex is to form allegiance to your Elemental in the first couple years and to have support as you undergo the Change. Ahna has a single thread of green, like an emerald vein, running up her neck and behind her right ear. I can't imagine the University Complex will stay closed forever, but what will happen when it reopens? Li won't return. I know Doran won't return either. And of course neither will I. Ahna would and probably a lot of others. My father said at breakfast the rumor was that Fire would most likely remain closed indefinitely while they continued to be investigated. A tribunal needs to be held. But the other Elementals will probably be able to return soon and continue their studies.

"It seems a shame to have to destroy it," Ahna says plucking the stone from my fingers. "It's so beautiful."

"I think having my identity back trumps the beauty of the stone."

"You act like you've lost something, Ka. You've always had an identity. It's not like you didn't exist before this whole thing started," Li points out.

"I know that," I reply, even though I disagree. I always felt like nothing. Well, not nothing exactly, but I always felt like I didn't fit in anywhere. And now I know why. I couldn't fit in any one place because I fit in all of them.

"You have to admit it's a pretty big deal, Li. I mean, all these secrets about her mom and who Ka really is. I can't imagine spending my life thinking I was one person, only to find out I was someone completely different."

"That's my point. She isn't completely different."

"Don't make it harder for her than it already is!"

Li stops swinging and turns to me, chocolate brown eyes boring into mine. "I'm not. It's just, some of us liked her fine the way she was." Abruptly, he gets up and walks away, heading in the direction of the Underground. We watch him walk away, slouched, moody posture, a shadow of the guy I used to know.

"Ignore him," Ahna says. "He's trying to figure things out.

He always knew he'd be a Fire and now he doesn't know what to do with himself."

"Yeah, I know the feeling."

. . .

Ahna and I walk toward the back of the small park, where it opens into a meadow with tall, silvery grass that whistles in the constant breeze. We find the spot we used to go to when we were kids, when we didn't want anyone to find us, including Li. It's a small, circular patch where the grass is sparse and the ground dips as if forming a little crater. We discovered it one day while we were playing tag. I was "It" and was chasing Ahna who thought it would be clever to run into the meadow where it would be more difficult to catch her. She disappeared; the grass taller than she was at the time. And then I heard her scream. I ran as fast as I could, searching frantically, until I found her. She hadn't seen the crater and had fallen, twisting her ankle. I had to half-carry, half-drag her back home. We didn't play tag in the meadow after that, but we did return to the crater often. Mainly, when we didn't want to be bothered. It was where we went as children to play dolls without Li being annoying or to talk about boys when we were older.

Now we sit inside the small crater, my lower back pressed against its side. I place the stone in between us.

"Precisely how did it work with the Fire stone again?"

"I don't know exactly. Sloan and I had tried everything. The matches didn't work. We were thinking fight fire with fire. But then he had this idea about water. So we went to the Water Building and threw the stone into underground lake where the Waters train. The stone sank. Sloan dove in and retrieved it. When he resurfaced, he grabbed my hand while the stone was still in it and our hands kind of fused together. Then the stone ripped us apart. A ring of fire formed around me...and it's a little fuzzy from there. I do remember the stone ended up disintegrating though."

Ahna stares at me slack-jawed. "That was really smart. The water would take heat from the fuel, lowering the temperature and it would make oxygen difficult to get to the fuel source. Impressive."

"Yeah, not gonna take credit for that idea. It was all Sloan."

"And here I thought he was a boring Universal History teacher all this time."

I feel my cheeks redden. "Yeah, he's got his good points."

"Well, obviously, water isn't going to destroy the Earth stone. And we already used up the vial. What's left in the sack Bina gave you?"

"A feather, a clear crystal, and the matches from The Old Tavern and the Sea."

"I've never heard of that place."

"Me neither."

We sit in silence a moment thinking it over. Three objects left, three stones left. The corrosive substance didn't destroy the stone. The Fire stone was destroyed by something not in the bag. "Do you think whatever will destroy it isn't in the bag, like the Fire stone? I mean, if the liquid in the vial was meant to destroy it, I think it would have."

"I can agree with that. Hmm. What would destroy an Earth stone? Fire and Water are kind of like opposites," Ahna theorizes. "So what's the opposite of Earth?"

"I'm not sure. Something not natural? Something man-made?"

"Or something from the sky? A feather is from the sky." She picks up the feather and runs it over the stone, as if it were a person that could be tickled.

I shake my head. "I really don't think it's something from the bag. There are three more stones and three more objects left to help uncover them or destroy them."

"Technically, it's your mother's stone, isn't it? And you've been to the Land of Earth. What do you think would be that Land's opposite?" Ahna is smart and she may be on to something. The Land of Fire was hot, fiery, and barren. Not a drop of water insight. Ash raining down from the sky. It was a mix of red and black. Doom and gloom. I recall how calm, peaceful, and beautiful the Land of Earth was and how fused with life: the bubbling brook, Cyan, birds, fish, tall green trees, even the wolf.

"Chaos," I say and then take a breath. "Death."

She raises an eyebrow. "Those don't seem like things that could destroy the Earth stone. They're too abstract. It needs to be something physical, like water or fire." Ahna, ever the logical mind.

But now that I've brought it up. I'm not so sure. My palms have grown sweaty and I have an uneasy feeling in the pit of my stomach. The stones are tricky; the magic in them runs deep. The fragments of my personality don't seem to want to return willingly or easily. Balance. Unbalance. Peace. Chaos. Life. Death. But whose?

...

That night I can't sleep, despite Ahna's even and slow breathing. Li never came home and it's strange not sleeping in my bed for the second night in a row. The pink light of the night shines through the window, which is open, allowing the warm Xon 9 breeze to rustle the curtains. When I do finally fall asleep, it's restless and fitful.

I dream of my mother. She's sitting by the brook, a turquoise-colored dragonfly rests on her shoulder. I'm watching her from far away. The sunlight caresses her head, bringing out the golden tones in her hair. It's as though she is somehow sitting directly in its beam. I watch as she dips her fingers into the brook. She is singing and I immediately recognize it as the song from my childhood.

You are many things to me
But of all the things you will be
Kata is my favorite
Loving, Steadfast,
Strong, Wise, and True
All of this is inside you
If you will just look inward and see
You are all these things to me.

Somehow this time it sounds different to me. All those years, I thought the lyrics were non-sense. Just words from a loving mother to her daughter. But now it suddenly makes sense: I am many things, but Kata—pure—is her favorite. I am Loving like the best of Fire, Steadfast like the best of Wood, Strong like Metal, Wise as Water, and True as Earth. All locked up inside me. All this time she had been telling me the truth. Since I was a baby. I had accused her in my head of keeping secrets, of causing my aimlessness, but if I had just listened more carefully I would have known. There were no secrets between us. As soon as I have the realization, she stops singing and turns from the brook, seemingly locking eyes with me. A small smile plays at her lips.

I see it before she does. The matted black fur and the glowing yellow eyes, the sharp fangs. He comes up behind her, soundlessly through the water. I want to call out, yell, throw something, anything, but it's as if I'm frozen to the spot, unable to intervene. She notices the panic in my eyes, and I watch helplessly as she turns and sees the wolf whose muzzle is inches from her own nose. The color drains from her face. The wolf opens its mouth, fangs dripping with red. Blood. Whose? Death. The Earth stone will be destroyed by Death. Not hers. Please. My own scream is swallowed up by the screams of my mother. I wake up sweating and terrified. My eyes dart around the room until I remember that I'm with Ahna, at the Solloman's house. My breathing begins to slow as I lean my head back onto the pillow and pull the bedsheet up to my chin. My father is asleep on the sofa downstairs. He is safe. I am safe. But is my mother?

I don't sleep the rest of the night. Instead I count the tiny air-pocket holes in the stone ceiling above the bed over and over again until morning finally comes. 346.

CHAPTER 14

I need to visit Bina. Sloan is off being Teacher 4, so I decide to take Ahna with me.

"Are you sure this is a good idea?" she asks as we head toward the Underground.

"It's not like you have to break your parents' rules and go to the Black Bazaar," I tease. "She's staying with Michaela."

"I know. I just mean with Sloan being at work."

I shrug. "I'm at a standstill. I need more information about the Imminent Darkness and my mom."

"What's with the sudden sense of urgency? Can't we just wait?"

I haven't yet told Ahna about my dream last night. I stop walking and turn to her on the sidewalk. "I had a dream last night. In it, I was in the Land of Earth watching my mom sit by the brook. She turned to look at me and the wolf, the same wolf that she had told me was the Imminent Darkness, attacked her." My throat catches and I stop there. No reason to go into detail and bring the vivid images flooding back.

We start walking again. "What will Bina be able to tell us?"

"For starters, she hopefully can tell me if my mother is safe."

We pass the wooden sign that marks the entrance to the Black Bazaar and keep walking. The homes and apartment buildings are closer together here. A mix of stone and metal. There are boarded up windows and crumbling front steps. Trash blows across the sidewalk. An older man sits on one of the crumbling stoops, his metallic threads sparkling in the sun, a brown paper bag containing a bottle in his hand. He leers at us as we walk past, causing us to quicken our pace.

We continue until the buildings become a bit further apart. Michaela lives on the outskirts of the Underground. Until recently, she lived in a trailer on the edge of the Underground, but her growing concerns about Bina's safety motivated her to move into a new place. Michaela's a Metal too, but not Unbalanced as most Metals are; therefore, she works in Xon 9's military intelligence. I'm not sure what happened to Bina to make her the way she is, she seems so different than Sloan or Michaela. I'm not sure if it's her becoming Unbalanced that gave her the Sight or the Sight that caused her to become Unbalanced.

I stop when I reach a building that's sleek metal and tinted glass. The building is one of the taller ones in the area. From what

Sloan told me, the bottom few floors are used as offices for the military, since the military only consists of Metals. Metals are both strong and strategic. But when Unbalanced they can be down-right destructive not only to others, but to themselves as well. I always thought the rest of our society corralled them into the Underground, but it turns out they put themselves there. Maybe they know something the rest of us don't. The rest of the floors are apartments.

The front doors to the building are unlocked, but we enter into a foyer that has an intercom and two sets of locked doors. One set leads to a lobby and the other set to a bank of elevators. Through the glass you can see a semi-circular counter and behind it sits a woman. "How may I help you?" Her voice crackles through the intercom.

"We're here to see Michaela Braden"

The doors leading to the elevators click open and we hurry through. There's a sign with a list of apartment numbers and first initials with last names. *M. Braden* is listed as apartment 411, which is the fourth floor. There are no apartments listed on floors one through three so I assume they're all military offices. The elevator doors open and we hit the button for the fourth floor. We quickly zoom up, the elevator doors open and we step into a dimly lit hallway. There are up-light sconces on the walls made of silver metal. The floor is a sleek, shiny black. All the doors are painted white with the apartment number clearly painted in black. Beside each door is another small intercom with a button. We turn right and easily find Michaela's apartment. As far as I know she isn't expecting us, so I press the intercom button.

"Braden." Comes the reply.

"It's Ka." The lock tumbles and the door is pulled open. Michaela has her blonde hair in a ponytail, and while her smile is cheerful, she has dark circles under her blue eyes. She ushers us inside and quickly closing the door behind us. "This is my best friend Ahna. Ahna this is Michaela."

"Welcome. Any friend of Ka's and Sloan's is a friend of mine."

Ahna shifts uncomfortably. "Well, I don't know about friend exactly. Former student."

Michaela begins down the hallway, indicating we should follow. "Same difference when it comes to him."

The apartment is small and kind of modern compared to other homes I've been in. The floor is a sleek black and Michaela has put down gray area rugs. The kitchen is small with modern looking appliances and is to the right as we walk down the short hallway which opens onto the living room, which is also small. It has a large window that looks out onto the rest of the Underground, I can even see the canopies of the trailer vendors in the Black Bazaar. There's a small couch big enough for two people, an over-sized armchair, and a small glass table. The kitchen counter is extended and there are two red metal stools. No dinner table. The hallway located to the left of the living room only has two doors, what I assume are the sole bedroom and the bathroom.

"Please, make yourself comfortable. I'll go get Mom. She was just taking a nap." I remember how when I first saw Sloan with Michaela, I mistakenly thought she was his girlfriend or something. Only later, when I really thought about it, did I put the pieces together: the similar noses, the same thin-set lips, her eyes a pale blue somewhere between her brother's and her mother's.

There's a shuffling and a grumbling coming down the hallway. "'Tis impossible to take a nap around here with yeh stompin' around like an elephant in here anyways." Michaela guides Bina by the elbow to the over-sized armchair and drapes a fuzzy blanket across her lap. She lays a gray eye on me. "'Tisn't often I get a visitor here." Michaela excuses herself and begins making tea in the kitchen.

"How are you feeling?" I ask.

"Much improved since the last time I saw yeh. My mind's a little on the fritz. Some things are missing."

I recall the pain of my memories being pulled from me, right up and out of my scalp. Plucked out forever. "How did your Sight save you?" Ahna asks. "I'm Ahna, by the way. Ka's friend. I've heard a lot about you."

"Is that so? Didn't think there was that much to tell. Well, Ahna, did ye say? The Sight, as ye know, allows me glimpses of things yet to come. All it takes is a touch, as Ka here can attest. But I'm old. I don't even need a touch anymore, just the energy a person gives off. They hooked me up to this contraption not realizing that the memories they were going to be pulling would be their own. They didn't like that much." She actually chuckles at the recollection. "They tried to increase the power, that's when things got a little fuzzy for me, but ultimately any pain done unto me was done onto them." Michaela returns and sets a tray of tea cups on the glass table. She hands one to her mother then sits on one of the stools with her own cup.

"We're lucky they didn't know that," Michaela says after a sip. "It worked in our favor, but it's taken some time to recover. There were a lot of mental barriers Bina had to put up so they couldn't get to her memories. As you saw, Ka, it left her in a fairly weakened state for some time. Not to mention the pain of the memories that were pulled, even if they weren't her own."

"Who would invent such a horrible device?" Ahna asks.

"You're looking at it," Michaela replies.

"Wait, you did?"

"Well, not me specifically, no, but the military intelligence."

"Why would they do such a thing?" I ask.

"Many reasons: alien invasion, criminals…it was created as a way to extract information. Literally. The problem is who is considered a criminal can be pretty subjective I suppose. Either way, the military intelligence is always coming up with these kinds of things. The Mindscape, the transport pods…are all inventions of the military intelligence."

"I didn't know that."

"Well, it isn't like they announce it, especially since all military intelligence are Metals," Michaela explains.

Bina adds, "And they'd rather ye think us as unfit and Unbalanced. But Metals are intelligent warriors, when working for the right people and the right cause." She takes a slow sip of tea and turns back to me. "Ye didn't come here to only check on my health."

I shake my head. "No, I didn't." I take a deep breath. "I was wondering about my mom. And I know there are certain things you can't interfere with, but I need to know if she's okay."

She nods. "The fear is evident in yer eyes." She closes her own eyes and after a moment reopens them. "Forgive me, but I'm still a little weak. Do ye happen to have something belonging to yer mother?"

I'm surprised to remember I have the map in my messenger bag. I feel around for it and pull it out, handing up the folded piece of paper to Bina. She doesn't open it, simply holds it in her hand. She closes her eyes again. The first time I met Bina was terrifying. I was a customer then, not knowing who she was or her relation to Sloan. She had grabbed my wrist and her eyes had rolled back in her head. Her words were ominous and I could tell they had frightened her as much as they had me. Now, though, it makes sense. Bina has clearly been a part of my life before I could even recollect.

She sways a little back and forth murmuring beneath her breath, her eyelids fluttering. It's only seconds, but it feels much longer before her eyes fling open. Her eyes dart around the room as if she's disoriented, before she remembers where she is and her eyes land on me.

"It's growing stronger. Seeping into other worlds."

"Who?" Ahna asks, but I already know.

"The Imminent Darkness. The balance is shifting. The world

is growing darker," Bina observes.

"But my mom, is she okay?" Images from the dream flash through my mind: glowing eyes, dripping blood, her screams.

"A life hangs in the balance. One must die for another to be born."

I feel my heart sink. "What? What does that mean?"

"I'm sorry. I could not see this time, only hear."

"Then who said that? Who said that, 'A life hangs in the balance. One must die for another to be born.'?"

She looks at me with an expression that's a mix of both confusion and sadness. "Your mother."

. . .

To further my confusion, the message is cryptic at best. It doesn't tell me whose life hangs in the balance, nor does it tell me who must die for another to be born. Even worse, is it literally balance or metaphorical as in the Balance. There's no way for Bina to differentiate between the two anyways. The only hope that I can cling to is that she said my mother told her this. If my mother was dead— the mortal part of her although I'm sure the Imminent Darkness could kill the immortal side as well—she wouldn't have been able to relay the message to Bina. As far as I know Bina doesn't commune with the dead. She's a Seer not a Necromancer.

She hands me back the folded up map and I finger its worn edge. "I did have one more question. But I'm not sure you can help."

"Go on then."

"I met a young woman. She helped me when I thought I was

in a place where no one would help me. She had gray eyes and was an Earth Elemental. Do you know who she could be?"

Bina reaches for my free hand and I place it carefully in hers. I swallow hard because I know she's about to tap into the memory. I didn't share it with anyone else but Sloan. She's going to see that I experienced what she experienced, at least sort of. But I trust Bina. She rubs the back of my hand gently and closes her eyes. I watch intently as her facial expression ranges from surprise to shock and then to wonder. I'm not sure exactly how her Sight works. I don't know if she sees through my eyes or bears silent witness as in the Mindscape. Either way, I suppose it doesn't much matter.

Finally, she let's go and sits back in the chair. She takes a sip of her tea before speaking. "I did see the young woman. There are several possibilities, of which I cannot be sure. Her name appears to be Kesara." The name sounds vaguely familiar but I can't recall where I've heard it before. "That's the best I can do for now."

"Thank you, Bina." I am grateful because even though all my questions were not answered, I am leaving with more than I came in with.

I slip the map into my bag. Ahna and I stand to leave. Bina looks drained of energy and there's a rosy flush to her pale cheeks. I turn to Michaela as she walks us to the door. "I'm sorry if I've exhausted your mother. But she's been incredibly helpful to me, if a bit enigmatic."

Michaela smiles. "I don't think she'd have it any other way."

"Wait!" Bina calls just as we're about to step back into the main hallway. She is standing near the kitchen and using the wall to help herself along.

"Mom, you really shouldn't be moving on your own yet," Michaela protests gently.

"If I waited on yeh every time I needed to get up or get something, Michaela dear, I'd be dead. It's important." She shoves past Michaela and grabs my shoulder. I'm surprised by her strength when only moments before she seemed in such a fragile state. She leans in close and her breath is warm on my ear. "Listen carefully, Impossible Girl. Things may not go as planned, but you must not lose sight of your purpose. Do not be afraid. Use the power of the Fire within you, the anger and the determination. Return your Earth to you and use its wisdom. Remember the Elements work together. They *balance* one another. Understand?"

There's that word again. *Balance.* The Universe is out of balance, darkness seeping into other worlds. Elementals can be Balanced which is good, or become Unbalanced, which is too much of a good thing. The Elements work together. You'd never know it looking at Xon 9.

I nod and she lets go of my shoulder, shuffling back inside the apartment. Michaela wishes us well and closes the door behind us.

"Well, that was one of the weirder encounters I've ever had," Ahna offers.

"Not even the tip of the iceberg," I reply.

. . .

I'm glad that Ahna doesn't ask me about my mother's message or about the girl with the gray eyes. It's late when we get back to the Solloman's house, past dinner time. We walk inside and Ahna immediately stops which causes me to run into her. I turn to see what caused her abruptness. Sitting around the kitchen table are Sloan and Mr. and Mrs. Solloman. But not my father. Maybe he's working late again. I nudge Ahna into the kitchen and close the door behind me.

"Where's Dad?" I ask. Mr. and Mrs. Solloman exchange uneasy glances. Sloan gets up from the table, comes over and puts an arm around my shoulders as he leads me to the living room and sits me down on the couch He sits down beside me. An uneasy feeling has begun to form inside my gut.

"I don't know how to say this, Ka, so I'll just be forthright. Your father didn't come home from work. Not last night and not today."

My stomach gets all fluttery and my heartbeat quickens. "I don't understand. I thought he was here this morning."

Mrs. Solloman comes in and sits on the edge of the table in front of the sofa. "We didn't want to upset you, Ka. We figured your father was working overtime. The Council has been putting a lot of demands on its workers lately. There are whispers of the Imminent Darkness. People can feel it. We see the people in cloaks, the so-called Citizen Law Enforcement. The disappearances." She glances up at Mr. Solloman who now stands behind her.

"I stopped by Council Hall and no one had seen your father

since yesterday evening. I assume shortly after he left here."

There's a choked feeling in my throat. *Things might not go as planned.* This isn't exactly what I thought Bina meant. First my mother, now my father. "It's the Imminent Darkness," I blurt out.

"It might be," Sloan says gently, "But we don't know that for sure. With your mother gone, maybe he set out on his own."

The MindCleanse was in the basement of Council Hall, right beneath our government building. My father works in that building as a Liege to the Council of Leaders. They are our trusted leaders, a board of five Woods, four males and one female, revered for their yieldingness, steadfastness, compassion, and ability to be both flexible and rigid when needed. Wood is also the least likely to become Unbalanced.

"No. No, he wouldn't go anywhere without telling me." I should be sad. But I'm not. I'm angry. None of it makes any sense. *Use the power of the Fire within you, the anger and the determination.* Somehow Bina knew. She saw that my father would go missing and she knew it would piss me off. But she also said to use the wisdom of my Earth and I don't have that yet, nor do I know how to get it.

"Ka, I'm so sorry," Ahna says kneeling in front of me and taking my hands in hers. "We'll find your father."

"He isn't lost, Ahna. He was taken."

"Now, we can't be sure of that," says Mr. Solloman.

"But we can. The Council of Leaders. They can't be trusted. Members of the Imminent Darkness run around right in front of their eyes. But they haven't put a stop to it, have they? Which tells me one of two things. Either they don't care or they're part of it."

"Ka, surely, you can't be suggesting…" Mrs. Solloman says.

"You're just upset," Mr. Solloman adds. Sloan and Ahna say nothing. Because they know. They know I've seen unimaginable and unspeakable things. They know I've traveled to other worlds and know that I've seen the Imminent Darkness for myself. A bunch of blokes dressed in cloaks is not the Imminent Darkness. The Imminent Darkness is ancient and it is formless. It can take on any form it wishes to fulfill its purpose. If it can be a mummy or a wolf, why can't it be a person? Or a group of people. Maybe it spreads like a disease, poisoning the mind. Mr. Solloman continues, "We all know the Council has our best interests at heart. Your father will show up. I'm sure of it." I wonder if his words sound as unconvincing to himself as they do to me.

"With all due respect, and I appreciate your hospitality, Mr. and Mrs. Solloman, but I think I'm going to stay with Sloan. It just seems really dangerous to stay near home and…" *And he's taken an Everlasting Vow to serve as my protector until the end of time or my mortal death, whichever comes first.*

"And maybe he can help you find some leads on your father, or take you around to ask people, or whatever. I agree. There's no point in staying here without your father," Ahna interjects.

"Are you sure, Ka?" asks Mrs. Solloman. Ahna disappears upstairs and returns with a small bag which she hands to me. I peer inside. Some of my clothes and a couple of her books.

"I am. There's a lot I need to sort through, and if the

Imminent Darkness is indeed attacking my family one-by-one—"

"Oh, my dear, I highly doubt that," Mrs. Solloman chuckles nervously, also not sounding very convinced of her own words.

"But if they are, then there's only one person left on their list. Me."

CHAPTER 15

"Do you really think that's what's happening?' Sloan asks me once we're alone.

"Truthfully? I'm not sure. But remember what building I came out of after they tried to MindCleanse me?"

"You said you were in the basement of Council Hall."

"Exactly. And I had a really eerie feeling about it. It made the hair on the back of my neck stand up. I have the same feeling now." We need to pass the University Complex to get to Sloan's from my side of town. As we walk, I think I catch a glimpse of something blue fluttering in the evening sky, the white moons reflecting off its wings. Cyan. I do a double-take, but she's gone. Or she was never really there.

I look around noticing where we've stopped. We're standing in front of the entrance to the University Complex, the familiar *Divide et impera* arch marking the entrance way. Divide and conquer. Cyan. Mom. Earth.

"Wait a second," I find myself saying. I feel around in my messenger bag for the book. *The Five Goddesses.* I flip to the part where the codger tricks the sisters. "Here, right here." I point so Sloan can see. "The codger says to the sisters *'divide et impera.'*"

"Okay," Sloan says slowly. "But what does that have to do with the Council of Leaders?"

"Don't you see? The codger is wearing a cloak like the modern day Imminent Darkness followers. But the Imminent Darkness is ancient and formless; therefore, it can take on any form that it wants. Who erected this arch?"

Sloan shrugs. "I'm actually not sure."

"Could the Council of Leaders have created it?"

"It's probable."

"Then if the codger represents the Imminent Darkness, why do we walk beneath an archway with its motto as we enter the University Complex? And what does the University do? It divides us into our respective Elementals. Divide us and conquer us. It's how the sisters were tricked."

Sloan gives me a dubious look. "You don't think that's a bit of a leap?"

"You think that it is? I can't figure it out, but I don't think that it's a coincidence we live the way we do."

"Societies have always been divided up. Caste systems go back thousands upon thousands of years. Eventually they evolved to more modern social classes, but the same concept."

"I went to see Bina today. She told me, 'A life hangs in the balance. One must die for another to be born.' And then she told me to remember that the Elements all balance each other. What if by making us choose they're perpetuating the imbalance of the Universe, which is exactly what the Imminent Darkness wants?"

He frowns. "I'm kind of stuck on that 'one must die for another to be born' part of what you said."

"Hard to explain. I had a dream about my mother last night. The Imminent Darkness was in wolf form and attacked her. It seemed so real. I just…had to be sure." My voice waivers and he puts an arm around me.

"Let's go home. We can talk about all this more tomorrow. If you're right, and I'm not saying you are—yet. But if you're right and your father is being kept in Council Hall then we'll need a plan."

I nod. Usually, Sloan is really supportive, but maybe it is too far-fetched. For some reason I can't chalk it up to simply being a coincidence. There's a reason that phrase is used in the story and there's a reason that it's placed in such a prominent part of our colony.

I flip the book closed and a small piece of paper flutters out and lands on the ground at my feet. I slide the book into my messenger bag and then bend over and pick up the piece paper. Immediately, I recognize Ahna's handwriting. All it says is: *Novea.= Anuja = Kesara..*

My heart beats just a little bit faster, but my brain has yet to put it together.

"'What's that?" Sloan asks.

"I'm not sure. I think some of Ahna's notes." I slip the paper into my pocket, snug against the turquoise stone that's already nestled there.

. . .

I don't want to be rash. Sloan's right, as usual. We can't just march into Council Hall and accuse them of being part of the Imminent Darkness. We need a plan. But first Sloan needs convincing.

"Come on, you've experienced the Imminent Darkness firsthand, you don't think it's strange that they have MindCleanse technology in the basement of Council Hall?"

"Just because the technology is right beneath their feet doesn't mean the Council itself knows about it or is part of it." Sloan sits cross-legged on the couch. It's been a long day and he's nursing a cup of hot tea. My own mug sits, still untouched, on the small coffee table, probably gone cold as I pace back and forth chewing on my bottom lip.

"That's just it! Hidden in plain sight! A lot of people trust that the Council has our best interests in mind. That's why the Council was formed in the first place. Who would think that the very thing that wants to destroy us is made up of the same people we've entrusted to help us?"

"You, obviously."

I flop down on the couch next to him. "Is there any way that you'll be convinced?"

He considers this. "Not without actual evidence, no. But you know what I'll help you do even though I'm not convinced?"

"What?" I ask, still disappointed that he won't just trust my instincts.

"I'll help you find your dad," he says. "We'll start with Council Hall and then if that doesn't help us, we'll go to the Wood Building. Deal?"

I sigh, resigned to the fact that Sloan will remain unconvinced for now. But if we can find my father, maybe my suspicions will be confirmed. "Deal."

"We'll wait until dusk. It will be easier to go unnoticed. Safer."

"How will we get inside?" I don't have Li's cloaking cuff anymore.

"Trust me. There's always a way."

. . .

After the moons are high in the sky, we head toward Council Hall. The hall is centrally located. The building itself is like a giant glass box. There are no people around and the building is dimly lit with security lights. The design is sleek, similar to the military building where Michaela lives. An elaborate stone fountain stands sentry in front. It draws water up from beneath the ground's surface. In the fountain's center is a man wearing one of the Council Leader robes, his left hand is open as if to say he has nothing to hide and the water flows out of his palm and back into the pool of the fountain.

The other hand is holding up a stone torch lit with a flame that always burns. The fountain is the only structure on Xon 9 representing all of the Elements. In the moonlight, the stone statue's face has a sinister look to it. I never cared much for the fountain or the building itself.

During the day Council Hall is busy with the comings and goings of Lieges, citizens, and other workers. Now with all the lights off, the building almost looks abandoned. Sloan leads me around to the back of the building, which isn't glass like the rest, but brick. The steel door has a sloppily hand-written sign with the words: DANGER. KEEP OUT. Sloan ignores the sign and tries the handle. It opens. You'd think they'd have fixed the door after the fire, but I guess they had other things to worry about. Sloan leads the way and we make our way down the narrow stairwell. He pulls a small flashlight out of his back pocket and turns it on. When we reach the bottom he sweeps the beam around.

The first thing I notice is the smell. It's a weird acrid, smoky smell. We turn the corner and the beam of the flashlight lands on the wooden table with leather restraints. My skin crawls at the memory of being strapped down and unable to move. The table is singed. He swoops the beam to the right and up. A cock-eyed curtain rod and some burned up shreds are all that's left of the curtain. He then drops the light beam to the floor and there's a burned up chunk of metal: the crown. Without thinking I walk over and kick it as hard as I can, as if to make sure that it's no longer alive. It clangs off the wall with a harsh, metallic sound. It won't hurt anyone ever again, but it's little consolation for the pain it has already caused. Sloan comes up and puts a hand on my shoulder. His hand slides down my arm to find my hand.

"Ka, look," Sloan whispers swinging the beam of the flashlight back toward the curtain. Its charred remains reveal that it wasn't simply a hideous decorative statement, but for concealment as well. Behind what's left of the curtain is a wooden door with an arched top and a visible pull latch. Sloan goes over and easily pulls the latch open. No squeaks. No moans. The door must be frequently used. The dark opening reveals another stairwell. He shines the beam down into the darkness, but all it reveals is wooden steps leading to a concrete bottom. He takes a few steps down, grasping my hand and pulling me along with him. The light bounces in time to our steps. And that's when I hear it: a soft groaning sound. I press tighter against Sloan as we reach the bottom of the stairwell, both hopeful and afraid of what we might see.

The stairwell ends at a wall, but the space to our right is open. Sloan moves the flashlight so that it illuminates the space. I almost wish that he hadn't. In the space are rows of cages, but instead of animals, they hold people. They shield their eyes from the glare of the light. Sloan averts the beam, but it's too late. I've already seen the dirty faces, tattered clothes, and the hollowed eyes. And the smell. It smells of filth and waste. "Is it some sort of prison?" I whisper.

"I'm not sure," he whispers back.

It's like we're frozen to the spot, wanting to move forward, but afraid to find out more at the same time. The space is vast. There are easily a hundred cages down here. Sloan slowly begins to shuffle down one of the rows and I squeeze his hand tighter and press even closer. He keeps the beam of the flashlight angled at the floor. Most of the people back into a corner, afraid as we approach. A few stay closer to the entrance of the cage and stare at us with blank expressions. One young woman with metallic threads along her face reaches out a hand, so bony it easily slips between the bars. I want to reach out to her and offer some kind of comfort, but I'm afraid she'll grab me and not let go.

Sloan doesn't think twice, he pauses and reaches a hand out toward her. Water is both intuitive and compassionate. She wraps her fingers around his and begins to cry. "I'm sorry," he says. She makes a gurgled sound. It seems as if her mouth can no longer work to form words. How long has she been down here? What crime could she have committed that this was the consequence? Obviously poorly fed, living in darkness with no human interaction besides the others.

Finally, her words find their way out. Her voice is raspy and unused. "He said you would come."

"Who?" I ask softly.

"The Wood man. Further down. He made quite a commotion when he was brought in a couple days ago, saying his daughter would find him. That's you, isn't it?" She is still squeezing Sloan's hand as if he is her lifeline back to the above ground world.

"Yes. It is me."

"Such faith your father puts in you." But I've stopped listening. My father is here. I begin to run down the aisle. Faces become blurs as I pass.

And then I hear it. One word: "Kata!"

I run toward the sound, rounding a corner. My feet feeling unsteady beneath me from the shock of what I'm seeing all around me. I hear the sound of Sloan hurrying after me.

"Daddy!" It comes out as both an elated cry and one of anguish. His face is dirty and there's a bruise blossoming on his left cheek. But he's alive. Thank the moons, he's alive.

My father's hands are too big to fit between the bars, so he wraps them around the metal and I wrap my own around his. "What is this place?"

"It's the prison. Well, not the military prison. A different one. Not to say everyone who is down here belongs here. The Imminent Darkness has a warped perception of the law."

"I'm going to get you out of here."

"How? The guards only come down once a day to check on us and feed us, but there are no keys and we're surrounded by iron bars."

I don't have an answer. He's right; each cage is locked with a sort of electronic key pad. Plug in the magic code and the door unlocks. Wait. "Stand back." He obeys and steps toward the back of the cage. I place my fingers lightly over the keypad and close my eyes. I think of all the things about this situation that infuriate me. My father being kidnapped and thrown into a dank prison. The Metal woman who is so frail her bony hand so easily slipped through the bars. The smell. I can feel the anger percolating just beneath the surface, a buzzing in my fingertips. My mother keeping secrets from me. Tristen causing me to hurt Li. Sloan for not believing me that the Imminent Darkness and the Council of Leaders are most likely one and the same. I conjure all that has frustrated and irked me in the last few days. My fingertips begin to grow hot and the keypad begins to spark. Not a fire this time, just some sparks. A malfunction. The keypad begins to beep and I hope to myself that it doesn't cause the cage to become permanently locked because I have no backup plan. A slow beep that becomes faster and faster until it's a steady hum and then it stops. One loud click. Sloan yanks the door open and my father steps out and scoops me into his arms, swinging me around like I'm a kid again.

"That was brilliant!" he says.

When he places me back down I turn to Sloan. "But what about the others? I don't have enough energy to release every single person." I also don't know who committed actual crimes and who is innocent, but I reason, if they were actual criminals they'd be in Xon 9's real prison, not this secret one. This isn't a prison, it's a holding cell for death.

"It's true." I turn and in the cage behind me there's a dark-skinned man staring at me wide-eyed. "The Impossible Girl." His hair is close cropped and white, golden filigree lines his face. "I've been a Fire some seventy-two moons, and never have I seen that before. Ever." He pauses, clearing his throat. "And if it's true, and you actually are the Impossible Girl, then don't you worry about the likes of us. Because everything is gonna be alright. You may not save us today, but you will be the one to save us. Every last one of us."

A murmur starts up at his words: Is it true? The Impossible Girl is real? How does he know it's her? Who is she?

The man laughs at the commotion and at first it sounds small and a bit broken, but then it cascades into a hearty, hopeful laugh. "She is all possibilities and yet she is none. She is the Impossible Girl."

CHAPTER 16

It isn't easy to walk away when you know something isn't right. Once in grade school Li saw this really popular girl, Diadona, making fun of me. I don't remember what exactly she said to me—Diadona antagonized me from year one up through Pronouncement—but what I do remember is that Li walked away. One of my best friends didn't stand up for me. At the time I didn't understand and was angry. Friends should stand up for you! That's what they do for crying out loud! I felt hurt and betrayed. But now I think I understand a bit better. Sometimes it's just too painful to watch. That's how it feels to leave all those people in the prison cells beneath Council Hall. I have to walk away and hope that the man is right: that I will be the one to save them all. It doesn't mean it makes it any easier.

"Ka, come on. We have to go!" Sloan urges, grabbing my hand and pulling me along.

My father follows close behind. We fumble along, sticking to as many back alleys that we can as we make our way to the Black Bazaar—probably the one place my father will be safe. No one would expect him to go there. We turn at the wooden sign and head down the steps and into the Black Bazaar. It's so late that most of the vendors are closed. I'm not sure where he's headed, but Sloan seems to be sure. We pass Bina's vacant trailer and head further away from the rest of the vendors. The silver trailers with their large service windows, slowly begin to turn into smaller house-like trailers.

We reach a small trailer a bit separated from the rest. There's an awning over the front stoop, beneath it a small stand full of trinkets that are probably for sale. To the right is a small patio with two chairs in front. The patio has a worn canopy over it. It looks vaguely familiar but I can't quite place where I've seen it. Maybe I'm wrong and I have been down this street before. But when?

Sloan knocks on the door.

"It's late!" I whisper. "Are you sure this is a good idea?"

He ignores me and waits. The door opens a crack. It's on a small chain. A short woman with acorn-colored skin and tired brown eyes stares back at us. She wears a purple bandanna over her hair and familiar metallic threads mark the side of her face. At first I think she's going to tell us to go away and get lost, but then her eyes register a familiar face. "Well, this is quite unexpected," she says.

"I'm sorry to disturb you, but we need your help." Sloan

glances back toward my father who's standing a bit behind me, unsure of what's going on.

She nods as if understanding without further explanation. "Of course. Please, come in." She closes the door and unhooks the chain, allowing the door to open wider. Sloan steps in, pulling me inside behind him, and my father follows. The woman shuts and locks the door behind us. I notice that not only does it have a chain, but it has several deadbolt locks as well. The amount of security has me curious, then again this is the Underground. She follows my glance. "Sometimes you need protected from your own kind."

Footsteps come down the hall. "Mom, do you have any idea what time it is? Who could you possibly be talking to at this hour? If it's that lady from down the street again, you need to tell her to find a hobby…take up knitting or something…" The voice stops as the person reaches the end of the hallway. Tall and thin, unruly hair forming a halo around her head. "Ka?"

It's Zora.

. . .

Sloan explains. "Mrs. Chatfield acts as a sort of safe house for people being targeted by the Imminent Darkness. You know Zora of course, Ka. Mr. Waylon, this is Zora and Chanice."

Mrs. Chatfield waves off the introduction. "The less I know the better. Zora, honey, show Mr. Waylon the shower. No offense, dear, but you smell something fierce."

"This way, Mr. Waylon." My dad follows Zora back down the hallway.

Now I remember the house. Doran brought me here. Zora is both my tattooist and his sister. I haven't seen Doran since my first trip to the Elemental Abyss when he helped me retrieve the Fire stone. "Is Doran around?" I ask Mrs. Chatfield.

"Are you one of his friends?"

"We were both initiated into Fire at the same time. And Zora did my tattoo."

"She does good work. I'm very proud of her." She pauses and when she speaks again there's a bit of resignation in her voice. "Doran, he comes and goes. Currently, he 'goes.'" She chuckles. "He's a lot like his father. Unpredictable, stubborn, and too loud-mouthed for his own good." I smile because that sounds exactly as I remember Doran. She looks at me and says, "He'll be back." But it sounds more like she's trying to convince herself than me.

She instructs us to make ourselves at home. I remember the pea green carpet from my last visit and the worn sofa. There's an armchair across from the sofa and it has a crocheted blanket draped across its back. We sit down and Mrs. Chatfield disappears into the small kitchen.

"You did the right thing back there," Sloan says softly.

"Then why was it so difficult?" I sigh.

"The right things often are. If they weren't, it wouldn't be a learning experience, would it?"

I smile. My father and Zora return just as Mrs. Chatfield emerges from the kitchen with a small tray full of steaming mugs. "Hot chocolate."

"Mom always likes to make sure her guests are well-kept." Zora grins taking two mugs off the tray and handing one to my father.

We all sit and there's an amicable moment of silence as we sip our hot chocolates. The scent is comforting and somehow I think Mrs. Chatfield knew just what I needed.

"I don't mean to pry, Mr. Waylon, but how exactly did you get in the prison?" Sloan finally asks. It's a question I've been wondering myself.

My father thinks for a moment and then slowly explains. "I went to work yesterday and everything seemed normal enough. But then I was on my way home, two men wearing the hooded cloaks approached me. One asked if I was Absalom Waylon. I said I was and the next thing I knew everything went black."

"Yeah they're quick with the black-out juice," Zora says. I look over at her and she catches my eye. "You see a lot in the Black Bazaar."

"When I woke up I was in that cage where you found me with no recollection of when or how I'd gotten there. That man across from me told me it was going to be okay. He said there wasn't much food or light, but that the other people down there with us were nice enough. I asked him why we were down there and he said, 'Do you have hope?' I thought that was an odd response and I thought about it and told him that I did. 'Then that's reason enough. You see all these people down here, that's what we have. And as long as we have that they can't get what they want.'"

"Who's 'they'?" Sloan asks.

"He never said."

"It's the Imminent Darkness. Right beneath the Council Hall. Isn't that a bit more than a coincidence?" I ask.

"I wouldn't have believed you before, Kata, but now…now I'm no longer so sure."

"It makes sense," Zora adds. "The Imminent Darkness located right beneath the Council Hall. Hiding in plain sight. No one would suspect the Council Leaders of kidnapping or MindCleansing its own citizens."

"I've worked for the Council of Wood for a long time. And I've never suspected a thing," my father objects. "That said, after finding out I went to work every day right above where innocent people were kept in filth and darkness, I'm willing to risk saying not much would surprise or shock me at this point."

"That's exactly what they'd want, isn't it? If no one suspects a thing then they can continue with their agenda and their rise to power," I argue. "Sloan, even you said yourself the Imminent Darkness operates in secretive ranks."

"They do. True. And no one seems to know who's at the top. At least from what I could tell."

"It's like they're all operating on their own agenda," Zora adds.

Mrs. Chatfield finally speaks. "All this talk. It's getting late. You all should be getting some rest. Mr. Waylon, you can use my son's room. Ka, you can sleep with Zora." She stands collecting our empty mugs. "And Sloan...."

"The couch is fine for me. Thank you, Mrs. Chatfield."

My father and I follow Mrs. Chatfield and Zora down the hallway. She shows him into Doran's room and we say good-night. Then as I'm about to follow Zora into her room across the hall, Mrs. Chatfield grabs my arm gently. She leans in so close that I can smell the hot chocolate still lingering on her breath. She whispers softly into my ear. "I will give this piece of advice before I retire for the night. Just be sure what you want to see doesn't cause you to be blind to the truth. Seeing isn't always believing."

. . .

Zora snores softly beside me and I lie awake staring at the ceiling of the trailer. There's only a single, small window that allows in the night's light. This return home has been an epic mess. The MindCleanse and the strange woman with the gray eyes, Li being all weird, my father getting kidnapped, and the peculiar Earth stone. Crap. I'd completely forgotten about the Earth stone. I'm still wearing the same pants, so I reach down into my pocket. When I pull out the smooth turquoise stone, a small piece of paper comes out with it. The note from Ahna.

The moons' light from the window falls across the note in my hand. *Novea = Anuja = Kesara.* Novea is my mother's name. I remember how in *The Impossible Girl* my mother was called Anuja. Another of her names must then be Kesara. The name vaguely rings a bell, but where did I hear it? I carefully twirl the stone between my fingers, like a worry stone, trying to think of where I've heard the name Kesara. Raspy words return to me: "Her name appears to be Kesara." Bina. When I asked who the young woman with gray eyes was, the woman who had freed me and saved my life, she had said her name was Kesara. I can still see her eyes in my mind: intense, yet calm at the same time as she undid the straps fastening me to the table. The green vines curlicued up the side of her face.

The words come tumbling back into my mind: *The Land of Earth is filled with lush greenery, bubbling brooks, and various animals that could have been found on the Planet Earth. Some even theorize that planet Earth was the Land of Earth given to Anuja/Kesara/Novea, but archaeologists have yet to prove this to be true. The Earth Goddess is also known in various other myths as the Maiden, Mother, and Crone.* The recollection is jarring. I grip the stone firmly in my fist. Could it be a coincidence that the woman who saved me was an Earth Elemental and goes by one of the names of my mother? But the woman was young, a maiden. That would somehow mean my mother reversed her incarnations. The thought is almost too complex for my brain to understand. I have a strong inclination that this coincidence is about as coincidental as the Imminent Darkness housing torture cells beneath Council Hall.

I feel a little flutter of hope in my chest that Kesara could be my mother. That would mean that she's safe and the wolf in my dream didn't kill her. But why hasn't she come to find me? And why didn't she save Father—the man she became mortal for? I hold the stone up so that I can see it in the light. Cyan. Maybe she doesn't want the Imminent Darkness to know she's here in order to protect us. Hidden in plain sight.

Chapter 17

I'm not sure where to begin. How can I possibly find Kesara? Sure I know she's an Earth, but she could be anywhere in the colony. If she actually *is* my mother, no one will know. I understand her need to hide, but at the same time I feel a bit betrayed. I thought that retrieving the Earth stone—her stone—would somehow bring us closer, but if anything it's only brought up more hurt and confusion.

I pull a hooded sweatshirt over my head and quietly step out of Zora's room and into the hallway. The rest of the house is still asleep. I tiptoe to the small living room. Sloan is asleep on the couch, an arm slung over his eyes.

"Hey," I whisper. "Come with me."

He surprises me by pulling me down and kissing me. My heart does a little happy dance in response to his lips pressed to mine. He pulls away and opens his eyes. "Man, I've wanted to do that for, like, two days now. The timing just never seemed right given the circumstances."

"It still isn't," I quip.

"True." He sits up and stretches. "But did I tell you lately how glad I am that you're still alive? Actually, how you're alive is still beyond me."

"Yeah, I don't know either. But come on, we need to go."

He gets up with no questions asked and quietly follows me out the door. As we walk in the pink light of the early morning, the moons having already set, we don't talk. Sloan must be as much inside his own head as I am in mine. We enter into the back of the Black Bazaar. It's quiet. All of the vendors still closed. No customers to be had. We pass a bench where I shared my first kiss with Li and my stomach does a little roll. Change is supposed to be good, but I somehow feel as if I'm on the periphery. I want to change, want these changes for myself, but also want to bring certain pieces of my past along with me. Only those pieces are going through their own changes as well. Changes that I'm not a part of.

We exit out of the Black Bazaar and I stop, unsure of where to go. We can head back toward Michaela's and the edge of the Underground. Or the University Complex. But to be honest I'm not sure which is best.

"Where exactly are we headed?" Sloan finally asks as I look back and forth between the various directions in which we could head.

"I don't know. We're looking for an Earth woman named

Kesara."

"That name sounds familiar. Didn't I read that was one of the names of your mother in that *Mythology of the Ages* book Ahna had?"

"Your memory is better than mine," I say taking out the note and handing it to him.

"Okay, so let me see if I got this right. Your mother used the key to escape the cage in the pyramid in the Land of Earth and you haven't seen her since. Then a young woman rescued you from the electrical fire at Council Hall. Who told you her name was Kesara?"

"Bina."

"Which I must say is sound counsel, but I may be biased," he grins. "And then Ahna gave you this note when?"

"Yesterday before we left. It was stuck in the book she gave me. At the time I didn't understand it so I just shoved it in my pocket."

"So where do you suppose Kesara is hanging out?"

"That's my problem. I don't know. But what I do know is that if Kesara is an incarnation of my mother, the Imminent Darkness is following her. If I find my mother, I find the Imminent Darkness."

"And if you find the Imminent Darkness they also find you."

He has a point. So either way both parties get something they want. I sigh and take out the stone. I hadn't had a chance to show it to Sloan in its new form. "Ahna and I found out that the plain rock I had was just a sort of armor for the Earth stone." I hand it to him. "This is what it really looks like."

He takes it from me. "A stone of many disguises." A funny look comes over his face. "Does it always pulsate like that?"

"Huh?" I have no idea what he's talking about.

A flush creeps up his cheeks like he's embarrassed. "Pulsate. It's like it has its own heartbeat or something." He hands the stone to me and I cup it in my hand and close my eyes, trying to feel whatever it is that he feels. But it just feels like a cool, smooth rock and nothing more.

"No. Nothing." I hand it back to him. Now it's his turn to close his eyes.

"I definitely can feel it. It's like the faint pattering of a heart. *Ba-dum, ba-dum.*" He opens his eyes and I shake my head. He frowns. "Maybe it somehow has to do with the Everlasting Vow."

"Maybe." But neither of us sounds convinced. He extends his hand to give the stone back to me, but I shake my head again. "No, why don't you keep it? Maybe it's trying to tell you something."

"Like it's communicating with me?"

"Yeah, kind of like how when the Fire stone was activated it would grow hot in my hand." He gives me a dubious look. "Hey, weirder things have happened."

He shrugs and drops the stone into the pocket of his t-shirt. "So how do we find Kesara?"

"No idea. Let's go that way." I point toward the University Complex. "Maybe she's at the Earth Building."

"Isn't that where your mom's a professor? Doesn't seem like a good idea to go and visit all her old haunts in case the Imminent

Darkness is waiting or something."

"That's exactly why it's a good idea because everyone else thinks it's a bad idea."

. . .

Did I mention how much I love the Earth Building? I'm not sure if it's the way that its little glass dome conceals the labyrinth of tunnels beneath or if it's the magnificent waterfall, but every time I come here a part of me feels like it's coming home, and I suppose it actually is. Because the extensive library can be used by citizens of the Colony, the door is open.

"Where should we begin?" Sloan asks, taking a backseat and letting me lead the way on this part of the adventure.

"I don't know." I've actually never been to my mother's office. I've no idea where classes are conducted. I've only been to the library and to visit Ahna. Then I remember the books on her desk. "I know she researches food sustainability. I don't know if that would help us or not."

"The library is open. Let's ask."

We wind through the tunnels and the giant wooden doors come into sight. A hand-written sign hangs on one of the doors indicating that the library is open. Sloan pulls open the door and I head toward the giant desk in the center of the library. The first time I was ever here I just breezed past, searching for Ahna. Now, I take the time to appreciate the magnitude of the library. I take in the stone walls and the wooden floor-to-ceiling shelves of books, aisle upon aisle. My mother would have studied among these stacks. I never thought of her like that before and it's interesting, given all that I now know, to remember her as normal. Just Mom, and not a daughter of the Universe. The front desk is circular and made of thick wood, its front is lined with shelves housing more books. The stone and wood is in direct contrast to the modern levitating computer screen that hovers above the surface of the desk. A woman stands in front of it, glasses slid down her nose, peering at something on the screen.

We startle her as we approach. "Hello."

"Oh, my!" She exclaims, placing a hand over her heart. "I wasn't expecting anyone to visit this early. Especially with the Complex still on hiatus."

"Sorry, but I was wondering if you could help us?"

She smiles, gesturing at the surrounding library. "That's what I'm here for."

"Well, we aren't actually looking for a book. We were looking for a person. Can you tell me where professors' offices are located?"

"Oh, that's easy. If you head back out the way you came and cross the courtyard to the other side of the waterfall you'll find the Earth offices. Is there a particular office you're looking for?"

"Food sustainability?"

"That's an easy one too. That would be part of the Agriculture Department. Just go down the first hall you see and it's the last door on the right. All the professors' offices for that department will be located there. Is there a particular professor you're looking to find? Some of them have been working from home due to the hiatus."

Word gets around fast on Xon 9, so it would seem, and I don't want to use my mother's name in case the woman has heard about the attack. "Nah," I lie. "Just conducting some research. My boyfriend here's a teacher."

Sloan clears his throat. "Um, yeah. I want to collect some information for my Universal History course on food shortages and its effects on societal decisions."

"That sounds fascinating! Well, I hope you find what you're looking for!" She smiles before turning back to her computer.

"Thanks for your help." We turn and head back out the way we came. Once the door is closed behind us I turn to Sloan. "Food shortage effects on societal decisions?"

He blushes. "Hey, you put me on the spot. And it's a valid topic. No food equals no civilization it's as simple as that. Some countries even resorted to population control in order to ensure their people had enough food."

We head back toward the waterfall and it's nice to be able to enjoy the sounds of the rushing water without being lulled into a dreamland where I could potentially sleep forever. We head down the first hallway and pass the doors for several different departments: Astronomy and Astrology, History, Modern Civilization, Medicine, until we reach Agriculture. Fire is all chemistry, communications, and the arts. Earth is about both our past and careers that nurture and help our society run as best it can. I reach for the door, but Sloan reaches out to stop me. I turn and his eyes are riddled with questions.

"What if she's not here?" he asks.

I'd thought about that and to be honest I wasn't sure. I know I hope she'll be here. But it probably wouldn't make any sense for a seemingly completely different woman to be traipsing around my mother's office. At the very least maybe she'll leave me a clue of some kind, letting me know where I can find her. "If she's not here, then hopefully she left something behind so that we can find her."

He nods and let's go of my hand. I turn the knob and pull open the door. There's a narrow hallway with small offices divided by wooden half walls. Each office has a plaque with a last name. In the first office on the left is a gray-haired man bent over a book. He peers up briefly and smiles in greeting then returns to his book. Three offices down on the left we find *Waylon*. Mom. She's not there. My heart sinks a little, but I can't say I'm surprised.

Her desk is piled with books and papers, as are the shelves above it. A little green plant with spines and a pointy red bloom looks like it could use a little t-l-c. I pull open a drawer, but it's just full of random office supplies. What are the odds that her desk at work would also have a secret compartment? Not likely. A small board with memos catches my eye and I scan it looking for any signs that could be a message left for me.

"Ka." Sloan puts a hand on my shoulder. I look over my shoulder and he's standing behind me with the turquoise Earth stone in his hand, green eyes wide in his angular face. "It's pulsating."

"You said that already. Earlier," I reply about to turn back around.

"No," he says and there's a bit more urgency in his voice. "It's quicker. Like before it was like a faintly beating heart or something, but now…it's grown steadier."

I put my palm out and he places it in my open hand. Nothing. No beating. No pulsating. Nothing. I frown. "I still don't feel anything." I hand it back to him.

"Strange. I noticed it as we got closer to the Earth Building, but thought I was imagining it. Do you think it means anything?"

I turn my attention back to the memo board. "I don't know. But if I've learned anything from the Fire stone, they seem to have a mind of their own." That's when something catches my eye. One word. The handwriting definitely belonging to my mother: *Cyan.* My heart does a little flip. "Sloan, look. She was here." He leans in over the desk and follows my pointed finger to the note.

"So she was here, but where is she now?"

"I don't know. Is there another clue or something?" I unpin the note form the memo board and turn it over. On the back is a series of numbers. 36-22-68. "What do you suppose these mean?" I hand him the piece of paper.

"They look like coordinates for something. Or some sort of combination." The paper has me stumped. Obviously my mother was here and left this note for me. I made up the name Cyan and no one else knew about it, so it was a secret just between us.

"Or page numbers. They could be almost anything." I plop down in the desk chair. "It's like the closer we get the further away we get."

There's a rustling and then some footsteps. The gray-haired man from the first office appears. He's holding an old wooden box. "Are you Professor Waylon's daughter?"

His question catches me off guard. "Yeah, I am."

"Some young woman came by the other day and left this box with me. She said if Mrs. Waylon's daughter, Ka, came by that I should give this to her. So, since that's you, here." He awkwardly hands me the box, gives a small smile, and shuffles away. We hear the door to the department open and close behind him.

"Well, that was weird." I set the box on the desk. It's heavy and carved with intricate flowers and leaves along the sides. The top is carved with an ornate tree, branches in every direction and stopping at the edges. The latch is metal and has a keyhole that reminds me of my mother's skeleton key. I try the lid. It's locked. "What good does a locked box do me?" I groan.

Sloan tries the lid even though it's useless. "It looks like it takes a really old key."

"I think you're right. It looks my mother's key would fit perfectly inside it." I run my fingers along the branches, tracing them like a family tree. "We have a pulsating stone, a note with coordinates or a code, and a locked box with no key. How is any of this useful?"

"Maybe your father would know?"

But I shake my head. "The less my father knows the better."

"You not including him isn't going to keep him any safer you know," Sloan says gently.

"It does in my head." It's hard when just as I begin to find out more about who I am, my family seems to be crumbling around me and I'm left grasping at the pieces.

"You could be looking at this all wrong, you know?" Sloan pauses, picking up the box, turning it around, and inspecting it. "Your father could be an asset. He has to know your mother's true identity. And if I were him, and let's be honest, I very well could be." He stares at me intently. "Then I'd want to know if you were back, no matter what form you were in: maid, mother crone, dragonfly." He smiles.

"What if he doesn't know?" But even as I ask the question it doesn't feel true on my lips. Sloan's right. If it were me and him, he would know. He does know. Granted, he knew even before I did. As I'm beginning to learn with Sloan—and even with my tumultuous friendship with Li—it's all about give and take. Sometimes you have to let something go in order for it to circle back around again. My mother was willing to risk her own immortality in order to be with my father. I imagine a secret like that could potentially put a damper on a marriage. Any strong relationship should be constructed on a foundation of truth, not lies. But I'm starting to see that everyone has their secrets because we want to protect the ones that we love. And then a thought dawns on me, like a light blossoming in the shadows. Something I was thinking in the back of my mind, but that had to rise through the murkiness in order to break the surface. *If my mother was willing to risk her immortality to be with my father, what did my father risk in order to be with my mother?*

Chapter 18

When we return to Mrs. Chatfield's Doran is there. He's sitting in a chair next to the stand of trinkets, working a piece of metal wire with a mandrel. I find it both awkward and relieving at the same time to see him. He's engrossed in his jewelry making and looks up in surprise when we approach.

"Ka." He stands and gives me a quick hug. "Your dad didn't think you'd be coming back."

Sloan holds up the wooden box. "The puzzle deepens."

"Nice box." Sloan hands it to him and we take a seat in a couple of canvas chairs beneath the canopy. "The carving on this is really good. Did you do it?"

"Nope. It was given to us."

"It looks like it opens with some sort of skeleton key. Good luck finding one of those." I bite my lip, not wanting to explain the entire story again. He continues to mess with the box, not meeting my gaze. "I heard about your mom. I'm sorry."

"Word gets around fast."

He looks up. "What can I say? My mom's in the know."

"She worries about you," I blurt out.

He turns his attention back to the box and shrugs. "She'll get over it."

The door to the trailer opens and closes and my dad steps out. "I thought I heard your voice out here." Doran pulls another folding chair out of a storage compartment on the side of the trailer. My father thanks him and sits down. He catches sight of the wooden box Doran has set by his feet, having returned to his jewelry working. "Find out anything interesting?"

"Yes and no. We went to Mom's office." I reach in my pocket, pull out the note, and hand it to him. "This note was on her memo board and some guy brought us this box." I pick up the box from by Doran's feet and hand it to my father. He's quiet for a long moment. "I haven't seen this in a while."

"Where'd it come from?"

"It was a wedding gift."

"Really? From who?"

"Your mother's parents." So Raj and Katayun gave the box to my parents in honor of their wedding. I can only imagine what could be inside. What do immortal parents get their immortal daughter?

"What was inside?"

He laughs. I haven't heard my father laugh in a long time, least of all since the attack on my mother. "That's just it. I have no idea. We could never get it open."

"You've had this box for over eighteen years and never got it open?" Sloan asks.

He chuckles, "Oh, believe it. Not for trying. Eventually, we gave up and I hadn't seen it since."

If I've learned anything about my mother from our trip to the Land of Earth it's that there are no coincidences. Everything is done with a reason, whether it be mine, hers or some force greater than us. Each action, each person, everything has a purpose. What's the purpose of this box? More importantly, why did she leave it behind? Maybe she's expecting that we'll need it.

"Do you think Mom will come back?" I know my thoughts on this obviously. I'm pretty confident that my mom has somehow taken the form of the maiden Kesara. Novea, at least as my father and I knew her, I think is gone. I'm not sure if she's gone forever, but I know that she's at least gone for now. Really, I'm using this question as bait to find out what he knows.

He bites.

"To be honest, I'm not sure. I want her to come back, with my entire heart. But I know it won't be easy for her. As you may already know, she had to make certain sacrifices in order to marry me. Those kinds of sacrifices cannot be easily undone."

I know he's referring to her immortality and the

consequences if she returned to her true home.

"What if she found some sort of way around the agreement she made with Raj and Katayun?" My father hides his surprise that I know this as well.

"Like a loophole?" Doran interjects, and I have to give him credit considering he's missed a substantial amount of developments since our visit to the Elemental Abyss together.

"I don't know. I don't want to say it's impossible, because as we know firsthand just about anything is possible. Kata, you have to understand that I've only known your mother in one form and, like any goddess, she can take on many."

"Like a dragonfly? Or a young woman?"

He nods. "Exactly."

"I think I've seen her." I almost regret it when I say it, only because of the hope that springs in my father's eyes.

"Then you probably did." He pauses, tracing the carved designs of the box. "I can feel her. She's here. She's trying to keep you safe."

"This stone," Sloan pulls it out his pocket. "It seems like it has a pulse. When we were in the Earth building it became stronger, but when we come here it grows fainter."

My father takes it from Sloan and turns it over in his hand. "I haven't seen this since you were a young girl. Your mother went to great lengths to keep you safe. Unfortunately, we can't keep you safe forever. There would come a time where you'd have to learn to keep your own self safe. Obviously, that time is now." He hands the stone back to Sloan. "You're correct. The stone is inextricably linked to Ka's mother. Sloan, perhaps you have a bit of your mother's gift?"

Sloan flushes. "Yeah, a little here and there.'"

"Then you have enhanced perception. The stone would pulsate no matter whose hand it's in, but only someone with enhanced perception would notice. It's good. The closer you are to Novea the stronger it should beat. Like a heartbeat."

"But I have to destroy the stones to return that part of my personality. What will happen to Mom if the stone's destroyed?"

He lets out a tired sigh. "That's a good question."

. . .

My father recommends that we travel to the perimeter, the land in between the colony and the entrance to the cavern concealing the Elemental Abyss. He theorizes that she could have been given a very brief grace period, due to the kindness of Raj and Katayun given the uniqueness of the situation. Obviously, Raj and Katayun would never want anything bad to happen to me, their only grandchild. At least not of their own doing. He said they have little to do with the creation of the Imminent Darkness. It's simply the natural order of the Universe.

"The Universe needs balance." He'd said it as if it were so simple. "But just as with the Elementals and our own physiology, the Universe can become Unbalanced. That's where you come in. I'm sorry that we deceived you, Ka. Hopefully you understand that it was out of the deepest of our love. You're unique. There's no modern precedence for a half-mortal, half-immortal of the Universe. There's not another person in the entire Universe with your gift. It's a lot of responsibility, but as I've often found in my life, the things requiring the greatest responsibility are often also the most rewarding." He told us to take the box and the stone and travel to the coordinates on the note. "That's what these numbers are. They're coordinates, and if my memory serves me correctly, they're near the Elemental Abyss. She wrote it as three sets of numbers, but really it's two: two sets of three numerals. It's not 36-22-68 as you see here, but 362 and 268. Your mother loved creating codes and solving puzzles." He'd smiled. "She was very good at it too. Although, I suppose she may have had an unfair advantage. Feel the heartbeat of the stone and you will know you're on the right path. I don't know what's in the box, but I have the sneaking suspicion it too is one of your mother's puzzles. Take it with you." I think of the map, tucked safe in my messenger bag, with all of her notes only appearing when wet. I always thought my mother was so serious. Apparently, she was also playful as evidenced by both Cyan and her puzzles. How come I had never taken the time to notice?

"Aren't you coming with us?" I'd asked. "Don't you want to see Mom?"

But he'd shook his head. "The memory I have of your mother is the one I want to keep. To see her in a different form, it wouldn't be the same."

"She's still the same on the inside," I'd objected. Again, he'd simply shook his head.

Now, as we walk in silence, Sloan on one side of me and

Doran, who'd insisted on coming—I had no objections; he's saved my butt on more than one occasion—on the other, his words bring tears to my eyes. It wasn't that he didn't want to see her; it's that it would be too painful. She can never come back. I can't enter back into the Land of Earth through the portal, once I've gone through and retrieved the stone it's sealed closed. I swipe at my cheek. It's the song of every story isn't it? As soon as you find the truth in something, in someone, it flutters away. The realization is always a moment too late, the escape always too soon.

We walk for a long time. I fill Doran in on the things I've learned. He listens, but doesn't give me much of a response about the things he's been up to. I know that something horrible happened to his father, to their relationship, but not what. I know his father became angry, violent even, and I'm pretty sure he became an Unbalanced Water. He doesn't talk about it. I suppose he's not ready. I'm not sure he ever will be. The newly developing filigree on the side of his face reflects the pink light of the sun, contrasting against his dark skin. He lives back among the Metals, but Fire still rages through his veins. As soon as we leave the limits of the colony, the wind begins to whip up, stirring up the terracotta-colored earth. In many ways Xon 9 reminds me of a desert. Outside of the colony it's vast, with the mountains in the distance. There's no vegetation. No nothing.

"We're getting close," Sloan says. "The stone's pulse is growing stronger."

"It's hard to see with the wind whipping around the dirt." I squint against the wind. I can't see anything but barren land in every direction.

"There. What's that over there?" Doran points in the distance. Through the duststorm I can see what looks like a shadow. It could be anything.

"The stone's getting stronger."

The shadow begins to take form and I can see that it's a figure wearing a hooded cloak. I'd like to trust the stone and believe that it's telling me this is my mother. But I also know the Imminent Darkness can play tricks on me by its ability to also take any form: human or otherwise. "Be careful." I say to Doran and Sloan, but more to myself than anything. As we approach I realize the figure is also approaching us. It doesn't appear to be walking, but almost floating along with the wind.

"It's a steady pulse now. No longer a beating."

The figure pauses as if waiting for us. I still don't want to get too close. The figure seems to sense my hesitation and continues slowly toward us. Now that it's closer I can see that the figure is small and slender. My heart surges in hope that this is my mother, this is Kesara. The hood hides the figure's face. I need a sign. A sign that only my mother would know. As if reading my mind, a small dragonfly flutters through the air, fighting against the wind. I stick out my index finger and it lands on it briefly before dissolving into a sparkle of cyan and being swallowed by the wind.

We stop a few feet from the figure and I take a step forward. Sloan puts a solid hand on my shoulder, reminding me to still be cautious. The figure looks up and large gray eyes peer back at me from the hooded shadows. Mom.

CHAPTER 19

A young maiden's face. Her cheeks are flushed and her lips are pink. If ever my mother looked like a goddess in the mortal realm, it's now. She pushes the hood of her cloak back, revealing tumbling chestnut-colored curls.

"You got my message," she says. Her voice is soft and melodic, like a song in the wind.

"We did," I reply.

"Sloan. It's good to see you. I admire the fact that you take your Everlasting Vow so seriously," she smiles but her face quickly turns grim. It doesn't lessen her beauty which seems to radiate out of every single pore, as if the entire Universe is somehow encapsulated inside her and longing to pour itself out. "Unfortunately, it is only going to grow more difficult with each retrieval of the stones." She closes her eyes and tilts her head, as if sniffing the air.

"What do you mean?" Doran asks.

She opens one gray eye. "And who are you again?"

"Doran. He's the one who helped me retrieve the Fire stone."

Her face softens. "Oh, yes. I do recall you. Such tragedy…but such bravery forged because of it." If her words were meant to stir a reaction she doesn't get one. Doran's face is as impassable as the Earth stone. She continues. "What I mean is that as my daughter grows stronger, so too does the Imminent Darkness."

"I thought as Ka grew stronger, the Imminent Darkness would grow weaker, to restore the balance."

"That's just it. The Imminent Darkness isn't what's causing the Imbalance. Ka is. As she grows in strength, the rest of the colony will realize that they too can hold all of the Elements. This will cause a gross imbalance, in our favor of course. But as above, so below, good and evil, and all of that. So in order to defeat the lightness, the illumination that comes with knowledge, the darkness will seek weak links in the chain of evolution in order to harness its power and fulfill its own agenda. Surely, Sloan, you know that. Think of any war or any dictator. So many cultures make so many marvelous technological advances as a result of war. And we cannot know peace without war. It's the way of the Universe and always will be." She looks around as if noticing something for the first time. "Your father?"

I shrug. "He didn't want to come."

She puckers her lips in a frown. "I can't suppose I blame him. He only ever knew Novea. The only way I could return to help you was to take another form."

"Kesara."

She nods. "Kesara. But you must understand, my dear daughter, I will never be able to return. I can sense that Raj is displeased that I even risked one of my other incarnations. Immortality is a lofty responsibility, and I admit I lead more often with my heart than with my head." She closes her eyes and sniffs the air again, her nostrils flaring. "We don't have much time. Do you have the box?"

Doran steps forward, looking at me first. I nod. *Give it to her.* He hands it to Kesara. She lifts it up to inspect it. "Hello, old friend."

"Dad said it was a wedding gift from Raj and Katayun."

"That it is. Funny, they have a way of knowing just what I'll need and when, but not a moment too soon." Her smile fades and she turns serious. "Now, Kata. Listen carefully. The map, the ingredients can be bought in the Black Bazaar, but for a price. You can harness the power of the Elements, however once I'm gone for good, they may not be as responsive. The ingredients should help. My sisters have grown more cautious and they fear the Imminent Darkness and what it can do to their own Lands. That's where the ingredients will come in handy. Also, no matter what happens, know that I will always be with you."

"Are you leaving already?" I feel a swell of emotion in my chest. It's as if all the other times I knew deep down that I'd be seeing her again, but now I have the same knowing that I won't be seeing her again. Possibly ever.

She pulls her key from a pocket of her cloak. "Don't fret, Kata. You and your father…this mortal life. I could never have asked for anything better. In all my years of existing and of all my years to come nothing can ever surpass it." She wraps me in a hug and I bury my face in the softness of her cloak. I'm not a crier, but I can't seem to stop the flow of tears that streak my face. She takes my chin in her hand and looks deep into my eyes. "I will always be near, Ka. I promise you. It may not be in the form that you know me. But I will be there, watching, and protecting you." I nod even though I don't really understand. Even a dragonfly like Cyan cannot replace my flesh and blood mother.

She sets the box on the ground and kneels beside it. "Stand back. Oh, and remember, the stone is your key." I have no idea what she's talking about, but just nod numbly. "I'm sorry to leave just when you'll need me," she's saying as she puts the key into the lock. A perfect match. "But I'm afraid I've already interfered a bit too much." She turns the key and the box flings open. "I love you, Ka. Always remember to follow your heart, it will lead you to places and people you never could have imagined."

Her words are sucked up by a burst of air that rushes out of the box. A beautiful bird with a long-feathered tail soars out of the inside. Its feathers are red as the Fire that flows through my veins. It soars up and then comes swirling back down, leaving a golden trail behind it. It flies to my mother and lands on her outstretched arm. "Tell your father, I love him." The bird's talons grip her arm, leaving an imprint on her cloak. I nod. But I won't tell him because I now realize what my father risked in loving my mother. She risked her immortality, but he risked something far more fragile: his heart.

This time when the bird spreads its magnificent wings and soars upward, it's in a swirl of sparkling golden light. My mother soars with it, up into the red sky of Xon 9, growing smaller and smaller until there's a blindingly brilliant burst of light. An explosion. Golden sparkles rain back down to the ground, covering our heads in a sort of glittery dust. A single red feather from the tail of the bird floats down and lands at my feet. My mother is gone.

. . .

I pick up the feather. I draw it across my skin. It feels silky. Doran's face is slack-jawed.

"Since meeting you, I've seen some pretty whacked out things, but what the heck was that?"

Sloan steps forward and wraps an arm around me. He takes the feather and carefully ties it into my hair. "It was a phoenix. A mythological bird that is reborn from its ashes." He tucks the feather behind my ear. The symbolism isn't lost on me, what with my mother being the maiden, mother and crone. "The stone has gone still."

The stone. "It still needs destroyed." Sloan hands it to me and it's cool and smooth in my palm, like always. Somehow it hasn't quite sunk in that my mom is gone forever and that I'll never see her again. This whole time I think I secretly hoped the box contained something to make her stay, but it didn't. It was her ticket out of here. I look around. The box is gone too. No more key, no more box. Just a turquoise stone that needs to be destroyed somehow and a map of the Elemental Abyss is all that remains of my mother.

"Remember how your mom said something like sorry to leave just when you'll need me?" Doran's voice cuts through the cloudiness of my thoughts.

"Yeah."

"Well, I hate to be the harbinger of bad news. But we're not out here alone."

Sloan and I look up. In the distance something approaches. The wind still whips the dirt around, there's nothing out here to stop it until it reaches the mountains. I can't tell if it's human, but what else would it be? Although, it approaches faster than a normal human could walk and has a strange, lop-sided stride.

"What is it?" I ask.

"I don't know," Sloan replies and there's an edge of uncertainty to his voice.

"Do we run?" The hair on the back of my neck prickles.

"To where?" Doran asks. "There isn't anywhere to go. If we run back to the colony, we have to pass it. If we run to the mountains, we have to climb them."

"What if it's dangerous?"

Sloan's eyes narrow and his hands involuntarily ball into fists. "I'm pretty sure that it is."

The dust seems to clear, as if making a path for what approaches. And once I can make it out, my stomach convulses and I want to throw up in the dirt at my feet, but I swallow it back down, the bile burning my throat. It's hideous.

It's the head and torso of a woman, but where two legs should be is a long serpentine tail. Because of the tail, the creature has a sort of loping, hopping gait, like walking on one leg and a tail at the same time. It's grotesque.

"What do you think it wants?" Doran asks.

"What else? The stone."

"Or to kill you."

"Gee, thanks for that vote of confidence."

"No problem." His gulp is audible enough to hear from Sloan's opposite side.

"Get behind me," Sloan instructs.

"No offense, but you're not the most powerful one of the three of us."

"I took a vow."

"A vow. Not a death wish."

The argument stops as the figure comes into better view. Shoulder length, blonde hair, an angular face with sunken in cheekbones. A pert nose.

"Tristen." Doran says and there's so much contempt in his voice. She's the one who broke him, or rather continued to break what was already broken.

She pauses a decent distance away. Close enough that I can see the reptilian scales that run up her chest and down her slender arms. It's like I want to look away, but can't. "Sweet, Doran," she coos. "I never thought I'd be lucky enough to see you again."

He says nothing. Just spits at the ground.

"And Ka. A pleasure."

My blood is boiling. I can feel my Fire being stirred up inside me. It's percolating just beneath the surface, the only thing stopping it the pliable mattress of my skin. "It's not likewise. I'm surprised to see you, Tristen. I thought you were on the naughty list."

She flicks her tail. "I was. But." She shrugs coyly. "Now I'm not."

"You look a bit…different than the last time I saw you." Her Fire markings are gone, replaced with the same burnt tattoo that mars Li's skin. Punishment for her error?

"Ah, yes. Well, the Imminent Darkness was very displeased. What you did to the Army of Fire was very bad, Ka. Very, very bad. And since it was my idea, well, let's just say that I begged for my life to be spared and this was the compromise." She flicks her tail and slithers a bit closer. I take a step back, backing up into Sloan. "The Imminent Darkness is very powerful. It can take many forms, you know. Animal, person, even the smallest microorganism Can you imagine being able to exist as virtually anything? Amazing." There's a hint of awe in her voice. Despite, what's been done to her, she still holds reverence for the Imminent Darkness.

"Why are you here?"

"To redeem myself of course. After receiving my new form, I decided that I shouldn't consider it a limitation, but an asset. I knew you were traveling to and from the Elemental Abyss so I decided to wait. Each evening I have waited until the right moment."

"So you're planning on killing her?" Sloan finally asks.

"To put it simply, yes. But you take all the fun out of it when you say it like that."

The rage boils over for Doran before it does me. "You, bitch." It's not a scream. Not even a yell. Monotone. Deadly. He lunges for her, but he's not ready for her new form, her punishment from the Imminent Darkness. She bats him away with her serpentine tail and it sends him flying away, landing on his back, sprawled out several yards away. I pause, waiting for him to move, but he doesn't.

That's it for me. I feel the snap as the anger boils to the surface and feel the sparks burning in my fingertips. Tristen gives me a sinister smile. "Come, Ka. Dance with me. I never got the pleasure."

"That's because you and Eoin bailed. You almost killed my friends."

She cocks her head to the side and it has an odd jerky movement to it. "You care more about the death of your friends than your own?"

"Yes, I do." My mind's racing. I don't know what to do. How can I get in close enough to zap her? I'm not strong enough to conjure fire balls on my own.

"Peculiar." And before I can decide what to do, her tail whips out and flings under my feet, knocking me down. The tip wraps around my ankles. Sloan grabs my arms, but Tristen is pulling me in the opposite direction and its having the effect of some sort of medieval torture device.

She continues to wrap her tail around me, coiling up my legs and squeezing so hard that I already feel the pins and needles.

"Take me instead," Sloan says. His fingers are slipping from mine.

"No!" I object. "Don't take him!"

"I haven't feasted in a while. First, the girl. Then you. And sweet Doran for dessert."

As if in response to his name, Doran comes flying in at a running leap, aiming at the human half of Tristen. He knocks her over and her tail unravels its hold on me, locking around Doran's waist instead, encircling around him.

"Ka!" he calls.

"Here," Sloan unsheathes a knife from his waistband and hands it to me. "Snakes aren't in my repertoire." I stare at him. Like they're in mine? He shrugs. "I'll try and distract her. Stab her tail. If you can, pin it to the ground."

I nod to show I understand

"Hey, Tristen. I've been in the ranks of the Imminent Darkness. Killing Ka won't be enough. The stones will still exist."

She pauses her squeezing of Doran, loosening her grip just a little, and he coughs gasping for breath. "No girl, no stones."

"Yeah, but you'd have to destroy the remaining stones too to truly destroy her. It's like trying to kill a man by cutting off his arm, if you know what I'm saying." He holds up the turquoise stone and it glints in the rising moonlight. Shiny and beautiful.

"You make an interesting point." She loosens her grip on Doran and moves jerkily toward Sloan. Doran crab crawls away. I make a run for it, knife raised ready to plunge it into her scaly tail. But she senses me and as I go to stab her, she whips the knife out of my hand. "*Tsk, tsk.* Tricks aren't very nice." Her tail curls around the knife. She turns to Sloan. "I'll have to take my chances."

The knife waves around wildly. I've run out of ideas and from the look on Sloan's face so has he. Tristen comes loping closer, the knife raised high. I backpedal away, my heart pounding in my chest. She's too fast and I can't get away. *The stone is your key.* "The stone!" I yell and Sloan hurls it at me as Tristen raises the knife and brings the blade down. I catch the stone and the tip of the knife cuts into it.

First, as with the box, a rush of wind whistles out of the stone. It immediately begins to swirl around Tristen. She bats at it blindly. As the wind continues to swirl, it seems to swoop her up. I can no longer see her, but can hear her screams of protest. Before I can even blink it sucks her back into the stone, the echo of her painful howls all that's left.

Then the stone bursts into a million tiny pieces, raining down speckles of turquoise, intermingling with the gold dust particles form earlier. The stone is destroyed. I feel the Fire raging inside me pause and I'm filled with a sense of peace and loving support. It wells up from my heart and coalesces inside my veins with the rage and passion of Fire, the Earth returning to me and kissing the Fire like a long lost lover, soothing it. I feel weak and begin to fall to my knees, Sloan catches me before I hit the ground. I smile before I pass out. My Earth has returned to me.

CHAPTER 20

Steadfast. Nurturing. Reliable. Compassionate. Grounded. These are the traits that I've been missing, that had just been a trickle in my veins. But, as with every good thing, Earth has its bad qualities too. Stubbornness. Narrow-sightedness. Narcissistic. I can see now how my mother ruled the Land of Earth because I can see these qualities in her.

Sloan helps me to my feet. There's no trace of Tristen. Little turquoise colored stones are scattered all around us. Doran limps over, an arm wrapped around his middle.

"I think she broke a couple of my ribs. That was one strong snake," he says.

"Are you happy she's gone?" I ask.

He shrugs. "Who knows if she's really gone for good? Maybe that stone whisked her away somewhere for safe-keeping. But am I happy that hopefully she can't hurt another person for now? Then yes, I am happy that witch is gone."

I'm a bit unsteady on my feet and Doran drapes his free arm around my waist. With Sloan's help we walk slowly back toward the colony. The wind has disappeared and everything has gone still. The quietness is almost palpable, the only sound is our boots against the dirt.

When we're back inside the colony, it's closest to go to Mrs. Chatfield's. So we walk Doran home. "Mom can take care of me better than any hospital can," he insists. She opens the door, takes in the sight before her, bites her lip, and says nothing. She ushers us inside and gets busy in the kitchen, creating concoctions.

My father doesn't ask about my mother. I don't suppose I should expect him to. I don't tell him that her last words were to tell him that she loves him. Somehow I feel like that would be grinding the pieces of his broken heart further into the muck. To be honest, I think my father got the crap end of the deal. My mother was going to live on even after my father died. Sure, her heart may have been broken, but surely after so many centuries or millennia it would heal, become whole again.

Mrs. Chatfield brings me a sweet smelling cup of tea. "It will help your body acclimate to the return of the Earth Elemental: cinnamon, tumeric, ginger." I don't ask where the spices come from. In the Black Bazaar you can find everything and anything. "Good for circulation."

I take a sip of the strong brew. "Will Doran be okay?"

She gives a slight shake of her head. "Doran will always be okay. He'll need to rest. Not much you can do for broken ribs. They usually heal on their own in a few weeks. But good luck keeping that boy in one spot." She smiles and disappears down the hallway probably to check on Doran.

Remaining in the living room are myself, Sloan, and my father. He lets out a long sigh. "So you destroyed the second stone. What happens now?"

A simple enough question. Go after the third stone. But something is nagging at me. Tristen is presumably dead, but the Imminent Darkness is still out there and they have more than just a revenge-seeking snake-woman on their side. From what Sloan's said, the ranks are deep and vast.

"Dad, those prisoners, what kind of crimes had they committed?"

My father leans forward, placing his elbows on his knees, and clasping his hands beneath his chin. "That's an interesting question, Kata. I never could quite gather. Besides the Underground there isn't much crime, and even that is petty, more deception than anything. As far as I know there's not much violence in the colony. We're a fairly small group, reliant on our interrelationships with our fellow colonists. We do have a prison, but it's in the Metal part of town, by the military facility, as you may already know. But what you may not know is that it's almost more of a fort than a prison. Non-stop surveillance. And once you've been found guilty, well, there's not much you can do to get out and see the light of day again. Some of our highest levels of security are used for that prison."

"With only several thousand people, how many prisoners are there?" Sloan asks.

My father shrugs. "A few hundred maybe. If that." He turns back toward me. "But to answer your question, Ka, I do believe that prison beneath Council Hall was a different type of prison. One not known to the general populace, if it were it would never be allowed. It's barbaric. I gathered from my limited discussion that the people in those cages had somehow challenged the Imminent Darkness in one way or another."

"But if the Imminent Darkness is so powerful, then why do they need to imprison people? All those families not knowing where their loved ones went. Children without a mother or father. Or a son or daughter gone missing. Just like that." It would be horrible if I hadn't found my father. At least I know where my mother has gone, but if I hadn't found my father I think the not knowing would be the worst. "Why. Why do they do it?"

"It's actually rather simple, and a tactic used for thousands of years. To create fear. Not only in the prisoners, but in the people left behind. Once you instill fear there's no limit to the power you can wield." I feel a bit nauseous at this proclamation, but as soon as it's said I know it to be true. When people are afraid they do things they wouldn't normally do; they turn against one another. They distrust. Power is the prize and fear is the currency.

"Then I know what I need to do next."

"What's that?" Sloan asks. He's been so quiet I thought he

may have fallen asleep, but his green eyes are alert and attentive.

"I need to save those people. We need to go back to Council Hall and set those people free. We need them to return to their families and tell them to not be afraid. And to tell them the Impossible Girl is real and that she's fighting on their side. Because the Imminent Darkness is real too and I don't plan on letting it win."

...

We leave the Underground when the twin moons are high in the sky. Mrs. Chatfield had some hooded cloaks similar to what the members of the Imminent Darkness wear.

"Long story for another day." Is all she said as she handed them to us.

Doran stays behind because he's useless if he gets injured worse. He wasn't happy about it either. I think he's one of those people who needs to immerse himself in chaos and adventure, anything to avoid having to deal with reality. But it will catch up with him sooner or later. It did with me.

My father insisted on coming with us. But I can't say that surprised me. "For a short time, I was one of those prisoners. I was lucky. You knew where to look and you came for me. Others were there much longer and no one came for them. As far as their families know, they're dead."

Council Hall looms in the distance. The cloak I wear is too big for me and drags on the ground with a slight scraping sound. The creepy statue in the fountain leers in the moon light. The water trickling softly, a soothing juxtaposition to the fierceness of the statue and the torch held high over its head, the ever-burning flame flickering in the constant breeze that wafts around our colony. The hair on the back of my neck stands up.

"Is that statue of anyone in particular?" I whisper to my dad as we follow Sloan around to the back entrance.

"No one really knows, actually. Rumor has it that he was one of the original 3,000 inhabitants of Xon 9, but no one knows his lineage and he was never matched to any of the original files. My best guess is he just represents a member of the Council." The Council of Wood has only one female member, and I can count on one hand in the last several hundred years the other female members. That's it.

Despite my father's explanation I know I've seen the face before, I just can't place where. We reach the door and it has a new electronic key component. My specialty. I'm getting better at controlling the energy of my Fire. I don't want to only summon it with rage because rage is uncontrollable and unpredictable. I visualize the heat coursing through me and when my fingertips are warm I place them on the electronic pad. Almost immediately it begins to smoke. It lets out several short beeps and then one long final beep before the red light turns green and the lock tumbles.

"Excellent," Sloan grins in the moonlight. My father goes in first. He uses a small flashlight to illuminate the stair way. We reach the first sub-level. Everything looks the same, but the smell has subsided and been replaced with a chemical cleaner smell. The giant curtain has been straightened and is hanging neatly. The rest of the room is empty. No crown, no table with restraints. As if it were never there at all. My hair would beg otherwise.

My father sweeps the curtain aside and the wooden door with the arched top is still there. He pulls the door open and it makes a soft groaning sound. "Dad, how come we never see any sort of guards or anything?" I ask before we head down the second set of steps leading into the sub-sub-level.

"They only come once a day to check on and feed the prisoners. I suppose they assume they aren't much threat. Like I said they aren't truly guilty of any crimes except maybe knowing too much or challenging a particular way of thinking. They didn't strike me as a violent bunch." He swings the flashlight down the stairwell.

We make a sort of Ka sandwich as we make our way down, my father leading with me in the middle, and Sloan bringing up the rear. I forgot about the stench. I've heard before that if you experience something really excruciating, like say childbirth, that your brain forgets about it on purpose. A sort of self-preservation response. The mix of filth and feces fills my nostrils and I try not to gag. As we reach the bottom of the stairs and turn the corner, I can hear some whimpering and moaning. Why torture the prisoners when they're being starved to death and living in their own filth? An influx of patients at the sole hospital will probably arouse suspicion, but this is something I have to do. I'm sick of feeling like a pawn in some sort of messed up game. It's time I make a move of my own.

"Are you ready?" my father asks. "It's going to take a lot out of you. There are a lot of cages."

"Maybe there's some sort of main connecting line. The

electricity to work the locks has to come from somewhere. If I can find it Ka can just destroy that and it should open all of the cages."

My father hands him a second flashlight. "You find that. Ka will start unlocking cages and I'll begin herding people out in small groups."

Sloan nods and disappears, searching along the walls for a sort of main circuit box. I head for the first cage. Inside is a very thin man with shaggy black hair. His clothes are torn and he backpedals away frightened. My father talks to him in a gentle, soothing voice while I get to work on the lock. My fingertips are still warm as I conjure up some heat. Pretty soon the pad begins to beep and then the lock tumbles. I yank the cage door open and at first the man just stares dumbly, eyes wide, unsure.

"Go," I practically choke out, overcome with an emotion I can't quite describe. "Go home. Back to your family. Back to your life."

He scampers forward in an animalistic way. How long has he been down here? His face has soft folds, but he doesn't look very old. He is thin and dirty. He puts a bony hand on the arm of my cloak. "Thank you, young lady." His voice cracks, either from emotion or lack or use. Or both.

I swallow back tears and nod dumbly. If I cry now the work will never get done. I move on to the next cage. And I keep going one after the other, getting faster as I go, but there are still hundreds of cages. I reach the woman from before, the Metal woman I was afraid of. "You came back! Bless you!" she says when she sees me.

She grips the bars of the cage excitedly. "The wise man said you'd be back. And he was right!"

"I'm sorry I wasn't back sooner," I reply as I set to work on the lock.

"I found it!" Sloan calls and his voice is like thunder in the darkness. The woman's lock beeps and she pushes the door open, flinging her bony arms around me in a thankful hug. I give her a quick hug back then urge her toward my father who is taking the first group up the steps and back out into the world.

I run down the row toward the direction where I heard Sloan's voice. I find him several rows over standing beside a metal box on the wall. "There's several sets of switches for lights and for the electronic pads. Look, they're even labeled." He shines the flashlight inside the metal box: L1, L2, L3. C1 C2 C3. "The C stands for cell. The numbers are the row for the cages." He points to a large Y-shaped lever. "This is the master switch. Do you think you can do it?"

"Yes." My lips say even though my mind thinks *hopefully*. What choice do I have?

"I'll leave you to it then. I'll go to the stairs and help direct people out. If all the cells open at once there's probably going to be a lot of confusion." He looks down at me and smiles. "Have I told you how amazing you are, Ka Waylon?" He kisses me before I can reply and disappears back into the labyrinth of cages.

My fingers are already hot now. I wrap my hand around the Y-shaped master switch. My stomach is jittery because I'm unsure what will happen. Will it explode? I close my eyes and try not to think about it. Instead I think about all these people. Innocent people treated inhumanely, locked up for crimes they didn't commit. Locked up for no reason at all except challenging the truth. The master switch begins to spark. They're families assuming their loved ones are dead. What will happen when they return? The switch grows hot in my hand. What will happen when the Imminent Darkness finds out what I've done?

Sparks begin to fly overhead. There are crude lightbulbs along the ceiling and they're creating a rain of sparks. I begin to hear sporadic beeping, then more beeping. "You're doing it, Impossible Girl!" A hysterical laugh. "She's doing it!" I recognize the voice as belonging to the wise man in the cell across from my father.

More voices. Voices filled with hope. "She's doing it!"

A laugh erupts somewhere from within the labyrinth of cages. "You can do it, Impossible Girl!"

"Thank you! Thank you for saving us, Impossible Girl!"

I swallow the lump in my throat. I find my voice and call out as loudly and clearly as I can. "Call me Ka!:

My name soft at first then growing louder. "Ka! Ka! Ka! Ka!" A chant rising from formerly hopeless hearts. There's a resounding click as all the cell doors simultaneously unlock.

I hear the first *whoop* of freedom. And then I hear the soft pad of feet. Sloan's voice directing people up the steps and toward my father who's waiting to lead them away from this hellish place.

The lights overhead continue to rain sparks and I run up and down the rows, making sure that all the cell doors have been unlocked and that no one is left behind. I'm almost done with the last row when I see something. Rather, a someone. A small, someone with knees hugged to her chest. Rocking back and forth. Sobbing softly.

I kneel beside her. "Come on," I urge. "Let's get you home."

"There's no one left," she cries. "I was the last one." I don't know what she means and I don't have time to find out.

I'm about to scoop her up into my arms when I have a chilling thought. The Imminent Darkness can take on any form. Wolf, mummy, human. Tristen even said it could take the form of a microorganism. The hair on the back of my neck prickles. The little girl lifts her head up and her eyes are glowing yellow. "I've been the last one for a long time. It gets lonely you know." The voice that comes out of her mouth is not that of a little girl, but of a very old, sinister-sounding man.

I jump away, squatting in a defensive position, unsure what to make of this situation. Sloan and my father are upstairs. All the prisoners are gone. I'm alone.

"Such bravery leads to foolishness," the girl says and she leaps onto all fours, like an animal. Like a wolf. She opens her mouth and reveals fangs. "I've grown hungry over the centuries. Your mother was a little taste, but you, you will be a feast to keep me satiated for at least a thousand years."

The girl leaps at me, snarling, muscles in her arms and legs spry like the most elite athlete. She lunges at me, red sparks raining down, eyes glowing. I hear the softest whisper inside my mind. *Earth.* It's my mother's voice. I throw my hands up to protect my face and when I do long green vines shoot out of my wrists and wrap around the girls ankles, waist, and wrists, stopping her in mid-air and causing her to fall to the ground like an anvil.

The vines keep coming, wrapping, and coiling around her, forming a sort of cocoon. Then the vines stop flowing from my wrists as quickly as they started. The girl laughs, an ominous old man laugh that grows louder and louder as I run toward the steps. Sloan is half-way down the steps already. "Are you okay?" His voice fades as he sees the little girl with glowing yellow eyes wrapped in vines, laughing manically in the row behind me. The laughter reaches a crescendo then in a puff of putrid yellow smoke the girl is gone.

"What the...?"

"No time. Let's get out of here." He grabs my hand and practically drags me up the steps. We run through the sub-level and up the steps to the outside. The last of the prisoners are but specks in the distance, heading to their homes, to their families, hopefully back to their lives. We continue to run, Sloan's hand sure and solid in mine. Real. Not something or someone pretending to be someone else. Solid and real.

My father waits at the crossroads in front of the Hall that leads to the different areas of the colony: the University Complex, the Underground, the Military Building, the Agriculture Houses, and the School Grounds. As we run past the fountain I look back over my shoulder and catch sight of the statue in its center. For a second I think its eyes are glowing yellow, but I blink, and they're back to normal. And then I remember who the statue reminds me of: the codger from *The Five Goddesses*. The Imminent Darkness.

CHAPTER 21

Mrs. Chatfield's house is abuzz with activity. Word has quickly spread about the freeing of the prisoners. The small trailer is crammed with people, bustling about the kitchen, helping to put together small baskets of homemade herbal remedies, Mrs. Chatfield's own concoctions to help the malnourished prisoners. "I just cannot imagine. Cannot imagine." She keeps mumbling over and over again as she moves about.

Doran comes meandering down the hallway. Mrs. Chatfield takes a kitchen towel and swats it at him. "You should not be up! Back to bed!"

He rubs the stubble on his chin. "Who can sleep with this racket?"

Zora pops her head out of the tiny kitchenette. "Ka freed prisoners that were being kept beneath Council Hall."

"Council Hall? What were prisoners doing beneath Council Hall?" He scratches his head.

"That's what I'd like to know. From the few people that I spoke to who were being kept down there, they were opponents of the Imminent Darkness," my father replies.

I help Doran over to the living room where Sloan has taken the map out of my messenger bag. He's sprinkled it with water and is tediously writing down the various ingredients that we'll need to get from Bina. A young Metal man in fresh clothing is fast asleep in the armchair, snoring softly.

"That's Jock." Doran says jutting his chin toward the man before allowing me to help lower him to the couch. He adjusts a pillow behind him.

"Is that his actual name?" I ask.

"Well, no. I think it's Charles or something, but as long as I've known him he's been called Jock. He's a solider. I'd heard he'd gone missing, but I never thought…" Doran's voice trails off and he shakes his head. "That's messed up, man."

I reach into my messenger bag and search for the *The Five Goddesses*. I find it and pull it out, flipping to the part of the story where the codger tricks the sisters. The small, hand-drawn illustrations throughout the book are done in ink and are nothing compared to the full-blown watercolor portraits in the back of the book, but the author illustrated this scene with a sort of floating head in the margin of the page.

Almond-shaped eyes set far back in the face, a wide flattened nose that comes to a point like an upside down triangle, elongated ears, and a small mouth with an upper lip that is almost non-existent. The hood casts a shadow across the face making it seem menacing. Either way it definitely is the same face as the statue in front of Council Hall.

"Dad, look." I show him the page from the book. He's walked past that fountain with the statue almost every single day for the last however many years.

He takes the book and looks at it closely. "Why does that face look so familiar? Like I've seen it before."

Sloan glances over his shoulder. "It kind of looks like the man in the statue in front of Council Hall. You know in the weird fountain where his palm is open and his other hand holds the torch."

"Yes," my father agrees. "It does appear to resemble the statue." He glances at the book's cover. "It's been a while since I've heard this story."

"You know it?" I'm surprised. I know he knew my mother was immortal, but I wasn't sure how much of her story he knew, considering I had to do a substantial amount of my own research to figure it out.

"Well, when your mother first told me who she was, naturally, I wanted to see proof. She'd shown me several books in the library confirming her identity." He flips to the back, to the portrait of the Earth Goddess. "Look how young she was."

"You should have seen her as the maiden who saved me from the MindCleanse. She couldn't have been much older than me.

Maybe Sloan's age."

His mouth folds into a thin line and his eyes seem to mist. He rubs at his eyes, closing the book, and handing it back to me. I feel horrible. And angry. Sure my mother had an agreement, but to leave my father behind seems so unfair. I never realized how much he loved my mother. They were never overly or outwardly affectionate, but maybe sometimes you don't have to be. Not when you're risking things like your immortality or simply your heart. A thought occurs to me. I'm half-immortal, but does that actually make me completely immortal? If so, then Sloan and I aren't that different than my mother and father, except I don't have any stipulations on my immortality. But Sloan is mortal and that means that I'd have to live on forever without him. The thought makes my stomach ache and I push it aside, tapping the book as if the sound can make the thought shatter into a billion tiny pieces.

"Do you think it's a coincidence the codger and that statue so closely resemble one another?" I ask, feeling like I'm rehashing the same argument over and over: Council of Leaders equals Imminent Darkness.

Sloan folds up the map and hands it back to me. "I don't know if I'm completely convinced yet, but I don't think the argument for them not being connected somehow is exactly working in their favor."

"There's a statue to the Imminent Darkness standing in front of our Council Hall!" I protest. "Does no one else find that ironic?"

"Ironic, yes. Guilty, no." My father says. "I'm afraid you're going to need more evidence, Kata."

"Yeah," I mumble, "Hopefully I can get it before anyone else is hurt."

. . .

After a couple days the hubbub has died down. Sloan and I helped deliver care packages to families with known escaped prisoners. To say word gets around is a bit of an understatement. Unbeknown to me, there has been some unrest in the darker corners of Xon 9, in the corners that no one dares peer in because of what they may find there. The Unbalanced. They've known and they've watched. Waited patiently in the shadows. Forced to choose an Elemental then injected with its powers, the physiological affects interacting with their own unique body chemistry. I've always known that Metal was the most likely to become Unbalanced, a delicate equilibrium between strong and forceful, the ability to defend and the ability to abuse or manipulate. I always accepted it as truth that Metals had more Unbalanced Elementals, so much so that they formed their own community within the colony, erroneously thinking that the rest of the colony shunned them to this existence.

"It's complicated," Sloan explains. "Why was my mother Unbalanced and Michaela not? I can't say."

"What about your father?"

"I didn't really know him all that well. He..." There's a slight hesitation in his voice. "...disappeared when I was young. All I truly know is that he was an Unbalanced Metal who worked in Universal Intelligence."

"I'm sorry." I feel like Sloan's telling me a half-truth, but who am I to question what he remembers about his own father?

"It's okay. Like I said, I was really young when it happened. Mom didn't talk much about him after that. Michaela is a bit older, so maybe she remembers more, but she never really talks about him either. I have a couple of fuzzy memories, but sometimes it's like he didn't even really exist."

"That's sad." Is that what I will do with my mother? Will she eventually seem as if she never existed at all? I know that's not true for my father.

He shrugs. "I think the Underground has known for a long time about the Imminent Darkness. They believed, more than anybody, that there was truth in the stories, the legends. Which probably made them seem all the more crazy to everyone else. There are several Mrs. Chatfields throughout the Underground. And now that the missing have returned..."

"What will happen now?"

"Just don't be surprised if you start to notice some changes." He looks out the window. "We should get going." He waves the list of ingredients he recorded from the map the other day. "We need to get these items from Bina's trailer before it gets dark. And we should pay her a visit before we head to the Elemental Abyss for the third stone."

"You're coming with me this time?"

"Yeah. I wanted to come with you last time, but it didn't quite work out."

"Not worried about interfering with my own free will?" I ask, repeating the words he once said to me.

He zips up a backpack and looks at me, his green eyes deep as the sea, swirling with unreadable emotions. My stomach stirs and I feel heat spread through my entire body. "Not anymore." He leans over the backpack and grabs me by the waist, pulling me in close. He kisses me carefully. "Or should I be?"

"No. I wouldn't want anyone else to come with me."

Someone clears their throat behind us and I turn around. Doran's leaning against the couch behind us. "I'm glad you want him to go and not me. Because I think hanging out with you, will get me killed sooner rather than later."

I smile. "Are you sure?"

"Three's a crowd anyways." He holds something up that catches the light from the window. "I, uh, made this for you. As, like, a thank you for not leaving me to die…numerous times." He limps around the couch. I take a couple strides to cut the distance and he drops a small object in my palm.

It's a small silver ring. The band is simple and delicate. The stone is triangular. It's turquoise. "Doran, thank you."

"It's from the Earth stone. I picked up a few of the pieces after it shattered. I mean it's kind of messed up since Tristen got sucked up into it, but I figured it would make you think more of your mother than anything. You know, since she's gone and all." He shifts awkwardly from one foot to the other, a pink flush flowering across his coffee-colored skin.

"It's beautiful." I slip it on to my left index finger. The turquoise seems to glow in the dim light of the room.

"So, now even though she's gone, your mom will always be with you." I don't know the entire story of Doran's father, and maybe I never will, but I can't help but wonder if he has any pieces left by which to remember him. That is, if he even wants to remember him.

"I won't ever take it off." I give him a hug and he blushes even more. "You're a good friend, Doran."

"It wasn't anything, just a, you know…"

But it is something. It's a piece of the stone that I retrieved with my mother. It's also the stone that saved me and finally destroyed Tristen. Its color reminds me of Cyan, the carefree adventuress, a side of my mother that I'd never even known existed before. It's much, much more than simply a ring. It's a reminder of where I came from, of who I am, and what I am here to do. Even though I chose Fire, Earth now also runs through my veins: grounded, nurturing, and supportive. It's a reminder of the sea and sky in the Land of Earth and the fine balance that is needed in order for something to work and, more importantly, for it to last. It's a reminder that even though my mother is gone, she lives on somewhere else. Lives on for all of eternity.

The stone is the key.

CHAPTER 22

"Dad!" I'm running down the short hallway and pounding on the closed door to Doran's room. "Dad! I found a way! There's a way for you to visit Mom!"

He opens the door and rubs the sleep from his eyes and for the first time I realize with a tinge of horror that my father looks old. There are slight folds in his face and creases around his brown eyes. There are several days of peppered stubble across his chin.

I push open the door, sending him stumbling back. The room is small, a mattress on the floor and a small round window. There are sketch pads, jewelry making tools, and bottles of paint scattered about. I practically trip over a small pottery wheel that's on the floor, packages of clay stacked beside it, dry bits crumbled over the top. My father sits on the edge of the bed.

"It's the stones. She said, '*The stone is the key.*' I thought she meant in getting rid of Tristen. But she meant it literally is the key. Like her key. The stones are transport objects!"

"I thought you were going with Sloan to Bina's."

"Dad! Don't you understand what I'm telling you! You can be with Mom again!"

He shakes his head sadly. "I'm sorry, Kata, but it just isn't meant to be. This life of your mother's is over and she's moved on elsewhere."

My heart sinks. "She's still the same person. No matter what she looks like on the outside. She'll always be my mom just like she'll always be your wife." His grief has him not thinking straight; I'm sure of it. With the key she simply put her hand over mine. The ring is on my finger so I grab my father's hand in mine, close my eyes and imagine the beautiful white castle and stained glass window, its vibrant colors dancing across the stone floor.

"Kata, what are you doing?" he asks, his voice already sounding far away.

But it's too late. Everything goes black and it's as though we're hurtling through time and space. I see bits and pieces of my father's memories: the sad groans of the voices around him as he waited in his prison cell, my mother's smiling face, him watching me from his seat as I pronounced Fire and the black box appeared to go up in flames. All of these images come fast and furiously. Some are entire scenes sped up, others are glimpses of moments in time: a smile, a hug, a kiss.

We hit the ground hard. Really hard. Because the ground is

stone. "Absalom! You came!" A young woman's voice floats over to me and there's the sound of barefeet slapping against stone. I open one eye and turn my head slowly so that my cheek rests on the cold floor, trying to reclaim the breath that's been knocked from me.

Kesara kneels beside my father and her face radiates a joy that makes my heart ache. The rainbow of colors from the stained glass illuminate her face giving her an even more ethereal quality. Her brown hair cascades down around my father's face.

"Novea?"

"Yes, it's me. Novea, Anuja, but in this form, Kesara. Oh, my dear, husband I didn't think you'd ever come." She picks him up and cradles him in her arms. "And you, Kata!" She exclaims looking up at me, as if noticing my presence for the first time. "You understood."

"Yeah," I grumble sitting up slowly. I hold up my hand with Doran's ring. "It took me a minute, but I figured it out."

. . .

"This place is magnificent," my father says. We're seated in a small cluster at one end of a very long wooden table in an immaculate garden. Vibrantly colored flowers and green leafy vines grow all around and hang from the trellis above us. My mother conjured up my favorite meal of roast chicken and root vegetables. Carrot cake is for dessert.

"I never conjured up meals at home of course," she smiles. "I always did the cooking myself." That explains a lot, I think.

"You look so young," my father says admiring her gray eyes and smooth, almost porcelain skin.

She puts her hand on his cheek. "And you look as I've always known you." I wonder why my parents never seemed to look at each other like that back on Xon 9. Did they not or did I simply not notice? Was their worry over my safety so heavy that a bit of their original spark had dimmed? "You will stay, won't you Absalom?"

Dad glances at me. I shrug. "I didn't exactly bring you here to say good-bye."

"The Earth stone is a bit different than the key. It remembers where it came from. It has a living memory, almost a sort of link between the Land of Earth and Xon 9."

"So I can return whenever I want?"

"As long as you need me, the stone in the ring will bring you here. But as soon as you stop needing me, it will no longer work and simply be a ring that your friend made."

"What about the other pieces? Tristen was sucked into the stone and the pieces went everywhere. Doran took only a few which is how he made me this ring."

"The stone's magic is a bit more than I can comprehend. But Tristen should not be able to cause anyone harm ever again."

"Is she dead?"

Kesara smiles. "More like floating about in the cosmos somewhere in about a billion pieces." She turns her attention back toward my father. "And what about you, Absalom?"

My father lets out a long sigh. "Of course I will stay, Kesara." I knew that would be his answer but I can't help feeling a tinge of disappointment. Hasn't he felt the call to something greater? Freeing the prisoners and leading them to safety, doesn't he want to help keep the rest of the colony from a similar fate? "But, I too want to be able to go back if Ka decides she needs me or if she's in danger."

"Don't forget the passage of time is different. Here it feels like days or even weeks, but on Xon 9 only a short time will pass. You'll age." Kesara reminds him gently.

"Yes, I am mortal. That's a truth I cannot outrun or hide from, but my responsibilities are to my wife and my daughter. I took the vow of til death do us apart, and I do plan to take that quite literally," he smiles stroking Kesara's hand gently. "Tell me there's a way to be in two places at once, my love."

Kesara nods. "Your ring, Ka?" I slip the new ring off my finger and slide it across the table toward her. She takes a small knife, still set on the table from dinner. She dips it in her wine glass, then wipes it off with a linen napkin. She draws it across her finger tip, slicing through the skin. She squeezes a droplet of blood out of the tip of her ring finger and it falls directly onto the stone. It sizzles and then disappears, sinking into the stone. "Flesh of my flesh. Whenever you need your father, truly need him, the ring will send out a call to him and he will appear."

"So not only is this ring like my ticket from home to here, but it's also, like, a calling card to the Universe that I need my dad?" I pick up the ring, slipping it back onto my left index finger. It doesn't feel any different.

My mother laughs, that melodious chiming laugh. "Something like that."

I look at dad as sternly as I can. "And you'll come right?"

"Any time of the day or night." He smiles and I can't help but wonder if I hadn't brought him here how often I would have seen that smile back home. The heart that he risked to be with my mother, her immortality that she risked to be with him. I can only hope that I can have a love like that. Sloan took his Everlasting Vow before he even knew who I was. He's risked his life to protect me ever since. He's slowly chipping away at the hardened shell that's my heart. The heart that was unfeeling for far too long. Maybe not unfeeling, more like indecisive, but that's the same thing in my book. Indecision is the lack of feeling. And what am I willing to risk? The same as my father. My heart. The possibility of immortality. Everything.

"Sloan's waiting," I say, rising from the table.

"Just place your fingers over the ring and think of him. The ring will take you there," my mother instructs. She gets up, coming around the table and giving me a hug. "Thank you," she whispers in my ear. I realize I had it all wrong. I thought my father was the one with the greater risk, but my mother's heart was just as damaged without my father by her side.

My dad stands up and enfolds both my mother and me in a hug. "Thank you, Kata, for seeing what I needed even though I couldn't see it for myself."

"I love you," I whisper and choke back the tears that threaten to overflow. My parents take a step back and I place two fingers from the opposite hand over my ring, picturing Sloan's deep sea eyes and shaggy brown hair, the glistening of his scales. My heart swells and I'm back hurtling through time and space.

. . .

I land with a soft thud. At first, I'm confused, but then I remember that we left from Doran's room. I roll over on the mattress and Sloan, having been seated on the floor, is scrambling to his feet. "Everything ok?"

"Great," I say. "Best landing yet."

"You know what I mean." He comes over and sits beside me. "Did he stay?"

"Yeah, but my mom gave me a way to reach him if we need him." I wiggle my finger with the ring at him. "Universal calling card."

"And you, you're okay?" He pushes a piece of hair that went askew as I hurtled through the dimensions back behind my ear.

"Yeah," and I realize as I say it that it's true: I am okay. "His heart couldn't have handled being apart. I'm not sure hers could have either."

Sloan wraps a hand around mine. "I know what you're thinking."

"I hate when you do that."

"No not because of some seer-dream thing," he laughs. "Because I think the same thing."

"You do?"

"That you're my half-immortal girlfriend who's supposed to save the entire planet from some ancient evil force and that you may or may not die in the process? And if you did, how would I deal with the guilt?"

"Or the complete opposite," I say. "You took an Everlasting Vow. You've been risking your life for me before you even knew who I was!"

He takes my chin and gently turns my face so that we're looking each other in the eyes. "And I wouldn't want it any other way."

"Me neither," I say and I mean it more than I've ever meant anything before. It's not the Fire and it's not the Earth, it's me and only me talking.

"That's what love is. The reward is greater than the sum of all the risks." He whispers and before he can kiss me, for a change, I kiss him, pressing myself into him until he almost falls over and back onto the mattress. I can feel his smile beneath my lips. Fear, risk, chance, love. That's what love is.

This is what love is.

CHAPTER 23

It's a little surreal being in Bina's trailer. Clothes, papers, and other things are tossed about, scattered across the floor as if an afterthought. One of the metal folding chairs from where she does readings has been tossed aside, lying in the living room area. After the attack, more time was spent nursing Bina back to health than redecorating her home. It wasn't long before she was staying with Michaela full-time. Better. Safer.

Sloan flips a switch and the kitchenette light comes on. He's standing on a wooden dining chair and starts pulling open cabinets, searching for the various ingredients my mother listed on the map. He begins pulling out boxes of various items and tossing them aside. Behind the food items, deep in the back of the cabinets are the ingredients he's looking for. The back of the cabinets are full of glass mason jars with labels. "What am I looking for again?" he asks.

I read from the list re-written when we were still at Mrs. Chatfield's. "Medeis Seaweed, Zephyrus Seeds, and Ignis Flos." I read trying to pronounce the words as best as I can. I didn't do that great in Ancient Languages.

"Here's the Medeis Seaweed." He hands me a mason jar. I peer inside. It's greenish-brown, murky water with brown-green chunks floating in it. I slip the jar into my messenger bag, along with the original map, the book, and the sack that now only contains the crystal, the feather and the matches. I try not to gag. Maybe that's how it stops the waterfall's enchantment; the song stops because it's trying not to throw up from the seaweed.

He continues rummaging, moving jars this way and that. "And here's the Zephyrus seeds." He hands me another mason jar. This one contains tiny, oblong purple seeds. Supposedly, they're going to help me summon the wind. I slip the jar into my messenger bag and it makes a clinking sound as it rolls up against the seaweed jar.

"What was the last one again?" He peers down at me.

"Ignis Flos."

"Ah, yes, that's right. Fire flower."

"You speak Latin?"

"I'm the Universal History teacher. I speak lots of things." He grins, his head disappearing back inside the cabinet. He pulls out a jar and frowns. The shaky hand-writing clearly says Ignis Flos, but unfortunately the jar is empty. "Guess she ran out and never filled it. What's that one supposed to be for?"

"It's supposed to 'appease the beast in the chasm.' Huh, the Fire Beast likes flowers. Who would have thought?"

"Kind of a big deal?"

"Yeah, kind of. It'll get old spitting or bleeding every time I want to summon him."

Sloan climbs down off the chair. "You cut yourself to summon the Fire Beast?"

"Well, it was Doran's idea, but it worked. You know, like Fire for Fire, calling on one of our own." I hand the list back to Sloan and he folds it, then puts it in his back pocket. "How do you think we find some Ignis Flos?"

"I have no idea. But I know how to find out." He heads out of the kitchen and I follow him to one of the back rooms of the trailer. There are only two rooms and a bathroom here. Bina's bedroom and another room. Neither of the rooms have doors, instead they're partitioned off with thick, dusty curtains.

Sloan slides the curtains of the room to our right to the side and I'm surprised to see that the room is full of books. Everywhere. Five metal shelves, seven shelves high, almost reach the ceiling and they're doubled-up with books. There's books on the floor and books on a chair. There's a small desk, like a student at school would use and it too is covered with books and old magazines.

"We just have to find a book on herbs or magic."

"Or magical herbs."

"Exactly."

"There must be a million books in here," I say. "How do you

suppose we find the one we're looking for?"

"I don't think there's any rhyme or reason to it. I'll start on the left side and you take the right. Just scan for titles that might fit the bill."

I shrug. Ahna would love this. And she'd also probably be able to find the book in a matter of minutes. She's that good. I begin scanning titles. Some of the books are about planet Earth and the solar system, some are about ancient religious figures from Earth like Jesus, Muhammad, or Buddha, and others seem to be made up stories for entertainment purposes. I've never seen this many books outside of school or the library.

"Find anything?" I ask.

"I never understood the phrase 'looking for a needle in a haystack,' but I think I have a better idea now."

I return to scanning the spines of the books when one catches my eye. *Agricula Flos*. I pull it out and it's a thick, leather-bound book. Its cover is brown and squishy, the letters pressed in a bright golden color. I flip to the table of contents where the flowers are listed by habitat which isn't very helpful to me, so I flip back to the index. The alphabet I can handle. I find Ignis Flos just as it should be beneath the *I* section. Page 182.

I turn to page 182 and there's a picture with a description. It's a spiky red flower that grows on a faded green plant the size of a barrel, with white needles sticking out all over. The red flowers seem to form a sort of crown on top of the plant. "Here, I think I found it!"

Sloan comes over and regards the picture. "If a plant could look mean, I think that plant has nailed it."

"It says it grows in dry, arid areas. That's, like, everywhere here. But I've never seen it before."

"Maybe it doesn't grow here."

"Would Bina know?"

"Bina is all-knowing. Literally."

. . .

After straightening up the trailer a bit, we reach the Military Building where Michaela lives. We stand in the foyer and a man with a blonde crew-cut sits at the front desk. "May I help you?" His voice crackles over the intercom.

"We're here to see Michaela Braden."

"Names?" Sloan and I exchange a look. The last time when I came with Ahna I didn't have to give my name and from the expression on Sloan's face he never has either. The guard notices our expressions. "Security protocol has been changed. I assure you it's for the utmost safety of our residents given the potentially sensitive nature of their work."

It's as though he's memorized the memorandum verbatim.

A million thoughts run through my mind. Is it because of the prisoners escaping? Is it because of what happened when they tried to MindCleanse me? The codger's face in the stone statue floats to mind. Even the guard could be the Imminent Darkness.

"Sloan Braden, her brother and—" He pauses for just a second. "Ahna Solloman."

I try to hide my sharp intake of breath. I've never heard Sloan lie before. The guard looks at a screen and seems to be confirming something. What if they have pictures of all the colonists or ask us to use some kind of biological scanner to confirm our identities? That wouldn't be typical Imminent Darkness though. The Imminent Darkness waits until you're close, close enough to taste it before it interferes or tries to take it away. The girl sitting alone on the floor crying, the memory of her laugh still makes my skin crawl. Her glowing yellow eyes. The Imminent Darkness can take on any form; it could be anybody or anything at any time.

The skin crawls on the back of my neck and I rub my hand there, noticing the new texture beneath my palm, the thick vines, like veins, and the silky filigree of the fire in my elemental star. The rest of the tattoo is still flat and smooth like the rest of my skin. Time seems to drag as the guard continues to scan his security screen.

The lock leading to the bank of elevators tumbles and I feel the air soften as we both let out the breath that we've been holding. "Have a good day." The guard says and smiles at us as we enter through the now open doors. The locks click closed behind us as we head to the bank of elevators.

. . .

"It's me." Sloan says into the intercom outside apartment 411.

The door opens and Michaela ushers us in. "You shouldn't be here."

"Well, it's a little late for that." She bustles us down the hallway and back toward the bedrooms. She opens a closet and pulls out a hooded jacket. She hands it to me.

"The new security. It's only a matter of time before they figure out who you are." She's talking to both of us, but she's looking right at me.

"Who am I?" I ask taking the hooded jacket. She obviously wants me to wear the hood as I leave the building.

"They know about the prisoners and their escape. And while I admire both your boldness and your bravery, you're in grave danger now."

"You mean you knew about the prisoners?" I accuse. I like Michaela, really I do, even if I did initially think she was Sloan's girlfriend before I realized she was his sister. And although she's always been helpful, she's also always been quiet. Not that I'm saying she's on the side of the Imminent Darkness, but the government and the military is obviously a major part of her life. I can't blame her if she doesn't exactly want her entire life uprooted, much like mine has been.

She pulls back her shoulders. "No. I didn't know about that particular prison. There are some bunker cells beneath this building that's the official prsion. From what I heard the prisoners you released were imprisoned for speaking out against the Council." She scrunches her face up, in a puckered way, as if she's still trying to sort out fact from fiction.

"They had her father, Michaela. Those people did nothing wrong. And the conditions of the cells…they weren't cells; they were cages. With little to no food, festering in their own filth, and in the dark no less! They left them in the dark. I bet even the prisoners beneath here have light!"

Her face clouds over. I get the impression it isn't often that Sloan stands up to his big sister.

"You need to go. I-I'm sorry."

"Where's Mom? Mom!?" Sloan calls.

"She's resting, Sloan."

"Well, before we leave we need to ask her about where to obtain Ignis Flos."

There's a shuffle and a thud. Bina's head appears around the corner. "Like I said the last time, it's impossible to sleep with this racket ye people cause." She takes in Sloan and her eyes soften, filling with pride. I notice something that I was oblivious to other times. Michaela may be the one who's taking care of Bina, but Sloan is her pride and joy. "Ignis Flos is located in the mountains of Xon 9. It grows on top of an Earth-Cactus style plant. Don't let the blooms prick yeh though, they're full of poison."

"Sounds like a lovely plant," I say trying to ease the awkwardness of the entire situation.

"Sometimes the most beautiful things are the most deadly." She levels her gray eyes at me. And I freeze. That's a loaded statement if ever I heard one.

"I'm sorry they woke you up, Mother, but they have to get going," Michaela says ushering us back out of the room.

"Eh, they didn't wake me, Michaela. Calm down."

"Mother, the security…"

Bina shuffles down the hallway and I follow sending a glance back at Sloan whose eyes seem to be urging me onward. She stops at the kitchen counter top and takes my hand, her wrinkled fingers run over the ring Doran made me. How old is Bina? I find myself wondering. Sloan is only a few years older than me. And Michaela only a couple years older than him. So either she waited a bit longer than normal to have children, or doing what she does has taken a toll on her.

"The latter," she mumbles as if reading my mind.

I smile. "I hate when Sloan does that."

Now she smiles. "He's got a bit of the Sight in him that one. He's a good boy." I nod. I know. He is. "The ring contains the Earth stone." I nod again. She moves my arm so my shoulder turns exposing the back of my neck. "Yer Earth is returned. Yer growing stronger, Ka. I can feel it. Yer hand?"

"Of course." I say and hand her my palm. I can remember how not long ago I was terrified of not only her touching me, but of her reading my future, of what she'd see. I realize now that what I truly feared was that she'd only see more of the same. That I'd continue to be ordinary and just continue to float through life with no clear sense of direction. Obviously, I was wrong.

She closes her eyes and surprises me this time by running her thumb back and forth over the back of my hand. Sloan puts a hand on my shoulder to let me know he's there and I can hear Michaela's restlessness at the entrance to the hallway, ready to usher us back out the door. I know she just wants to protect herself and her mother, her own livelihood, but the military is run by the government and if the government is corrupted by the Imminent Darkness…well, you get the picture. Michaela knows who I am and the vow that her brother took, but that doesn't mean she approves of it or that she wants to be any part of it. I think the special gifts somehow skipped Michaela.

Carefully, Bina lets go of my hand. "Good." One word is all she says.

"That's it? No doom and gloom?" I ask.

She laughs, a deep, bellyful laugh. "Is that how yeh think of my gift? Doom and gloom?"

"No, I just mean…" I feel my face redden. Sloan nudges my shoulder. "She's just messing with you."

"Yer mother and father are safe. Yer growing stronger and the stronger ye grow the weaker the Imminent Darkness will eventually become."

"But it's here. I see it. And it can change…it can take on any form it wants."

"'Tis true, the Imminent Darkness is the ancient shape-shifter. A dark shadow that can take any form, or lack of form that it wishes." She glances over at Michaela then her eyes come back to rest on mine. "But ye have powers of yer own, Child, that I know you're still discovering. Trust yer instincts, the ones that have been guiding ye all along. Yeh say that ye thought ye were ordinary, but I suspect deep down you knew just the opposite were true. Yeh were just waiting. That feeling. That's the one that will protect ye and keep ye safe."

Bina isn't a warm and fuzzy person. But she pulls me in close for a hug wrapping a thin arm around me. I can tell she isn't as strong as when I first met her and she grabbed my arm across the table. She's grown frail since her failed MindCleanse. "Jus' so ye know," she whispers softly in my ear. "Sloan may have taken the Everlasting Vow, but I see him in yer heart and know that ye protect him too." It's a bit cryptic, but I know it's also her way of saying thanks.

. . .

In the elevator Sloan turns to me. I'm wearing Michaela's jacket. We're about the same size. It's black nylon and I've pulled the hood up to better hide my face as we exit. "I'm sorry about my sister."

I shrug. "It's okay. She's just worried."

"It's not just that. Sure, she worries about Mom and I think me, but mostly she worries about herself. My mom's Unbalanced and my father was an Unbalanced Metal as well. I chose Water and Michaela chose Metal. And she's managed to stay Balanced. It's a thing for her. Because I'm so similar to Bina, Mom and I've kind of been really close my entire life." I recall the look of pride on Bina's face when she saw Sloan, as if she was lit from the inside out. "Michaela was sort of the odd one out, so this," he gestures to indicate the facility. "It's her life. It's her perfectionist world. And she doesn't handle anything that doesn't fit inside it all that well."

"She was just trying to be protective."

"Yeah, of herself." The elevator doors ding open and we step into the lobby.

"Didn't you say your dad was in Universal Intelligence?" I ask, trying not to pry. Sloan's never really opened up about his father, except what he told me that one time. But at the same time, I feel I deserve to know more of the truth.

"Yeah, he was in the military and specialized in Universal Intelligence."

"Oh." We push into the small foyer. "What did he do that made him, uh, you know, Unbalanced?"

"He stumbled onto some research and began making public statements about how the Council of Leaders was out to destroy us and didn't have our best interests at heart." Now I know why it's been so hard to convince Sloan of my theory…which is the exact same one his father had. "He said they were infiltrated by a dark force with an ulterior agenda. *They* deemed him Unbalanced. I don't know all that much after that."

We push through the second set of doors and are greeted by the warm breeze of Xon 9. I swallow in the air, without even realizing I'd been holding my breath as Sloan talked. Even though I don't think I want to know the answer, I ask anyway. "You said he disappeared. Do you know what really happened to him?"

He turns toward me and his green eyes have little fires in them. Anger. No, not anger. Hurt. And when he answers the irony is not one bit lost on me. "He's in the bunker prison beneath the building we just left."

CHAPTER 24

That night I have a dream. I'm on the beach in the Land of Earth, sitting on the shore. The sun is a large orange globe, unlike the garish red sun of Xon 9. It's hovering just above the horizon as though on a precipice of something grand and wonderful. The water shimmers lavender and melon in the setting sunlight.

I feel oddly calm as I lean back on my hands, the soft sand beneath them. The pyramid's in the distance, its golden tip glistening in the sun. But I'm not afraid of what lurks inside. I lean forward and gently rub my wrists. My veins have taken on a greenish hint at the underside of my wrists and I now have small incision type marks where the vines can unleash at will. Vines, electricity, it's all so surreal. It's almost ridiculous. Almost. I run my hand over the back of my neck feeling both the three-dimensional and two-dimensional parts of my tattoo.

I know that I'm waiting for someone, but I'm not sure who. I scan the water in front of me, looking for a bobbing brown head. I used to have so many dreams with Sloan in them, but I guess now that we're together, he doesn't have to try so hard for my attention. I'm also aware of the fact that his body is laying warm beside mine on the mattress in the small bedroom pod at his home, an arm wrapped securely around my waist. If he's walking in dreams, they're not mine. Not tonight.

A shadow appears down the beach. Even from the distance I can tell it's a woman. A voluptuous woman with a young swagger to her walk, long brown tendrils blowing in the sea breeze. Her dress is gauzy, strappy, and long, flowing in the breeze. My mother wears many faces: Kesara, Novea, Anuja, the maiden, the mother, and the crone. Tomb-raider style adventuress one minute, seductress the next. When she reaches me she plops down on the sand beside me as if we are old friends.

"I forgot to tell you that I like your new haircut," she says with an appreciative glance as she adjusts the skirt of her dress around her knees. Her skin sparkles in the sunlight. "And your father and I would never have approved of you getting a tattoo." She pauses. "But I like that too. It suits you."

"You're the one who brought me here?" Her feet are bare except for these elaborate bottomless sandals that have brown leather straps looping around her big toe and again at her ankle, tying at her achilles. They have large turquoise gemstones across the tops of her feet. Barefoot sandals.

"No, hello, I've missed you?" she scolds. She may look not much older than me, but she is definitely still my mother.

"Yes. No. Of course, I've missed you. How's Dad?"

It takes her a minute to answer. "He's adjusting. It took him a while to get used to my new appearance, but I'm still me. I think it's good for him here too. He seems younger. Not so much on the outside, but on the inside."

We sit in amiable silence for several minutes, the only sound the crashing of the waves against the shoreline. I don't want to rush her, but I know she brought me here, or came here depending on how you look at it, to tell me something important.

"Am I dreaming?" I ask just to be sure.

"Of course." She smiles and even though her face is different, her smile is still the same.

"Then how'd you do it?"

"Bina and Sloan aren't the only ones with special gifts. I am a daughter of the Universe after all. But it's not something I can do all the time." She lowers her voice even though no one else is around. "Only when it's something very important."

"Such as?"

"You know the Imminent Darkness is growing stronger." I nod. "But as you grow stronger, it grows just a bit weaker, which infuriates it, so it will continue to recruit…to feed…in order to grow stronger."

"Are you implying that it feeds on…it feeds on people?"

She nods. "It does. It can take on almost any form, as you

already know, but Kata, it's an energetic being. Just like you, just like me, just like this place. It feeds on people's energy. When it draws their energy, the people become suspicious, distrusting, paranoid. Possibly even aggressive."

"Tristen. It was using her energy that's why she became that, that hideous thing."

"Now, now. Don't go feeling sympathy for her. Tristen was more than a willing participant. But, yes, her energetic being somehow merged, quite physically, with the energy of the Imminent Darkness."

"That can happen to someone else?"

"It can."

"The heightened security and the military involvement Michaela was talking about…" Even though I didn't tell her, I sense that she somehow already knows. She's my mom after all. Of course, she'd still watch over me.

"The work of the Imminent Darkness. The reason I brought you here, Ka, is to tell you that even though you grow stronger with every task, risk, and stone you retrieve and destroy…each time you return home to Xon 9, it will be more difficult. The Imminent Darkness knows who you are and it will be watching and waiting."

There's a cool breeze and the hair on the back of my neck stands up.

"Be careful of who you trust because the Imminent Darkness can cause them to say or do things they wouldn't normally do. You have Sloan, but even Sloan can be affected by the Imminent

Darkness."

"But his Everlasting Vow?" The words come out in a rush. If I don't have Sloan, who do I have left? And right away my brain answers: Ahna. Li. No, I don't have Li anymore.

"You will. Just give him time."

"I hate when Sloan and Bina do that."

"Do what?"

"Read my thoughts."

"I didn't need to read your thoughts, Kata. I'm your mother. Your emotions are clear on your face. I'm not telling you these things to frighten you, but to empower you. Sloan is a strong man, he can take care of himself, but if you notice any changes in him, be leery and know it may not be him, but the Imminent Darkness. Remember how you learned about the pollution that ultimately overtook much of the environment on the actual planet Earth?" I nod. I do. The polluted waters and atmosphere contributed to using up non-renewable resources, dwindling food populations, and creating strange weather patterns. "It's like that kind of. It could just be the environment is polluting his energy." I nod. That makes sense. "Now, I know you suspect that the Council is somehow involved or linked to the Imminent Darkness. Since it feeds on energy that's quite possible and for how long I don't know. That topic hits quite close to home for Sloan, but his father can help you. I don't know if you'll be able to convince Sloan, but you need to pay his father a visit. And soon."

She looks out at the horizon just as the sun slips past. "We don't have much time. Let's see, the Imminent Darkness feeds on energy, talk to Sloan's father, what was the third thing….oh yes." She reaches into the pocket of her dress and pulls out a small green stone with red droplets on it. "Heliotrope."

"Helio-what?"

"Heliotrope, also known as Bloodstone."

"Gross."

"Not literally. Although maybe at one time. This stone will help protect you. It can clear energy blocks. Even you aren't completely insusceptible to the power of the Imminent Darkness, as long as the balance remains in its favor. Use the stone to clear the negative energy out. It's both a healing and protective stone. Keep it with you."

She hands it to me. It's cold and smooth. "Um, how will I get it home if I'm dreaming?"

She smiles. "It will be there. Just remember to look for it." Stars begin to appear in the indigo colored sky. Billions of them, as if every star in the Universe has decided to turn on one right after another. We don't see stars like that at home since the sun never sets; its light blocks out most of the stars, except the really, really bright ones. "You should go. It's almost morning."

We stand and she gives me a hug, kissing my cheek.

The next thing I know I'm waking up, Sloan's sleeping form next to me is still snoring softly. I peer out the little port window. I can see that the sky is growing redder, indicating that the moons are setting. I pull my hands out from beneath the cotton blanket. Empty.

I pat the pockets of my pants. Also empty. I flop back, my head hitting the pillow where I'm greeted with a hard *thunk* instead of a soft thud.

I reach my hand inside the pillowcase, knowing what's there before I even pull it out. A small, dark green stone with red splotches. Smooth, shiny, and cool in my hand.

The Bloodstone.

. . .

I'm not very keen on returning to the military facility, what with the heightened security and all. I pull Michaela's jacket tighter around my waist. Sloan told me not to worry about it because the entrance to the prison is a completely separate entrance.

My mom was wrong though. It was fairly easy to convince him that we should visit his dad before heading to the Elemental Abyss for the next stone. I mean he wasn't jumping for joy exactly, but he didn't exactly stick his feet in the sand either. He was willing to hear me out and when I told him about my mother's dream visit—I left out the stuff about the Bloodstone though and the possibility of Sloan becoming affected by the Imminent Darkness's energy—he agreed under two conditions: one, that the visit is short and to the point and two, that we don't bring up Bina or anyone else in the family. I saw no problems with that so we agreed to go first thing before hiking to the mountains of Xon 9, which will probably take the entire day.

Before we left, Sloan rolled some rope, a tarp, and some stakes along with some other things into a bundle and attached it to his backpack, which he's wearing right now. He takes me to the back of the military building and there's a secondary entrance, actually more ominous than the front. We head down a walkway and there's a large concrete blocked wall that surrounds the back. At the top are little metal poles with a live current running through them, blue streaks jumping from pole to pole. A Metal soldier stands at attention, a laser rifle strung across his shoulders. You don't see people with guns around Xon 9. The hair on the back of my neck prickles.

The soldier stares at us blank-faced as we approach, his silver threads seem to intermingle with his own veins in his forehead before disappearing in his hairline. He's wearing a pair of black glasses. "Please state your name and reason for being here."

"We're here to visit my father…Finn Braden. My name is—"

But the guard cuts him off as he pushes a button on the side of his glasses and slowly looks Sloan up and down. "Sloan Braden, twenty-two years old, height six feet one inch, weight one-hundred-and-seventy-five pounds, Universal History Teacher 4, son of Bina and Finn Braden."

He turns to me and does the same thing. I bite my lip hoping there's nothing about the attack on my mother or my kidnapped father. No word about who I truly am, just ordinary Ka Waylon. "Ka Walyon, eighteen years old, height five feet seven inches, weight one-hundred-and-thirty pounds, Student, daughter of Novea and Absalom Waylon." He pushes the button again and nods at us. He presses his hand to a scanning pad and the steel door he's guarding begins to slide open. "The guard on the other side will take you for check-in."

The door slides open and another soldier with another gun is waiting on the other side, a female with a short spiky hair-do that's dyed purple at the tips. Almost as soon as we step through the door behind us slides shut. "This way," she directs. We fall into step behind her. On this side of the wall, there are some benches and some silvery green grass. The space is long and narrow, running the length of the entire back of the building. Michaela chooses to live above this? Granted, I never even noticed it was here, and if I did I probably would have assumed it was some sort of top secret military facility, not a prison. You just don't hear about crime on Xon 9, not that I didn't think it happens. I just didn't think a lot about it.

There's a second steel door leading into the building. The guard puts her hand to a scanner and the door slides open. We enter into a glass foyer and the door slides shut behind us with a final thud. Immediately various colored beams emit, scanning us from every which way. More of the same type of scan the first guard did, but probably even more invasive. "Identities confirmed," a robotic voice announces, the glass door in front of us unlocks and we're greeted by a third guard, a dark-skinned male. The lobby is sterile and airy, windows high up near the ceiling let in some light onto the pristine white floor.

"You'll need to leave your backpack and messenger bag in a locker at the guard station." He leads us over to a small area where we place our bags in lockers. He then leads us to another area, a counter with yet another unsmiling guard behind it. This one doesn't have a gun. He hands us two identification lanyards and we slip them over our heads. They have our photos, taken from one of the scans, our name and the name of who we're visiting. "This way." The guard leads us to another steel door. This time he places his hand on the pad at the same time he pauses for a retina scan. The lock to the door tumbles and he pulls it open, entering first.

The hallway has a concrete floor and either side is lined with steel doors. Some doors have small windows, others have none. Our footsteps echo as we continue down what seems an incredibly long hallway. Sloan is behind me and I'm behind the guard. I can't help but wonder what he must be thinking or feeling. Has he visited his dad here? I know how it would make me feel to see my dad in a place like this, especially when he didn't really do anything wrong, except speak out against the Council. My fingertips prickle in response to the flare of anger.

We eventually make a right turn, I feel like we're heading further beneath the building. The overhead lights flicker as we stop at another set of doors. The guard scans his palm and his retina and then we're ushered through yet another door. This hallway is different. Every steel door has a window. Finally, we reach an area at the end of the hallway where there is a row of windows, partitioned into sections, with metal chairs on either side. The guard gestures and I realize this is the visitor area. Behind the middle window sits a man.

He's hunched over a bit, eyes downcast, brown hair cropped short. His cheeks are gaunt, but his nose is just like Sloan's, strong and angular. His metallic threads almost seem to disappear in the whiteness of his skin that last saw the light of day when? The guard pulls a second chair from one of the other visitor windows and gestures for us to sit. He takes a step back and I realize he isn't going anywhere. We sit. There's a small black box, a speaker with a single button. There's an identical one on the other side of the partition. My heart is saddened that Sloan can't even touch his father. I never asked exactly how old Sloan was when his father was imprisoned. I never asked if he's visited before; his words had been "disappeared." Sloan presses the button on the box and clears his throat. One word comes choked out. "Dad."

CHAPTER 25

Finn's chin shoots up, eyes wide and that's when I notice. He's blind. His eyes are strangely beautiful, and I can see if they once held true color, they were the same as Sloan's. But now they are a milky, faded gray-green. He feels around the ledge on his side of the partition until he finds the box. With a shaking hand he presses the button. His voice is raspy from non-use.

"Son?"

Sloan takes his finger off the button for a second. "He wasn't always blind." His face clouds over in an angry shadow. "You know, if you lose your eyesight, you can't conduct research anymore." Horrific. That's the only word to describe such a thing. I don't know how to respond so I just say nothing. I place my hand over his. There's no words that can heal that kind of pain for either father or son.

He presses the button again. "Yeah, Dad. It's me. I have a friend with me, Ka Waylon."

His father smiles. He too is missing a few teeth like Bina and I wonder if it isn't simply the result of poor hygiene. The hair on the back of my neck yet again prickles as if in response. I stifle a wave of nausea at the thought of such brutality and here, only a little while ago, I thought physical reprimand was no longer supposed to be used. Tristen and Everly. Tristen and Doran. The Council and Mr. Braden. The Imminent Darkness and Bina.

"A friend?" his father teases.

Sloan smiles even though his father can't see it. "Okay, okay. We don't have much time." His father nods as if as much is expected. Sloan exchanges a look with me before saying, "We were wondering if you could give us some information."

"Ah, information is my specialty." I turn and look at the guard who's standing off to the side, stone-faced and staring straight ahead at nothing.

"It's about the ID," Sloan says slowly placing a weird pronunciation on ID.

"Ah the ID. An impulsive, basic part of humanity. The dark side to the ego. Our basest and most primal parts."

I have no idea what he's talking about. They're obviously talking in some sort of code, but I'm not sure what it means exactly.

"We were just wondering if the ID could infiltrate other parts of the *body*," Sloan says.

His father considers this. "Yes. It could. If the body is not strong and is susceptible it could be infiltrated. The ID has been around since the beginning of time. It can learn a lot of bad habits in that many years. I'm not sure when the particular body you're referring to was infiltrated. Maybe since the beginning, but it's hard to say. The ID needs instant gratification and doesn't care much for the consequences, it's the nature of the beast. The girl who's with you, you said her name is Ka Waylon? Why does that sound familiar to me?"

"Oh, you know," Sloan says slowly, "Just one of Mom's *everlasting* stories she's always *seeing*." If the guard were truly listening he'd be picking up on the odd emphasis Sloan is using on certain words, but his expression never changes or otherwise indicate he knows what we're talking about. Maybe it's part of what makes a good combat soldier, not reacting to the inflection or tone in people's voices. I've gathered that ID stands for Imminent Darkness, but I'm not sure about all the ego stuff Finn is talking about.

Finn smiles. "Ah, I miss your mother's stories."

The guard barks. "Two more minutes."

"Is there anything else you need to ask me?"

"No. Just wanted to let you know we're heading out to get some *wood* and *stones*."

His father nods again. "How many were you looking to get?"

"We need three more."

His father nods again. Stones. They're talking about the Elemental Abyss. I'm his mother's story and the reason Sloan took an Everlasting Vow. His father must know about the legend.

"Well, be careful. Keep your eyes on the trees. The ID isn't the only thing that can lurk in the dark shadows and we wouldn't want any trouble."

Sloan nods, even though Finn cannot see him. "We should be going." The guard doesn't move, still as a statue. Almost imperceptibly, Finn slides a tissue thin piece of paper beneath the partition and Sloan quietly takes it and slips it into the inside pocket of his jacket. "Well, it was good seeing you, Dad." Sloan stands and I follow suit.

"You too, Son. And you keep a watch on him, Ka. Don't go letting him act all impossible."

He does know who I am and for some reason it warms my heart to know that. Sloan's dad is a good person. He shouldn't be in there for standing up for what's right. "I won't, Sir."

Finn smiles and takes his hand off the intercom box. Sloan places a hand against the glass partition, palm flat against the smooth surface and somehow his father must sense it because he places his hand up against his side of the glass, almost in line with Sloan's. And even though he's smiling a tear rolls down his cheek.

. . .

Once we're outside, back on the other side of the giant concrete wall, I realize that I was again holding my breath. Sloan doesn't say anything. Just takes my hand and starts walking in the direction of the perimeter. We pass Pax Park and continue walking, eventually passing Sloan's neighborhood until I can feel the breeze pick up more, turning into a wind as we approach the perimeter.

Finally, once we reach the perimeter and there's no one else around, just red earth as far ahead as the eye can see, I say: "Your father seems like a nice man."

Sloan looks at me sideways. "He is a nice man, which made it all the more difficult to deal with the situation. But what's done is done. The least I can hope for is justice to be served, at least for him to not die before it does."

"He doesn't seem that old."

"He looked old. Much older than the last time I went to see him."

"How often do you go to see him?"

"I don't." He turns to me cringing. "It's weak and pathetic of me, but it's just too damn difficult." His eyes well with tears and he looks down at his boots, still holding my hand.

"He loves you and knows you love him," I say without thinking, just knowing the truth of the words deep down. "He understands, Sloan. I could see it."

Sloan nods, still not looking at me, and it's odd because he always seems older than me, which he is, also having been my teacher, but in this moment he seems like a fifteen-year-old boy again. Unsure, insecure, hesitant, and afraid. I wrap my arms around him and he rests his chin on my shoulder. The wind whips Michaela's jacket causing it to make a sort of flapping sound and we just stand like that for a long time, his chin on my shoulder, my cheek pressed to his chest.

The past cannot go away no matter how bad we want it to. It

stays with us, like a wound or a scar. It's a reminder of both where we've been and where we are going. I cannot undo the scars that line Li's face or bring Everly back any more than Sloan can undo his father's blindness. We make decisions that not only affect ourselves, but the lives of others as well. Just as all the Elements are interconnected, so too are we.

My mom asked me just before Pronouncement: *Which one, Kata, heart or head?* Which one would I follow to make my decision? My mother answered heart and risked her immortality in the name of love. My father answered heart and risked his breaking. Bina answered heart and lost the man she loved. Finn answered heart and lost his family. Sloan answered heart and has risked his life in order to protect mine.

And me, I've risked everything to protect the people who've risked all these things for me.

Head or heart, Kata?

I didn't listen the first time, but now I know.

Heart. Always, heart.

ABOUT THE AUTHOR

Jennifer L. Kelly is a middle childhood educator. She resides in Cleveland, Ohio. When she isn't writing, she can be found fangirling over *Doctor Who*, doing yoga, spending time with her dog, taking photos for her #bookstagram, or making candles for her Etsy shop: TheBookishFlame. This is her second series for young adults. Her first novel, *The Prophecy: The Lucia Chronicles Book 1,* was published in January 2014. Visit her website **Skim.Scheme.Scribble:** www.jenniferlkelly.com Or say *HI!* :

info@jenniferlkelly.com

JenniferLKelly3

AuthorJenniferLKelly

AuthorJenniferLKelly

ACKNOWLEDGEMENTS

First, I'd like to thank the talented Joshua at www.JoshuaJadon.com for creating Ka's Elemental Star. He took my measly, cartoon drawing and turned it into something real! Its design exceeded my expectations. I'd also like to thank my Dad for always helping me and being supportive and my dog, Mennie, because she has to put up with all the craziness that is writing, editing, formatting, and proofing, but like a good furbaby she always keeps me company. I think someone deserves extra doggie treats. ☺ I'd also like to thank all my fellow #bookstagrammers who have supported me and been willing to be ARC readers for this series. You are amazing and I appreciate the discussions I have with each and every one of you.

Turn the page for the beginning of ...

GENESIS OF WOOD

The Elementals Book 3

03.07.17

PROLOGUE

There once was a naive, young woman named Novea. She was fascinated with mankind. Sure, she looked like she was human, except for the radiant skin and silky, chestnut-colored hair. Only she wasn't human; she was a daughter of the Universe, one of the five goddesses birthed of Raj and Katayun. The entire Universe was at her fingertips, until the Imminent Darkness, disguised as a codger, tricked Novea and her four sisters. He separated the sisters, drawing a wedge between them. As a result Raj created a Land for each one of his daughters: one each of Fire, Earth, Wood, Metal, and Water. Novea ruled the planet Earth, until her sister Celosia played a trick on her, gifting her the sun to create life, but then cruelly taking it away, for as we now know, the sun was a star. And eventually stars die.

Xon 9 is where mankind went to live before the Earth disappeared in a fiery inferno. That's where things get interesting.

Novea was intrigued by humankind, specifically their ability to feel so deeply and passionately. She would wear her golden cloak and wander the streets, sticking to the shadows, until one day she was noticed by a handsome young man named Absalom. Novea didn't intend to fall in love with Absalom, but soon she found herself wanting to stay with the mortal man. Raj and Katayun gave their blessing, under the condition that Novea would have to become mortal. If she returned at any time to her home, the Land of Earth, she would never be able to return to Xon 9. If she returned, she would die. All of time and space, given up in the name of love. She agreed.

They were married and eventually had a child, a half-immortal, half-mortal daughter. A seemingly impossible hybrid. Absalom knew Novea was a daughter of the Universe and he knew his daughter was bestowed with powerful gifts from each of the Elemental Goddesses upon her birth. But sometimes things don't go quite as planned. The daughter's birth created an Imbalance in the Universe, a Balance that had persisted since time itself began.

Now their daughter is grown and the Imminent Darkness has returned to restore what has been lost.

But not if I can help it. Who am I?

I'm the granddaughter of Raj and Katayun.

I'm the daughter of Novea and Absalom.

I am the Impossible Girl.

I am Ka.

CHAPTER 1

The familiar, constant breeze has gone still. I have blisters on the bottoms of both my feet and the palms of my hands are caked with dirt and dry blood. Somehow the surrounding mountains have blocked the breeze. The air here is humid and so thick you could cut it with a knife. Sloan and I pause to take a drink and swallow some nutrient pills. It's only been about two days' time and already his face has taken on a more angular appearance, his sea green eyes alert in the shadows of his face. The gills that line the left side of his face wiggle thankfully as his water equilibrium is restored.

"Don't look at me like that," he says replacing the cap on the bottle of nutrient pills and tossing it back to me

"Like what?" I ask slipping the bottle inside my messenger bag. It drops with a clunk beside my jacket, more bottles of water, a couple flashlights, an empty glass jar and the burlap sack Bina gave me. All that's left in the sack is a speckled feather, a pack of matches from the Old Tavern and the Sea, and a small crystal.

"Like I'm some alien just landed from outer space."

I push myself off the mountainside which I had been leaning against. "We are in outer space."

We're colonists on Xon 9. Not the original colonists, that was some years ago. But we are the descendants: the Elementals. The scientists discovered Xon 9 when they went out searching for other habitable planets since Earth was about to become toast, thanks to the dying of the sun. Xon 9 was good enough. Its two moons provided enough gravitational pull, the red sun never setting past the horizon, casting the planet forever in an eerie glow of pinks and reds. There's no surface water on Xon 9, but there is plenty in the planet's inner layers, nothing a state-of-the-art drill can't extract. Animals and crops from home are raised in storehouses run by the Earth Elementals from the Agricultural Department.

The only thing the original colonists hadn't accounted for once they set up shop on Xon 9 and decided to call it home, was the unique physiological affects the planet's Elements would have on our fragile human bodies. I guess these things can be overlooked when you're running against the clock of a supernova. There are five Elements: Earth, Fire, Wood, Water, and Metal. Over time, the colonists came to harness the unique gifts of each of these Elements. Earth is wise. Fire is passionate. Wood is steadfast. Water is nurturing. And Metal is strong. Which was all fine and dandy until they also realized the whole yin and yang of it all. If one is not careful, the Element can take over, and cause some to become Unbalanced. Earth can become stubborn, Fire impulsive. Wood can turn unyielding and Water unrelenting. And Metals can become aggressive. The Elements have a fine balance and it is up to the individual to harness and control it. Only, it's not that simple.

"Is that it?" I ask squinting and pointing a short distance up the path. Sloan turns and peers in the direction which I'm pointing.

"I don't think so. Remember Bina said Old Earth-Cactus style. Those just look like bushes." We keep walking, the thickness of the air pressing on us from either side. I'd always taken the constant 70-degree temperatures and ever-present breeze of Xon 9 for granted. I make a silent vow to be more appreciative.

What I mean when I say that it's not that simple is really that none of it makes any sense. All of the Elements affect each one of us, yet at the end of our schooling, as we near our eighteenth moons, we're forced to choose one Element. Choosing an Element is a Pronouncement and a lifelong label. I had the worst time deciding. I didn't feel connected to any of the Elements. I felt like nothing. Hollow almost, like an empty shell.

And that's because I *was* empty. But now I am becoming filled. Filled with each of the Elements. All of the Elements. I am the Impossible Girl of Legend. I am born of the goddess Novea and her mortal lover Absalom. I am the only grandchild of the Universe itself. Because of this, upon my birth, I was bestowed with many gifts. In fact, I was given one gift from each of my mother's sisters: the gifts of each of the Elements. Unfortunately, my aunts' generosity threw the Universe off kilter and now the Imminent Darkness is out to restore the balance that was lost. And not necessarily in my favor.

When I was young my mother saw my propensity for each Element and was afraid the ID (Imminent Darkness) would come for me. So in order to protect me she consulted a Seer, a Metal woman named Bina, who also happens to be Sloan's mother (more on that in a minute). The Metal woman told my mother that in order to protect me she had to throw five stones—one for each Element—into the Elemental Abyss, deep in the Mountains of Xon 9, and as I now know, not short on enchantments and obstacles. My mother did as she was told. With each stone trapped inside the Elemental Abyss, so too was that Elemental part of my personality, thus explaining the emptiness. Retrieve and destroy the stones, restore my fractured personality. Sounds simple.

Only the Imminent Darkness grows stronger as I grow stronger. And now with both my mother and father in the Land of Earth, I have to rely on Sloan. I watch his lithe form as he hikes up the trail in front of me, periodically pausing and scanning the rocky landscape for a bright red flower perched atop a plant with poisonous thorns. Sloan was my teacher and is now my boyfriend.

Now before you get all weirded out, he's only about three moons older than me. After Pronouncement, new Elementals attend the University Complex to become more familiar with their Element and to induce the Transition Phase. Even weirder still (I know, really, does it get much weirder? Yes, in fact it does.) Sloan is my protector. Not that I can't protect myself, because I totally can with my ability to conjure fire energy and my newest trick: green vines that shoot out from the inside of my wrists. I turn over my hand, inspecting the green tinge my veins have taken on. Normally, an Elemental develops the telltale signs on the right side of the face: a clear indication of your forever affiliation. Apparently, being half-goddess, and half-mortal manifests the Elements in a completely different way. But back to Sloan.

Before he'd even met me or even knew who I was, his mother had told him about her visions, about the Impossible Girl who would be coming to save the colonists from the deception and darkness of the ID. Sloan has some of his mother's gifts, like he can dream walk, and send these sort of weird messages, but he's also like his father, Finn. He's got a fierce allegiance to the truth, sometimes to a fault. While my mother was tossing stones into the Elemental Abyss, Sloan made an Everlasting Vow by the light of the twin moons, to protect the Impossible Girl no matter the cost, not so much *for* me but because *of* me. Because I may have all the Elements in my blood, but so too does every colonist of Xon 9. The notion that we must choose is a farce. We are all one.

Sweat drips down the back of my neck. I rub the droplets away, feeling the smoothness of my tattooed skin juxtaposed against the Fire filigree and tubular green Earth vines that now bulge beneath my fingers. My Elemental Star. With each acquisition of a stone, my tattoo seems to morph in response. Two down, three more to go. Only first…

"There!" I call out, seeing the glint of red just past Sloan's right shoulder.

"I see it!" He starts to jog toward it, veering off the path and heading into a small alcove. There's a cluster of three sturdy looking green plants. They kind of resemble people with a head in the middle and arms held up in an awkward surrender posture. White spines poke out every which way from the plant and nestled in the top, where I imagine a face would be, is a large red blossom.

"Ignis Flos," I breathe.

"The fire flower." Sloan takes a step closer inspecting the plant. He's about to reach out and touch one of the white spines, but I put a hand out to stop him.

"Bina said they're poisonous, remember?" The red flower seems to taunt us, its beauty protected by the poisonous spines surrounding it.

He nods and pulls a small knife from the pocket of his cargo pants. I reach up carefully, gently pulling the red, silken petals out of the way, avoiding the spines that surround the plant.

"And what about you? What if you get pricked?" he asks as he tries to maneuver around the numerous poisonous spines to get to the plant itself, which is nestled around an intrusive cluster.

"Half-immortal," I reason.

"Tsk. Half-*mortal*," he corrects. "That's the kind of thinking that will get you killed, Ka Waylon."

Ever so delicately he takes the blade and slices at the base of the flower which I pluck off the cactus. The blade of his knife slices through some of the nearby spines and a black substance oozes along the blade, dripping to the red dirt at our feet.

I pull out the empty glass jar and place the bloom inside it, careful to avoid the base of the plant in case there's any lingering poison.

"*Ignis flos to appease the beast in the chasm*," I recite the words from my mother's hand-written notes.

"At the very least, I hope it's appreciative," Sloan says dumping some water on the blade of his knife. He closes the knife and drops it back into his pocket, taking another long drink of water. "So, where to now Ka, Warrior Princess?"

I pull out the tattered map with my mother's notes, trying to orient myself. We need to get back to the cavern with the enchanted lake. I look up, and point in the opposite direction. "The Elemental Abyss is that way."

GENESIS OF WOOD

The Elementals Book 3

03.07.17